To the girls in my life, personal and professional. To Jen, for supporting me wholeheartedly without reading a word of this novel 'til now – just because. Kate and Sarah for supporting me wholeheartedly while reading and re-reading far more than you'd have cared to. And to Khaya, the best four legged sidekick anyone could ask for. You're still missed, my baby girl.

— Jeff

To 2 a.m. discussions in the Parsons living room, which may have been the the most educational part of college, and were certainly the most inspirational. To my mother, who didn't let being the only woman in the lecture hall stop her dreams, and told me to chase mine, wherever they led.

— Sarah

Fair Winds, always.

Jeffrey Cook

ISBN 149427650X

ISBN 978-1494276508

Dawn of Steam
Book 1: First Light

by Jeffrey Cook
with Sarah Symonds

Table of Contents

Preface by Dr. Cordelia Bentham-Watts
January 18th, 1887
London, England

When my dear husband of sixty-five years passed away last year, the day was treated as a solemn national holiday. It is always difficult to mark the passing not simply of a hero, but to most people's minds, the passing of an age. It also marked the beginnings of what was destined to be a nearly impossible task. I had always felt it was vitally important to organize his notes and memoirs to be presented less as something personal and more as a lesson in history as it happened, through the eyes of the one person who could truly claim to have been there throughout it all. But it also had to be my task. Amidst his many letters and journal pages and maps was a good deal that was always intended to be only between us. There were also the most personal details of the lives of his companions, and some corners would still prefer some information not come to light. Even now, I am quite certain I should be facing one such person quite soon.

For now, I am left with the daunting task of organizing history. I am certain some of my many detractors would state that I'm re-writing history, perhaps yet again. I am sure my regular readers would prefer another semi-scholarly diatribe into the worlds of international diplomacy and women's place in medicine, the worlds that have become almost as much my home as this wonder of technology, science, and manners we call the real world, a thing far removed from the niceties of international diplomacy, I assure you. This is not even my work, but the work of history. I'm equally sure some of my long-term detractors, who read my works for the pleasure of sneering, would prefer that I just set down my pen for good. I assure you, that will happen soon enough, and you will be forever free from the written thoughts of the first woman doctor, though I hope you'll grant me a few more years of being an overly busy old woman.

Instead, what lies within will begin as a familiar story to some people, the story of a tiny band of brave and noble souls who set out in 1815 to shine a light on the dark corners of the world. This is the story of how that band explored the western reaches of the American colonies, journeyed to the near-mythic East, helped to open Australia to expansion, and through heroic effort and sacrifice, played a significant part in the difficult times following the Napoleonic Wars. While this is that story, it is also so much more.

Many of the details of that journey have never seen the light of day. A good deal of this has been intentional. My husband never wanted to deal with some of the certain backlash that would come from putting his pages to wider print. I do not think he was worried so much of the eyes of the world and how they would judge him, but worried that parts of the world he cared very much for were not ready. Certainly there was also the concern for his companions. But with his passing, the risk that the truths of the very first dawnings of the modern age of enlightenment and technological wonder would be lost forever to age or accident has grown to be the greatest concern. And where my husband had a deep love for trying to please everyone, the very nature of the accomplished diplomat, and a deep sensitivity, I have the impish sense of humor given to an old woman who has long since grown accustomed to shaking the branches of the social order for all they're worth to see what falls out.

What you will read is the truth as I know it. My husband was not given to reporting falsehood, and at the time he very much thought of himself still as a reporter, the position he gained quite by accident due to a keen mind for remembering facts and details of even chaotic battlefields. In those places necessary, I may leave a few footnotes here and there, for the modern reader, but will endeavor to do my best to allow the chronicler to tell the story as it was intended, with some assistance from his fellow travelers. Where another source of the time may tell parts of this great story as clearly, or provide facts in a more organized fashion, I will provide those clippings as well. After all, Scotland Yard and the New York papers can provide glimpses of what happened when this brave group rubbed up against the larger world far better than my modest husband.

Notes on the Overseas Edition

My good reader, I hope you will understand when I inform you that the edition of this history for overseas print has been slightly edited. Specific locations of Military Bases and Advanced Mechanical Workshops have been removed, as have the few photographs showing dirigible controls or technical drawings. Colonial citizens may view more information on these topics at their local universities, should you be blessed with such, or at Cambridge. As always, complete information is at Oxford, and those who apply for clearance to study there may see the unaltered documents, as well as working models, in the Bowe Memorial Wing of the Second Coltrane Building. I do recommend at least three days for the visit, should you be in the area.
– Dr. Cordelia Bentham-Watts, 1891

Note from the American Publishers
July 1891
New York, New York Colony

The American Publishers of this history wish their readers to know that the spellings and punctuations have been modified from Dr. Cordelia Bentham-Watts's manuscript, and thus from the original documents. This has been done in accordance with the delineated differences between the two varieties of written and spoken English, as Codified most recently in the Cambridge English Dictionary, Complete Volumes, Issuance 1890. Additionally, the colloquial 'flingy' has been modified to 'slingshot' throughout the manuscript, although it apparently had not drawn the attention of that august publication, being merely an informal genitive gerund naming said item.

Gathering The Team
Leaving London

January 1st, 1815
London, England

My Dearest Cordelia,

My love, I wished you to be the first to receive the news of my excellent fortune, though I can scarce believe this opportunity myself. With the war ended, it seems the fancy of some men of station and wealth in the House of Lords has turned to gentlemen's bets.[1] Lord Donovan has wagered that the works of noted exploration writer Dr. Robert Bowe are not, in fact, works of fiction, as the general belief would have it. He believes that the journals are true accounts of exploration of a vast portion of the world. His opponent, more sensibly, has wagered that one man could not possibly have traveled so far, to so many unknown corners of the world, in a man's lifetime. As Dr. Bowe has long since disappeared, with many believing him deceased, the two gentlemen have each set about hiring a crew to follow the paths outlined in the journals to see if they have any merit. Despite my own beliefs on the matter, Lord Donovan has hired me, on the strength of my past work documenting the progress of the war with Napoleon, along with my experience with Oxford's camera device, to chronicle the journey of the crew he's hired.

Of course, such a journey is not without its difficulties. The first of which is that the crew he is intending to hire are not yet aware of the undertaking. His Lordship has asked me to travel with his representative to recruit the people I will be traveling with. You will, of course, recognize the first of these. To make such

---

1 The post-Colonial-War period was full of notorious bets, which would still have been spoken of in 1815. The war and its settlement brought great shifts in income, including catapulting up some of those of lower breeding into the upper scales of wealth. These men had become accustomed to making bets among the soldiers during the war and now had vast fortunes and little accountability, setting the stage for the bets in gentlemen's clubs that shocked the public, for example, 1000 pounds sterling on the first letter of a newspaper's headline. – C B-W

an undertaking even possible, such a journey would need both a highly capable leader, and a means to travel rapidly. Lord Donovan has accounted for both in sending me to recruit Sir James Coltrane, the famed war hero. In addition to the prestige that Sir James's presence alone would offer, Lord Donovan believes that the Coltrane family's personal dirigible, the *Dame Fortuna*,[2] is the vehicle best suited for covering such long distances with great haste.

After the Coltranes, we are to travel to Scotland. As if Sir James's name was not enough, the Lord Donovan also believes that he has the means to recruit Edward McBride, the Scot sharpshooter, to our company. Beyond those two esteemed names I do not recognize the rest of the company. I do know, however, that apparently most of the rest are believed to be in the American colonies, so our first adventure will simply be gathering the crew.

As excited as I am to even consider travel alongside the two greatest war heroes of our time, the trip itself promises to be even more exciting. Though we are not expected to come near to completing all of the tasks laid out in Dr. Bowe's many adventure journals, the possibilities make my head swim.

There has been mention of attempts to fund an expedition to explore the American West and find a land route to the Pacific, but all such efforts were cut off by the beginning of the war. Now, that seems to be one of our most likely *immediate* goals, once the ship is fully crewed. Just think, dearest: our *first* goal is to sit on the Pacific coast and sketch (or in my case, photograph) exactly what Dr. Bowe did.

---

2 The *Dame Fortuna* started the war as navy property, but was granted to the Coltrane family for distinction in service three years before Waterloo. While this was not the first war that England had used dirigibles, certainly a far greater number were produced and survived the Napoleonic wars than the American skirmishes. Eight were produced in 1774, and seven survived that conflict, the other being infamous. Fifty-two were produced for the defense of the realm in the early 1800s, and Napoleon's famed efforts were such that only twenty-four survived the war. – C B-W

Beyond the colonies, Dr. Bowe's journals include mention of lost cities in South America, savages and natural perils in Australia and New Zealand, mountains and monasteries in Asia, and all manner of wonders in Africa. I cannot believe that all of these things will be as described in the journals, but I am certain that what is in those places will be no less fascinating. Very soon, I shall be sending photographs of the truth of these matters back to England, along with my accounts of the trip. I will, of course, also write you at every opportunity to keep you abreast of not simply what we find, but of this incredible journey itself.

Tomorrow I will be meeting Mr. Toomes, Lord Donovan's assistant and my companion until such time as we have recruited the traveling company.

As always, my thoughts are with you and your health, my love. I have always admired your sense of wonder and willingness to believe in the impossible, so I can only hope this letter will prove an inspiration. Give your good father my regards. With luck, the money and fame from this journey will impress him sufficiently that he will give his consent to our marriage upon my return.

My love, always,
Gregory Conan Watts

Editor's note:

Tucked into Gregory's journal is an extraordinary piece of paper. It is the original listing of things which Lord Donovan intended the explorers to prove. The depth of the mission can be seen when one ponders that this listing is simply that, a list, originally printed as an index of Dr. Bowe's novels. One can easily see why credible sources think that such exploration is far beyond the capabilities of a man's lifespan. *The Journals of Dr. Bowe* were widely read in the 1810s as an escape when travel was restricted due to the war.

Those listings <u>underlined</u> were done so on the original list, presumably by Lord Donovan's hand.

– Dr. Cordelia Bentham-Watts

Bowe, Dr. Robert Set of matching volumes, with subheadings

North America – Primeval Florida – <u>The Northwest Passage</u> – <u>Brimstone and Geysers</u> – <u>The Great Mississippi</u> – Gentle Savages and Wild Men – <u>Walking to the West</u>

South America – The Magic Amazon – <u>Lost Cities and Civilizations</u> – <u>Navigating the River of Doubt</u> – There is No El Dorado – South South America: Cold, Ice, and Feathered Fish

Africa – <u>Timbuktu</u> – The Nile, Sourced and Mapped – <u>The Nile's Great Falls</u> – Ancient Egypt's Treasures – Small Hunters – Deepest Jungles – Inland Mountain Ranges – Crossing the Kalahari and Sahara Deserts – Into the Great Rift Valley – <u>Navigating the Congo River</u>

Australia and New Zealand – Australia's Unforgiving Nature – <u>Through the Blue Mtns</u> – Across the Desert – The Friendliest People on Earth – Reef the Size of England – <u>New Zealand's Eden on Earth</u> – The Deadliest People on Earth

Islands of the Pacific – Mysteries of 'Tiki' – Living on the Edge of Volcanoes – Tides of Life

Near Asia – Riding the Steppes – Russia's Court

East Asia – <u>Climbing the Tallest Mountain</u> – Monks in the Wilderness – Where Wisdom Rules – Forbidden China Explored

Tropical India – Tea Fields and Temples

Hidden Japan – <u>The Closed Land Open'd</u>

From the journals of Gregory Conan Watts,
January 2nd, 1815
Outside of London

It seems even the greatest of adventures sometimes have the most mundane beginnings. I met with Mr. Toomes this morning over breakfast. Though we were given suitably rich options, given the prestige of our sponsor, Mr. Toomes insisted on having only a single biscuit with jam and a cup of strong tea before spending the rest of breakfast watching me eat while he smoked his beloved pipe.

Since that time, the pipe has been ever-present, either in person, or in conversation, as it seems to be Mr. Toomes's singular hobby. By and large, Elliott Toomes is the most difficult man I have ever attempted to speak with. Though I have been told that I have a relaxed manner that puts people at ease, he has no use for small talk if it does not regard the smoking of pipes. I have learned more about tobacco blends from around the world, the subtle differences between mahogany and cherry wood in construction of pipes – though he favors nothing so much as his beloved calabash – and the origins of the different clays and materials used in construction of pipes. We have so far stopped the carriage at every township along the route large enough to possess a smoke shop, that he can sample the local blends.

Aside from this, he is an extraordinary fellow. Whoever first trained him in soldiery would be proud, for even at rest, he sits at attention. Were it not for the lingering odor of pipe blends, he could be ready for inspection at any moment. I cannot tell how long ago his training might have been, for he is so severe as to seem quite aged and worldly, yet so strong for his tall, reed-like frame as to suggest someone younger. At best I can guess somewhere between mid-forties and early sixties.

Regardless of his demeanor and habits, I have been assured that the estimable Mr. Toomes is quite well connected, and has considerable history with many members of the House of

Lords. Lord Donovan not only trusts him, but trusts him to accomplish the herculean task of putting this crew together. I may be along to document all stages of the journey, including its roots, and maybe I will be of some help to Mr. Toomes, but he is to be the primary negotiator when we approach Sir James and the others. Whatever aid I can be, I will, but I have already learned to be very guarded while under Mr. Toomes's squinting, disapproving gaze.

Still, I would weather far more than Mr. Toomes to be a part of this journey. The opportunity itself is staggering, but most importantly, I cannot imagine that Captain Bentham could object any longer to accepting me as his son-in-law after my taking part in a venture of this magnitude. Of all of the incredible sights we are certain to encounter in our travels, I look most forward to returning home to my love.

Mr. Toomes has unavoidable business in London and is waiting on correspondence from around the globe. I am awaiting his leisure in the matter of this adventure, for only he truly knows our first steps. While I feel slightly impatient, I understand this endeavor is a feat of planning, and must be done properly.

THE TIMES of London presents an opportunity to **SEE in PERSON** that about which you have only Previously **READ**!

Sir James Coltrane,

newly made Baronet of the Realm, Defender of our Mother Country against the aggressions of the World in the recent war of all European nations, will be exhibiting his invention, the near miraculous **Mechanical Battle Suit** in Hyde Park, this *Friday, Saturday, and Monday*, so that the Citizens of England may see the **Hero of Waterloo in Action!**

~ **Sir James** has stated he will **launch** from his custom modified **Airship**, *The Dame Fortuna*, directly to the **ground**!

~ Watch this Giant, **9-foot**, **Steam-Powered** behemoth **Walk** like a *man*, **Run** as fast as *horse*, and even **Jump** higher than *houses*.

~ *Ladies be warned*, he will exhibit the **powerful rockets** built into the suit, the overwhelming firepower he took to the **enemy**.

~ And one of our own brave *veteran marksmen* will fire at him, showing how **bullets dare not pierce** the suit.

~ See the **pure strength** of the *metal man* in person. Watch him **bend iron rods**, and *sign autographs* with the same hand.

~ **Be there**, *dear reader*, to see the **talk of the town**. Don't be the only member of your acquaintance to not see this **Oxford wonder!**

~ It is a day your children will tell their grandchildren about. Be there for **history**!

Editor's note:

Dear reader, I am quite certain that the concept of such an invention as the Coltrane steam-powered monster fills even the most educated modern mind with doubt, as nothing of the sort has ever been reproduced. However, as you can see from the photographic record included herein, as well as historical record of the Napoleonic wars with the continent, Coltrane's work, including the mechanical marvel described, is a matter of historical record.

Even should you doubt Mr. Watts's journalistic integrity, which I assure you, you should not, there is evidence from many reliable sources in the past to assure that at one time such a thing was a reality. Certainly, the world has advanced in leaps and bounds in recent decades. Steam-powered vehicles have become commonplace and machines of war have begun seeing ever greater advancement. But these leaps have their roots firmly entrenched in wonders past. While the world of 1815 was dark and primitive by today's standards, it had its wonders which even our most advanced science now struggles to explain.

– Dr. Cordelia Bentham-Watts

February 16th, 1815,
----shire, Southern England

Dear Sir,

As I have been instructed to do, I have begun my writing when encountering that which I consider extraordinary. Though I know the intent was to pen such correspondence upon reaching unknown shores and darkest reaches, I have encountered such an element as needs documenting within our very own home of England. As I am certain you are most curious about my traveling companions, or those whom I hope to travel with, I feel that I must document today's adventure.

With your trusted servant Mr. Toomes in attendance, we traveled to the location provided to us as to where we would find Sir James, himself. Though we found him not at the club for young men of station and monies, Mr. Toomes did entreat me to carefully look upon a small group of fellows gathered in one corner. At the time I was uncertain what concerned him, and he bade me not look too long, but he seemed quite certain they were up to some ill. In walking close to their table, I came to hear some hint of foreign accents, well disguised, but nonetheless present as the men spoke. I believe I picked out traces of both French and German. In this day and age, this is a poor sign. Though travel across the waters between ourselves and our mainland neighbors is watched quite closely there have nevertheless, been rumors for some time of men successfully breaching those defenses, as well as some natives of our own fair shores with sympathies for those who attempted to steal that which we have created through our own brightest minds and great labors.

When I assured Mr. Toomes that I had heard some hint of this, he agreed with my assessment and bade me follow them from some distance when they left. He was quite curious how such as they came to attend such an establishment, and he would remain behind to try to gain some understanding of who sponsored them to attend, for surely they were not men of society, but merely knew someone with the proper connections as to gain attendance. I fully admit to nervousness, but wishing to prove myself worthy of the tasks given to me and of the esteem granted me by assigning me such a task, I did as I was bade.

I am certain they were worried for being followed, for their path twisted and turned throughout the town, and I admit that I lost them entirely on not one, but three occasions, but each time found some hint solid enough to put me back on their trail, twice through my own device and doggedness, and once through sheer fortune. Indeed, the latter may be owed somewhat to my time with Mr. Toomes. His presence has so accustomed to me to certain scents that I was able to find the proper path by following the scent of a smoke not particularly common to this region, but which hung strongly upon one of these men. Without such experience as the past few days have provided, I am quite certain I would have taken no notice of such a thing.

In any case, as I should have guessed, their path led eventually to the local military supply depot. As you are well aware, while the country begins to prepare itself for the postwar era, many of these dirigible supply stations still exist, awaiting demolition or transition to a peacetime purpose. In this case, as in many, one of the decommissioned airships was in attendance.[3] It seems that these gentlemen had timed their raid with some foreknowledge, for the ship, while tethered to the ground, was amidst a test of its systems and looked fully inflated and ready to return to service. I am uncertain why we continue to test these vehicles. Perhaps it is simply some nostalgia among those who have recently served, continuing to tend these wondrous vehicles until such time as another purpose is found for them, or they are

---

3 Modern readers familiar with the wonders of air travel would do well to note that the standard architecture of a dirigible terminal was selected to disguise their origins as storage depots. This would explain the phenomenon in which, while great effort is being made to make everyone feel quite comfortable, one cannot help but feel a bit like one is being stored in between legs on one's journey. Such quirks of modern life... – C B-W

put out of service.

In any case, these brigands knew not only when this test would be taking place, but precisely the rotation of the guards, who after the considerable months which have passed since war's end, certainly saw no reason to suspect any such problem. As such, they quickly found their way through the defenses of this small station at the edge of town.

While I knew well I should cry out and warn the base, I found myself hesitating, for I had grown so close that such a deed would surely put them on me before the raiders could be dealt with. It was only when the last of them had disappeared from sight past the outermost perimeter that I found my voice and raised an alarm, shouting that intruders had entered the depot. This did not raise the attention I had originally hoped. A guard called 'Who goes there?' as one might imagine they have done far too many times, almost as if he was bored of it. I shouted my name, and repeated that intruders were within the base. It took precious seconds before he deigned answer me, only to ask if I was given to drinking.

At this point, there was some bustle deeper in the confines of the buildings, as I imagined soldiers began to concern themselves with the noise. When I attempted to rush in to make certain they understood the urgency of my words, I was quite quickly restrained and questioned repeatedly. I am certain that this opera could have gone on for considerable time longer, but a shot rang out from the building to which the airship was tethered. Moving along with a small crowd now, I rushed for that building without any further hesitation, hoping we would not be too late.

Tragically, we were just that, as one man in guardsman's uniform lay quite still, and another lay groaning, clutching at a wound which I have since been told would prove fatal. I still mourn for those young men, ashamed that I had not done more to save them in my own struggle to put voice to an alarm and my inability to explain myself in such a fashion as to not paint myself the villain.

The guardsmen and I rushed into the building to find flickers of light ascending a staircase. As the first bold man rushed after the hints of motion and sounds from above, he was shot at close range by one of the men I had been following. Happily, I understand that he will survive, but may never have the use of his left arm again. Regardless, eventually with some exchange of gunfire, we were able to give chase, only to find that the doorways to the roof had been breached, and three men with guns had quite substantial cover and guns trained upon our small party – after all, no one in these days expects to come upon such dangers in England, and few would think anyone insane enough to attempt to raid one of our military institutions. It seems we may not be quite so safe as we thought, and perhaps I might venture to say this location was somewhat undermanned.

Amidst this stand off, I became aware of a great deal of noise outside, like nothing I had ever heard. Had some alert gone up, I'd have expected shouting or perhaps gunfire, but it was nothing of that sort. Rather, it was a tremendous crash, repeated time and again. The men we were facing off with picked up on it as well not long after I did. From my vantage point, I saw glances exchanged, and heard unintelligible but clearly urgent words. Had I not been so distracted by this new oddity, I might have gotten off a clean shot, but I, and the men with me, were as distracted and dumbstruck as the men breaking in.

We would not have to wait long for an answer. Before our opponents had quite gotten over their confusion long enough to break and run, a giant metallic fist tore through the wall very near to them. More of the thick wooden structure was pulled away to make room for the rest of the machine attached to the fist. I am certain that you are well-aware of Sir James Coltrane's wondrous machine-suit, but I feel no story I have yet heard does justice to seeing it in person.

After Sir James tore away sufficient wall, he pulled himself through the gap and into the room, though the suit had to stoop somewhat within the confines of the roof. The men we had chased this far panicked at that point, and opened fire upon it. I heard the sounds of the ricochets, with the shots slowing Coltrane's mechanical monster not in the least. As he reached their fortified position, he knocked the first man's hard cover aside as if the storage crates weighed nothing, and hefted the man in one hand and discarded him like a child might a doll. I have not inquired after the man's condition, for my own sanity perhaps, but am quite certain that if he somehow survived, he will never be the same. It is not easy to see in England that which one had become accustomed to on battlefields in France. One of the others surrendered straight away, while his fellow fled up the stairs.

Unable to follow directly, Coltrane lost some time in returning out the hole in the wall the giant had created and climbing the remains of the building. My courage bolstered by such reinforcement, or perhaps my curiosity getting the better part of my sense, I left the awestruck and huddled men in my company and raced up the stairs.

There I found that the remains of the company of brigands had found the means to ascend to the airship, and were engaged with the crew of that ship. They had secured the ladder and pulled it up, and it seemed for one heartbreaking moment it would be entirely up to the brave but likely surprised crew and a few engineers to protect one of England's military vessels and the secrets of flight with it.

This was not to be, however. For though he appeared thwarted, the metal monster pointed an arm skyward. There was a crack like thunder and a small flash of light from a barrel along one arm of Coltrane's creation. Something exploded above us, and two fellows I recognized from their garb as being among the would-be thieves fell from the dirigible. Unable to draw another safe line of fire, Coltrane crouched down. From the legs of the suit there were sudden rushes of steam and sparks, and a metallic groan as springs uncoiled. With these combined forces, the giant of iron and brass was launched upward, arcing over the side of the dirigible.

I saw no more, save for two more falling bodies, and a third which did not so much fall as travel some distance straight away from the ship before gravity overcame him, screaming all the while. Regardless, I am certain you heard some account of these events, likely in the headlines which always accompany Sir James's exploits. Even with the war behind us, he has again stepped in to protect those secrets that proved so decisive during the conflict, and which remain ours alone.

Needless to say, I did not have occasion to speak with Sir James Coltrane that evening beyond a few words to the suit. Words he apparently heard, for a deep and echoing voice responded that he had been told of our presence, but was busy that evening – clearly. And myself and my companion should attend him in better surroundings, perhaps for tea the following day at his country home. The rest of the evening I spent somewhere between shock and giving my account of events over and over again.

By the time I returned to our temporary lodging, Mr. Toomes had tracked down the fellow who had been given bribe enough to betray his homeland. He had granted the saboteurs access to a room where they could make their plans, while watching the depot and its officers. This also allowed them to establish themselves among the locals. How Mr. Toomes managed to bring the man in, I remain uncertain, though likely simply notifying the authorities and informing them who he worked for was enough to establish him as good to his word. I can only hope that the traitor is dealt with in a matter befitting the murderer of those two brave young men and who knows how many others.

I am quite certain, Lord Donovan, that I will write you again to report success in recruiting Sir James Coltrane to our mission, and now having seen him and his wondrous creation in action, I am quite excited at the notion that he, and it, should be providing security for this trip. Surely a good omen of success, and a guarantee that the best wishes of England go with us.

Yours,
Gregory Conan Watts

From the journals of Gregory Conan Watts,
February 17th, 1815
----shire, Southern England

I am unsure to whom this information should be reported, but feel I must document my early experiences. Besides, I have had such extraordinary experiences today as to make me feel that I must record my thoughts to bring them to perspective and have a clear head for tomorrow. It promises to be a most unusual day.

The morning was spent as every other one in recent memory. Breakfast at an inn of sufficient quality as to not embarrass those funding our expeditions and show their esteem for our mission. A simple affair, particularly for my companion, who insists on nothing more than strong tea and a biscuit with jam to sustain him until a more substantial lunch. I can little question how he became so rail thin now when he eats like this, and with so little flavor or variation, but as I learned whilst on the front of the war, a soldier cannot be overly picky about what he is provided, and often goes many months without any change in the menu afforded him. It seems that Mr. Toomes, for good or ill, has never escaped whatever service he so dedicated himself to, and continues to treat himself as if he were on such a front.

Personally, I am quite happy to have escaped that aspect of the service, for while many of my experiences were quite amazing, including whom I served with, I find myself loath to forgo sausages and fresh eggs when they are available. Of course, when he has finished his coffee and biscuit, as I have but begun to consume my morning meal, he brings out one of his pipes and finds amidst his pockets and pouches some mix of tobacco and herbage to suit him.

We spent the first portion of the day in travel, heading towards the country home of Sir James Coltrane, knowing we dared not be late for such a prestigious invitation as this. I found myself disposed to flutters in my stomach a number of times. After all, soon I was to meet not only the man who many said would nearly deliver England to victory alone, but also the pilot of that monstrous wonder of artifice I had the fortune of observing in action only the night before.

We were delayed some bit by the local constabulary, asking us questions regarding those of the saboteurs whom were captured rather than killed, our testimony duly recorded. Indeed, they initially requested we report as witnesses, but Mr. Toomes had a few words with the officers, giving his credentials and assuring them that we were on a mission which could not be delayed. It was agreed that our sworn information would be sufficient, as there was little question as to their guilt. Given that our nation was recently engaged in a war with much of the European continent, it is little wonder that the law is not kind to foreigners suspected of sabotage.

And so we were off, this time in a carriage drawn by four horses, that we could make a proper impression upon our entrance to the Coltrane estate. I have certainly traveled in this fashion before, but most often it was little more than a rough wooden box with similarly rough seating, and the rider quickly grows sore enough as to almost volunteer to put in the extra days so that he could be allowed to walk instead. This carriage was luxury by comparison. I almost found myself drifting off into a post-breakfast sleep a time or two amidst the cushioned ride, with only the occasional jarring motion from the uneven roads waking me.

Certainly Mr. Toomes's conversation did nothing to discourage slumber. I have learned that he can make quite the impression through speech and stern glance when he feels the need, such as when speaking to the local authorities, but he seems almost bored by having to go to the effort of being social when he is not at important business. I think we would both prefer it if we did not need to make these extensive trips, that he could move from one business dealing of import to another, and I would not need to suffer these long stretches of what seems to me the same conversation, though he seems assured that discussing the clays on the banks of one region of France are quite entirely a different subject that the clays to be found on the banks of another, and they seem to him to produce a miraculously different smoking experience.

And so it only moved to highlight all the more when I moved from that most mundane of circumstance to the true events of the day. We arrived at the Coltrane country estate some two hours past the village where we stopped to take in the early afternoon meal, just in time for ideal visiting hours. The houses and lawns are almost precisely what one would expect, if one can ever call the splendor that is the new English elite's homes and lands as anything but breathtaking. If anything was surprising, it was that there seemed to be almost no servants about, save those absolutely necessary to the running of the home.

Once inside the home, and seated comfortably, we were brought tea. Soon after our tea was served, we were introduced to the first of the trio who would join us for much of the afternoon, and she was quite the sight. Indeed, she was notable for the contrast she made with everything else in the well-appointed room, for she was a subtle horror of sorts. She was pretty enough for a woman of the middle classes, but definitely not the willowy beauty so many women of station in these times aspire to be. She was fair-complected, with light brown hair. Broad-shouldered and wide-hipped, she defied her seamstress' every attempt to form her into a more fae beauty, but at the least she had a very distinct hourglass figure – generous of both hip and chest, if I may be so bold as to comment on such base observations.

She was dressed as a lady might be for receiving visitors, a fine visiting dress, but notable for being of unusually dark colors. The most peculiarly dark coloration was reserved, however, for first the hem of her dress, which appeared much as the dips of a broom used to sweep up dust. I have seen small girls, still sometimes given to running about in the dirt when told not to so soil their fine dresses such, but never a girl in her later teens such as this woman. Most odd indeed. Stranger still were her fingertips, which were that very distinct blackish blue as only ink stains leave upon the hands. And contrasting the shades of her dress, her house slippers entirely did not match. I am no expert in fashion, but even I could not help but notice that the shades were not intended to go together.

She greeted us in a most distinct accent. I learned from some of the soldiers that it is an American dialect, though I have not yet met enough of the colonists as to be able to easily distinguish between Virginian, the Carolinas or Georgian, though I am certain to a more trained listener they are as distinct as the modes of speech when listening to a Londoner versus a man from the country. She had the faintest tinge of proper English in her speech, as if she had spent not inconsiderable time with the locals, but was quite some way from getting rid of her regional touches in her speech. It was most odd to hear her offering the traditional greetings and welcomes and introductions in so quaint a speech, quite out of place, but clearly she was trying hard. This marvel of conflicting elements and small oddities, I learned, was named Harriet Wright, apparently a cousin of the Coltranes who had come into their service as Jillian Coltrane's lady's companion.

It was a bare few minutes at most past meeting Harriet Wright that the lady of the house herself appeared. Jillian Coltrane, James's younger sister, has ably managed his affairs and household since the tragic deaths of their parents some time past. As his fame and resulting fortune grew, she no doubt had a considerable task just keeping up with those asking after commentary from her heroic brother, not to mention the many young ladies who have had their eye upon this most eligible of bachelors.

Despite what must have been a busy schedule, she seemed to bear it all well, and looked nothing at all like her cousin. Miss Coltrane, indeed, was a mostly lovely woman. Slight and willowy, with the grace and elegance of someone obviously used to the highest of social occasions. That impression was echoed by the pale complexion of someone used to the indoors, while her hair was also light – a blonde with some darker hints, but still several shades lighter than her brunette cousin. In many ways, she reminded me very much of a doll. A bit fragile, but lovely in a way that was almost too perfect, with every hair in place and every move just so. The other detail which struck me as unusual quite quickly was that whatever perfumes she used had a rather stronger hint of the scent of lemon than I have ever previously encountered. I most assuredly did not comment on this, and, indeed, took quite some time before finding my voice. In the meanwhile, I was privy to a most unusual exchange.

Mr. Toomes initially looked upon her with the same expression I have grown so used to, with slightly pinched features and a gaze all ready to disapprove. His encounter with Harriet to that point had, perhaps, prepared him to expect the Coltranes to have picked up some bad habits, or show some fault in their hospitality. His ear perked at her entrance, and he greeted her with suitable decorum, but no warmth in his tone. She seemed oblivious to his bordering on the edge of impoliteness, showing a great deal of decorum and trained manners in every response. Her tone was crisp and civil, though I might not call it precisely warm. For the next several seconds, while observing manners above reproach, but no hint of welcome, the two verbally fenced with one another. I have grown used enough to Mr. Toomes to be somewhat certain he was seeking some flaw in her manners or responses, as if trying to gain some victory or upper hand. I am not certain what he hoped to gain, aside from being the sort of person used to certain elevated circles, with all of the accompanying games of one-upsmanship.

After a few rounds of this odd sort of game, it seemed to be Mr. Toomes who ended up at a loss. By the time she had taken her seat, assuring us that her brother would be joining us shortly, I saw something in Mr. Toomes which I had not yet witnessed – a hint of genuine surprise. His typical squint was lost, and there was no hint of sneer or scowl to be found. Whether intended or not, his stiff and very military demeanor shifted, bit by bit, to that of a gentleman used to attending the officers and Lords of the nation's highest social clubs. Any hints of the disapproval he expressed from the first impressions upon meeting Harriet had disappeared. Indeed, Harriet herself almost seemed to disappear at times now that her cousin had arrived and taken up much of the talking.

I was also struck, after a while, with the fact that he did not light a pipe at first opportunity. I suppose I shouldn't have been surprised, as doing so would have been impolite in these surroundings, but I have grown so accustomed to the habit. In time, the scent of lemon was even strong enough to cut through that of tobacco. Once the general mood relaxed, while remaining entirely ladylike, she somehow shifted the topic to asking after Mr. Toomes's business. He seemed a bit taken aback at first, but also found himself answering her as many others have found themselves answering to him. She explained that she had become rather well versed in handling her brother's affairs, and demonstrated this familiarity by speaking fluently on matters of politics and the concerns of post-war England in general.

This conversation had not gotten terribly far when, true to her earlier promise, Sir James himself attended us. I will here admit what I would not outside of my private writings – upon seeing that metal monster, I had imagined that the legendary war hero must be some sort of gnome of a man, small and compact, or perhaps spindly. That he had come to build the thing because he was otherwise unfit to serve, and thus turned his fine Oxford education towards finding a means by which to contribute to the war effort. My imaginings could not be further from the truth, for though he was shorter than I by a few inches, and only an inch or two taller than his sister, he was otherwise the very image of the dashing war hero painted by the stories of him. Muscular and fit, with a broad chest and flat stomach, and the same fair and refined features his sister possessed.

Indeed, looking upon the pair, they could be nothing but brother and sister, for their complexion is the same, the same refinements, and even their voices carried a similar lilt and pacing, though his, of course, had a deeper timbre. Where her voice was musical, however, his own commanding tone was insistent, and he could not be mistaken for anything but a man used to being listened to. Likewise, his small observations and greetings were given a certain gravity that is usually absent from the routine pleasantries of first meeting someone. If he was not, in fact, quite pleased to see us, I could not imagine it, for he seemed quite interested in everything we might have to say to him.

Despite this interest, he made it clear he would brook no imperiousness from Mr. Toomes, despite their shared military backgrounds and Toomes's superior age and experience. I have seen such exchanges many times when working among soldiers, where you can quickly tell those officers who serve through merit, courage, hard work, and the respect of their men, and those who inherited their station through no merit inherent to them beyond fortune of birth. And though both are considerable men, Sir James quickly set the pace for the meeting, would not be hurried or pressed by Mr. Toomes, and thought nothing of the intensity of my companion's gaze. By some few sentences in, meanwhile, I felt almost as invisible as Harriet had become amongst the company of her cousins. This fact eventually turned my reporter's mind from the enthralling conversation to the details of my companion in mundanity. Harriet seemed to be quite intent on watching Miss Coltrane directly, and quietly attempted to ape her seated posture, her composure, her every minute gesture, in much the fashion as I have observed young girls copying their sisters and mothers in the road to becoming proper ladies.

And in noting this attention to minute detail, I found a most peculiar thing. As they spoke, James and Jillian were exchanging the most subtle of glances. She was continually shifting her grip on her fan in the smallest ways, shifting her eyes more than seemed entirely necessary for attention to guests. Had I not been noticing Harriet trying to perfectly copy every motion of Jillian's, I would never have noticed, but it became quite clear that while Sir James was driving the conversation and no doubt would make the final decision, he was seeking input and approval from his sister, and taking her perspective into account. I quite quickly came to respect the obvious intelligence behind the woman that so distinguished a man as her brother would value her opinion, and the time it had clearly taken the pair to establish so subtle a language between them, while wondering just how complex this language shared by the siblings was, and how much of a message they could truly pass from one to the other through it. While I had come in marveling at the man and his obvious heroism, intelligence and contribution to the war effort, now I saw that his keen intellect must be common to their family.

Whatever exchanges they had between them, and however reserved they were about keeping their true thoughts to themselves, I got the distinct impression that they were most intrigued by the details of the mission being offered. Sir James asked many questions concerning where we were bound, and exactly to what purposes and what size of crew and passengers were being recruited for this venture. He seemed quite concerned that the airship he had taken so long to have custom-fitted for his needs when piloting the Coltrane battle suit, for such he called it, would be ruined by trying to crowd too many persons aboard. When Mr. Toomes assured him that there was only to be a small, hand-picked crew of myself, the Coltranes and Harriet, and a total of four others, and Sir James would be permitted to retain whatever pilot and engineering crew he wished, he seemed considerably comforted.

While keenly interested in everything we had to say about the venture, three topics seemed of particular interest to the Coltranes. The American West has been a topic of much interest to many in the halls of power. Now that France no longer contends so heavily with us for control over the eastern regions, many wonder what sort of resources and territory may lay west of the Mississippi. I understand that, before the war, some talk was put forth about trying to map the Colonial West, but such talk was shelved when England asked for help and men from our colonial holdings.

Secondly, Africa is a matter of great curiosity among the gentlemen of the Royal Explorers society. Trade goes on between those of the African coasts and Europe, aside from just the slave trade to those places that still traffic in slavery, including parts of the American Colonial South. But beyond the coasts, the only European who has even claimed knowledge of what exists beyond the few cities we have mapped is Dr. Bowe, as described in his extensive journals regarding this vast and mysterious land. Even if one were to believe Dr. Bowe's far-fetched tales, that we could be the first to explore large stretches of Africa, and the first to include photographic evidence of what lies there quite intrigued our hosts.

Finally, though all the details were still being negotiated with the Dutch, news that our mission might take us into some amount of limited contact with the closed nation of Japan especially took hold of Sir James's interest. Mr. Toomes could not miss the obvious look of enthusiasm in Sir James's gaze when the Orient was even mentioned in passing, and took pains to give Sir James as many details as he could on what dealings we might have there. Dr. Bowe's journals detail some amount of contact with the Japanese, though there is no record of anyone aside from the Dutch having had any diplomatic relations with the Japanese people for many decades. Because of their closed borders, this is one of the sections of Dr. Bowe's journals which draw the most skepticism. Apparently, however, some high official within Japan has expressed curiosity to their Dutch trading partners regarding English technology, which may have opened the door to some very limited contact during our mission Because the English liberated the Dutch from French occupation during the war the Dutch traders are currently disposed to doing us what diplomatic favors they can. Negotiations are apparently fraught with difficulties, but discussions were ongoing, and nothing else seemed to so excite Sir James as the possibility of seeing Japan for himself.

Eventually, I did voice my own thoughts on our likelihood of success. Which was to say that while I was certain Dr. Bowe had some knowledge of exploration, and had possibly done a fair amount of travel, no one could have possibly done all of the things the doctor had claimed to. Charting the American West, finding ancient lost cities in South America, charting the vast reaches of Africa, crossing the Blue Mountains of Australia and crossing the inland – in addition to crossing Europe and India, finding numerous islands, exploring the waterways of the American colonial North, scaling numerous other mountains, crossing innumerable waterways – it was impossible any man could have done it all in a lifetime, even with a dirigible, much less without one.

At this insistence, Sir James came especially alive. He did not seem displeased with me in the least, but clearly relished holding an opposing view. His belief was not so much that Dr. Bowe's accounts must certainly be factual so much as he held the absolute view that very little was impossible for a sufficiently determined and resourceful man, and he quite hoped that Dr. Bowe was one such man.

In this hope and point of view, Sir James appears to be the very picture of the modern gentleman after the war. So many who risked their lives on the mainland, then returned home, soon found that there was no challenge in day-to-day life. So those of means quickly found other risk and challenge. For many, it was their pounds and pence they put on the line instead of their lives. While before he had seemed to have a casual interest in our venture, now Sir James was suddenly quite animated, and insistent that we must venture forth.

It was as if by daring to state that Dr. Bowe's work was fiction (a matter which, under other circumstances I am certain he cannot but have agreed with, for any other thought is nonsensical) I had personally given him a challenge to put his life on the line to prove otherwise. It was too great an opportunity to not take up, and through sheer force of will, he would alter time and the world to ensure that Dr. Bowe the fiction writer had indeed not wasted time printing imaginative books and instead had turned three or four lifetimes towards exploring the globe.

It was a most remarkable turn of character and spirit to our discussion. To that point, Mr. Toomes had seemed to me to be growing somewhat frustrated with trying to get a commitment or even rise out of those he'd been sent to recruit. He looked upon me with considerable astonishment, and maybe, just maybe, a small hint of relief. With further assurance about Sir James's control of his dirigible and leadership of the expedition, it was agreed, and so that possibility of this journey, which had seemed little more than a fantastic thought inspired by a perhaps slightly inebriated bet, would now become quite real. At the time I was relieved. Now, with time and opportunity to put my thoughts to page, I find that this reality is fast making me quite nervous. But it is for the hand of fair Cordelia, and thus I shall not waver.

February 18th, 1815
Coltrane Estate

Dear Sir,

    I only just realized that in my descriptions of other people and places, I entirely neglected to consider that you might have some readership which would be curious as to who I am. I would not have thought of such a mundane detail, had not I been reminded of just this by Sir James Coltrane. For where Mr. Toomes has filled our long hours of travel with pipe smoke and his occasional snort or harrumph of disapproval, Sir James instead insists upon filling the time and travel with conversation. He has a keener mind than I could have imagined for such details, continually surprising me. I had thought that the distinguished Oxford graduate and inventor must surely be preoccupied with math and chemistry such as is beyond my limited understandings of these subjects, but he seems to much prefer to share war stories. And for each one he agrees to tell, with far greater color and detail than was ever provided by even the tallest tales of his deeds, and with the most gripping pacing and tone, he insists that I recollect one of my own experiences. Of these, I did have several, first as a young soldier before my literacy and memory for detail was exposed, whereupon I received a prompt promotion to company clerk, and then to aide de camp and occasional messenger, until at last I had somehow found myself given the unofficial station of documenting the war.

    A reporter for one of London's newspapers had been sent to speak to the general at a critical time, as a showdown with the forces of Napoleon himself loomed large on the horizon. By whatever ill fortune visits the people who are put to such cramped conditions as the front, he quickly became ill, and passed on without so much as a word sent home. He had a new device with him based upon the studies of camera technology. Apparently his company had purchased it at tremendous cost, and felt it a worthwhile investment to have the image of our victorious troops posted accurately to their front pages. While at first loath to even dare touch something worth far more than my own life ten times over, I believed I had come to understand how it worked in my conversations with the man at his arrival and on what passed for a poor sickbed. And in learning that I had gained my station by the fortunes of literacy and capability rather than station in life, the dying fool entrusted me with his camera, a mobile, but heavy box which could be made to reproduce any image which it had view of with touch of a button, a few flipped switches, and access to but a small bit of coal to power the secondary box[4] where I was told it subjected specialty paper to various chemicals which would allow the image it took in to be printed upon the page.

The newspaper sent contact eventually, a man who seemed quite amazed at the images I'd produced with this invention, and they offered me a supplement to my war income in order to continue to use this wondrous device and put words to the images it produced. And through this succession of small miracles, I came into possession of the camera and the station of war reporter alongside my duties as an aide to some of our highest officers. While I tried desperately to return the camera upon my return, not wanting to be responsible for a device of such value, as I could surely never replace it, instead they insisted that I keep it and signed me on to continue to work for them should work worthy of my record arise. Before this mission, it had not, owing to most people being more interested in the society pages and gambling, neither my expertise.

Beyond this unusual turn of events, I am otherwise an ordinary man by most accounts. I was born into unfortunate circumstance, the 'poor Irish cousin' due to unfortunate intermarriage. When my mother fell to consumption, I was adopted by relatives with some title and land but limited resources, the very definition of outcasts to the high ends of society, with the background such they could not be entirely

---

4 This is recognizable as the predecessor to the modern, crank-powered camera carried by reporters and photographic enthusiasts. As you will have noted from Gregory's known pictures, his only used a single lens, since stereographic cameras were not common until 1843 in London, and not portable until 1847. – C B-W.

excluded from consideration, but having squandered most of their connection and goodwill to time or ill luck or frivolous spending. Such families as these dot both the country and city, hanging on wherever they can.

However, the one place where they have some esteem is with the new money, such as was the case with Captain Bentham. A career navy man, his tactical brilliance and capability had led to him turning in multiple captured enemy ships for salvage and refitting, making him quite a considerable sum. However, having come from more common roots, long on courage and military tradition but short on coin, they had no particular prestige or title to call on to afford them better accommodation. Thus it was that I, the ward of my family with prestige of one sort, came into contact with Cordelia Bentham, whose family had much that mine did not, but needed connection and people of proper station to invite to dinner. The two of us grew up together, though my poor Cordelia was always a frail child and oftentimes was kept to her bedroom while she recovered from one childhood malady after another. Despite this, she was both my best friend as a small child, and when I became aware of such things, we made a compact on some romantic whim as are given to young girls that one day we should marry. Indeed, the older I grew, the more I was certain I desired nothing else.

However, when I broached such a topic, her father would have none of it. Not that he objected to me as a person – indeed, he has often purported to being quite fond of me, more so than the empty-headed dandies who have never had to work a proper day in their lives and only wanted his daughter's money, not his daughter. However, he was quite insistent that his daughter, only child, and only one he would have following the tragic death of his beloved wife when Cordelia was quite small, would not ever fall into hard circumstance with relatives asking and begging after pieces of her dowry to satisfy their debts. As such I would have to prove I could provide for her in the manner to which she was accustomed and earn such prestige as I could stand on my own as a man of good repute, for he would not have her slandered with my being nothing but cousin to someone who long ago had important relatives. I have no wish to try to rejoin the army and climb its ranks, even if its ranks were not currently swollen beyond need. Thus it is that I find myself so enamored of the bet placed before me, for while I have some acclaim in small circles due to my skills as a photographer and writer of things related to war, the past war is not enough, and I understand there are more of these cameras being made, and they will come into the hands of those more accustomed to photographing racehorses and flowers than I.

To fill in more concrete detail, for those few who might care, in build I am tall, and reasonably fit enough to have been sent to the front, but never a champion athlete. Despite the assurances of my stockier relatives, I never quite grew into my height, no matter how much I ate, my frame insistent on being simply tall, but at least I did outgrow the awkwardness of youth that seemed to cling to me some time past what is generally considered youth, proper. I have ruddy brown hair, and have tried several times to grow beard or mustache to try to help give my face some appearance of breadth, but they are consistently too stringy and faint to achieve this aim, so I go clean shaven. My ears are rather too prominent, another favorite target of childhood bullies looking for something to mock, but apparently their size has come with being sharp enough that I became well known on the front, eventually, for never missing a word. There was some teasing as well, as is so common among fellows put under difficult circumstance together, but it was always good-natured. Indeed, since reaching some semblance of adulthood, enough to join our armies, I have often been called one of the most agreeable fellows those of my acquaintance has met. Never much of a fighter, and only a passable shot, I found it easier, when combined with some degree of education and an intense interest in the spoken word, accompanied by a fair memory for detail, in finding other means to settle my disputes. I fear that I did disappoint those who first tried to make a soldier of me, for I am poor material for soldiering, though they seemed to let me pass when they discovered it was some instinct and capacity for aggression that was missing, and not will, courage or determination, for those I have in occasionally too much excess. Particularly so when my curiosity gets the better of me.

While I am certain if questioned, I would have more to say, in general, I am a normal young man who has been put to extraordinary circumstance, rather than anything unusual in my own right. I do hope that I am up to the task put before me, however, for the only thing which truly matters to me now – and for which I have already quite willingly risked my life – still lies ahead of me, and depends upon making something of myself, as this trip is certain to do.

Hereafter, I shall attempt to be a better narrator for the tale to be told, and keep as much of myself from my text as I reasonably may, but felt that some might have some curiosity as to the chronicler of events. I thank you for your patience in this regard.

Yours,
Gregory Conan Watts

February 19th, 1815
Coltrane Estate

My Dearest Cordelia,

Even in the early days of the war, when I was sent across the waters into France with the infantry, I have never felt so far from you as I do today. Unable to acceptably communicate with you further until I am suitable to propose to you with your father's approval, I will continue to pen these notes in hopes that something will arise, and you might have some understanding of the undertakings of this quest I have agreed to that you and I might be together. Previous to today, even when leaving the country, I had Britain close to my heart, for I left our shores as a soldier in our armies, even if I did not leave the service in quite that intended role, as you well know. This time, while still an Englishman, I go out for my own gain and reputation, and leave the shores on that personal crusade, and inspired not by national pride, but by a wager between gentlemen of wealth and station.

I have previously given you some of the particulars of the details of the wager, so I will trouble you no further with it. However, I thought you might be curious to know some of the details of my most unusual hosts. I have had the unique opportunity to stay a few days with one of England's most fabled sons, Sir James Coltrane. He lives here with his sister and their cousin. They have been far better company, I assure you, than Mr. Toomes.

Sir James is everything the stories have claimed of him. Though he is not quite so tall as I am, he is more sturdily built. Very much the dashing, picturesque individual the newspapers describe. I am including a photograph he was kind enough to pose for, though I can only hope that in receiving it, you do not forget about me entirely. Though well educated and conversant on many subjects, he takes time especially to talk of our shared experience, the Napoleonic Wars. Though he has more tales in all, and certainly more gripping ones than my own, he has insisted that for each story of his exploits he agrees to share, I must tell a story of my own or he will not continue. He has likewise engaged Mr. Toomes in a similar arrangement, and seems quite interested in Toomes's stories of his own service during the Colonial conflicts of the late 1700s.

Sir James also has quite a fascination with card games. Each evening, when supper is past, he retires to his study with the other men about to play at cards, drink and share stories. Notably, while this includes Mr. Toomes and myself, Sir James does not restrict these gatherings to gentlemen. Each evening, there are at least a couple of servants about. The Coltranes do not have many servants, but those they do have seem extremely fond of their employers. Given this unusual treatment, I can see why. Many are of somewhat rough character and uneducated backgrounds, but at least over card games, Sir James speaks to them less as his servants, and more as men about a game. I have also noticed that despite his fondness for these games, Sir James is either not very good at the games, or has terrible luck, for he seems every night to leave the table with a few less coins than he arrived with. A habit which also has further endeared him to his men, and left me with a couple shillings more than I first arrived with. Sir James's humor is never at all lessened by his losing streaks, being far more intent upon the exchange of stories, even the mundane ones of his workers, and the goodwill he can generate among them.

Miss Jillian Coltrane is an impressive woman in her own right. Though she is often out of sight, when I have encountered her, she has always been the epitome of grace and manners. She is most often attended by her cousin and lady's companion, Miss Harriet Wright. The pair make for quite the contrast, though they are obviously quite fond of one another. Miss Coltrane clearly has a knack for saying and doing the right thing, so much so that everyone but her brother seems to me to be somewhat rough and uncultured by comparison. Her cousin suffers more than most. It has become clear that Miss Wright very much would like to be just like her cousin, and if effort alone were enough to make a fine young woman, she would be one of the finest. Sadly, she has a knack for missing cues, trailing her sleeves through butter or jam at the table, mismatching clothing – particularly shoes – and so on.

Worse, the more minor mistakes she makes, any one of them easily overlooked, the more tense and prone to misstep she becomes. At the very least, she is genuinely friendly, and I have enjoyed speaking with her when we've had the opportunity. Likewise, in some ways, it's a comfort to have someone even more ill at ease with these surroundings than myself, even if I cannot help but feel for her. I have also included a picture of Miss Coltrane and Miss Wright with this letter.

The Coltranes keep the oddest schedule. They seemed at first hesitant to offer us hospitality, but beyond this brief hesitation, they have been most gracious hosts. Behind their primary home, they have a reinforced structure Sir James calls the workshop. Doubtless where he built, and now maintains his wondrous mechanical suit. I do not know how Sir James maintains his schedule. No matter how late into the evening we play cards, shortly after we are abed, a racket rises from the workshop, and great billows of steam can be seen rising from open windows and under the doorways. Red and blue light emits inconsistently from within, and the sound of metal scraping on metal continues throughout much of the night. I can but imagine he has been setting himself to repairing the damage sustained during his already famed battle not long past with the criminals trying to steal the dirigible.

Despite this, he is always already awake and at breakfast when we rise, even at the hours at which Mr. Toomes has accustomed me to rising. Even if Mr. Toomes himself insists on limiting himself to strong tea and his customary biscuit, for everyone else, much to my pleasure, breakfast around here is always a hearty meal. Sir James is not so talkative over breakfast as he becomes late in the evening, but he continues to press for details, and each morning, shows signs of having read some further piece of Dr. Bowe's journals or the instructions our employer sent with us, and questions Mr. Toomes about the new information at length while we eat. After breakfast, he and his sister both retire to the library. The doors are open to anyone, but the two of them keep to a strict schedule which includes time in the day for reading, and particularly for correspondence. I have come to learn that Jillian, in particular, is a woman of letters who corresponds with women of station in our own country, among the Dutch, and with other well educated ladies as far away as the Colonies and India.

While we have been waiting here, I also have learned precisely what it is that we are now waiting on. Apparently, now that we have gained Sir James's certain assistance, arrangements are in progress to send myself and Mr. Toomes to Scotland to recruit another war hero, the rifleman Edward McBride. Sir James has given me a letter to pass to Mr. McBride, for apparently the two are somewhat acquainted with one another.

I will write more as I have occasion, for surely if this past day has been any indication, there will be a great deal more worthy of note in the times ahead, even before our true adventure begins.

Love,
Gregory Conan Watts

From the diaries of Jillian Coltrane (Translated from Greek)
February 24th, 1815

James, I know you shared some of my misgivings regarding this mission, though it is almost precisely the sort of opportunity we have been hoping for. I assure you that I am making some discreet inquiries into Elliott Toomes, per your request. His name is not entirely unknown to me, and my limited research with the resources present here within the house indicates that he served with distinction during the Colonial conflict, and was not unknown to our father. Likewise, he has some presence in the Royal Explorers Society. Although all seems in order, he is quite difficult to read. I certainly did not care for the way he was looking at me and was grateful for at least the efficiency of lemon juice and the distraction of Harriet. I do not trust him, nor should you, though I believe that was abundantly clear. Pray, entertain him with drink and cards and see what more he might let slip in less guarded moments in the coming days.

Mr. Watts is entirely what he seems. I know you are passingly familiar with his work from his writings during the war. I have found numerous of his articles, and verification of his story regarding how he came into possession of the camera device. If there is something more to this offer than it first appears, I do not believe he is any more a party to it than we ourselves.

Whatever my concerns, I still believe this venture into the unknown is well worth it. Only a short time returned from the war, and already I have begun to find the court scene tedious. This should also allow me to further delay our search for suitable candidates for marriage a time longer. I will continue to keep in touch with numerous hopeful mothers, of course, in case something should catch your fancy.

The funding for the venture is secure, and I have already seen to making sure that our former staff are all available to continue in our service aboard the airship. I am certain the Fishers will resume their excellent works, and at least most of the engineering crew should still be available. Given how much we were forced to retrofit the dirigible to suit our needs, I would be loath to bring anyone new in now. I will be sure to let you know if there are any difficulties, though to be certain, you may want to pay some of the crew personal visits and make certain they know that their loyalty, and, of course, their discretion, will be well rewarded.

The other names on the list Mr. Toomes presented us with are still unknowns, but I am doing what research I may while we have all the resources of our library and files at my disposal. I will let you know what I find out. In the meanwhile, as you are better able to travel in society circles without need for extraordinary circumstances, I strongly recommend you make some inquiries of your own into Giovanni Franzini. That we are asked to work with a European seems odd, though Mr. Toomes assures me that he has connections and friends in places few Englishmen would, and such we may need. This may be the case, but if I do not trust Mr. Toomes, I am certainly not going to trust anyone else on his say so alone.

When all the research is done, be certain to pack well for the trip, and add a handful of concealed weapons to our list of supplies. If we are going to travel with so many unknowns with so many of our secrets close at hand, best we be prepared for any eventuality. Despite these cautions, I am quite excited to be involved. I remain entirely unready for our shared adventure to end just yet.

From the journals of Gregory Conan Watts,
February 28th, 1815
---- Base, Scotland

The trip to Scotland was more uneventful than the days in England proper, a fact for which I am grateful to the degree that my life has not been further threatened, and the countryside has its quaint charm. Therein lies the extent of my gratitude, for my companion, lacking saboteurs or war heroes of legendary status in their own time to inspire him otherwise, has been quite cross and eager to make up for the loss of face he seems to imagine he suffered when he could find no unkind word to offer Miss Jillian Coltrane. Just as savage beasts despise any sign of weakness, that I dared witness him in a moment of near neutrality, he has badgered me no end with small facts and geography concerning his sole habit of any interest. And when he is not speaking of quality smokes, he is most often splitting his attention between smoking determinedly and glaring.

While I am not certain what else might be my fault, and thus worthy of such sinister scrutiny, I am quite certain that he feels that I somehow did some portion of the job entrusted to him when my interjection into his conversation with Sir James did more for the recruitment effort than his entreaties and offers of fame and money. Indeed, it was quite unintended at the time, but it makes a certain sense to me now, that a soldier who has already achieved great fame and possessed considerable wealth and station before the war, and more after it, would relish a challenge far more than he would simply more coin to count. That succeeding at a challenge would add to his reputation may or may not have meant anything to him. I had hoped in the aftermath that Mr. Toomes would simply hold success as its own reward, and be relieved we had successfully recruited the help and resource needed for the effort on behalf of our mutual patron, but it was not to be.

I can be grateful for Mr. Toomes to one extent. My sense of smell, always reasonably precise, seems to have become extremely well attuned by its reluctant exposure to countless forms of pipe smoke. Just as I found our saboteurs purely by a distinctive variety, the long hours in an enclosed space with that military gentleman and his pipe made me certain to appreciate every scent in the Scottish air when we were released from our carriage. Inquiries with some of the locals acquainted me with at least five types of flowers, which I was able to tell apart and find by scent, and I was never so grateful for the aroma of grass and sheep as when first freed from our travel accommodations. That we were getting out at what had once been a hunting lodge and had been converted into a small military base for the mustering of troops from Scotland had no bearing on this. The Coltrane estate was pure luxury. The inns we had stayed at along the way since, in those couple times the train had needed to stop for the night for resupply and cooling had been no comparison, but were at least comfortable. The converted base, on the other hand, had plenty of bunks, and very little else to offer.

Now this place was largely serving like most of the post-war military infrastructure: there until someone found a better use for it. There were many troops still serving out their time, maintaining equipment, patrolling the extensive countryside for signs of foreigners, and converting resources back to the countryside. The last is especially slow in the case of those families who had lost their young men. The English government certainly feels a considerable debt of gratitude to these young and brave men. Despite that feeling of debt, many were lost in a very short time. Additionally, with the agreement to allow Catholics to serve, and the additions of large number of Irishmen, Scotsmen, and Americans, exactly how that debt would be paid and what may be owed to who remains occasionally hazy.

Upon our arrival, we learned that Mr. McBride was not on the premises, but out on one of the foot patrols, which he volunteered for as often as allowed. In the meantime, we were given serviceable but uncomfortable bunks with what privacy we could be permitted and would be allowed a meeting with him upon his return. During the while, I found myself inquiring of his fellows as to what sort of man Mr. McBride was. I admit, as I have before, that Sir James surprised me repeatedly in our meetings, shattering my illusions as to what he looked like, and proving every inch the dashing young hero he was purported to be. I have learned that such stories are most often exaggerated. And this time, I wished to be better prepared where it concerned Mr. McBride.

The first thing I quickly learned was that no one in his acquaintance for long was permitted to call him Mr. McBride outside of business dealings. And you could quite quickly tell if he had taken a liking to you or not. If he did not, and you had no business with him, then he would dismiss any man regardless of name or station, for which he had suffered a handful of reprimands, and weathered them without changing a whit. It seemed he did not suffer fools lightly, and considered many men to be fools. If he did not take a liking to you, but your business was legitimate, then Mr. McBride would do fine, and you might well think him simply efficient, for with such people, the stories said he was quite terse, set to getting his business finished quickly so he could move on to other pursuits. It had taken some time, but apparently the officers now in charge of this locale's post-war days had finally convinced him that they fell into this category. I can scarce imagine a soldier ever insisting such formality out of a superior officer, but apparently he was a special case. Indeed, the words special case, in reference to Mr. McBride, have arisen many times, so much so that I wonder if there is not some meaning I am missing. Regardless, there is a final category that he puts people into, which includes most of the men with whom he has served, every man in this company who has given a hand, leg or eye in their country's service, and some few people they say are lucky enough to find what sense of humor he has. And if you are one of those, you will know it, as no matter who that man is, he will tell him the same thing, and from then on will brook no other means of addressing him. Specifically, apparently, you know that you are, at least temporarily on the man's good side should he ask you to, and I again quote many references saying this precisely, "Call me Eddy."

Aside from this peculiarity, Mr. McBride came from

ordinary enough circumstance.[5] He was the son of the keeper of a hunting lodge, as this place once was. He grew up a lad accustomed to rich men of station, but not one of them. The McBrides provided one of those rare services their direct servants could not due to a matter of skill and training. His father, and Mr. McBride when old enough, maintained the land, maintained the guns, saw to the dogs and horses, and all those other duties necessary for a successful hunt. It was from this background that he is said to have learned the skills for which he has become a wartime legend second only to Sir James Coltrane – where Coltrane is known for his battle suit and its raw power, Edward McBride is considered by some to be the finest shot in the isles, though some of the riflemen of the colonies insist that there are better in America.

Nonetheless, many amazing feats of precision have been attributed to him, both for accuracy in dealing with small targets, and nigh unbelievable shots at great range. Secondly, he evaded the enemy time and again, and is said to be able to disappear like a ghost. Indeed, the French, Germans, and Italians all have their own nicknames for him, and each is synonymous with some local ghost story to their countries. While but a single man with one gun, the effect he had on opposing morale as he picked off one officer after another from seemingly nowhere – past their ability to find his hiding spot – was reputed to be enormous.

His greatest feat and story remains his deeds upon the death of his unit, however. Because each man who has told the story has told it slightly differently, I will not recount it here for fear of passing on false information. The facts of the matter are that he was with a unit of Scotsmen who, through some error on either their part or communications, depending on who one asks, ended up in the way of an enemy advance. Edward McBride was the only survivor, and suddenly behind enemy lines. For over six weeks, he evaded the enemy patrols, picked off opposing scouts, and eventually managed to sneak into an enemy commander's

---

5   Cornelius Jeffery Jones has written a thoroughly comprehensive account of the early life of Eddy McBride, available from St. Andrews University Press. – C B-W.

personal command tent and steal maps, plans and information regarding both supply lines and troop numbers. He then somehow crossed back into friendly territory, and passed this information on to English generals.

For this, after much debate, he was inducted into the much honored 95th rifles, though even then, it seemed his Scottish pride allowed him to accept this unique honor only if he was permitted to wear his tartan, in the colors of the Black Watch, even in English service. I am not certain how this was accomplished, but it seemed that as thereafter he would often operate nearly alone, this was eventually permitted. He was, also in this time, apparently given three things. The first was unusual freedom, told to select targets of opportunity rather than being instructed to look for specific persons or opportunities. Sometimes the pursuit of war, it seems, requires unusual compromise and improvisation or recognition of an individual's talents, be they a gift for literacy and photography, or a sharp eye for the points where a battle might turn.

More materially, it seemed that in support of the war effort, the minds at Oxford had devised an unusual method for reloading a rifle. Eight balls, already packed with wadding and powder, were loaded into a cylinder, which could then be attached to a specially made Baker rifle designed to accommodate the change. By means of turning a hand crank, the rifle could thus be reloaded in a small fraction of the time it took to reload one of those rifles, famed almost as much for their difficulties in reloading as they are for their accuracy at range. However, because of the gears in the crank mechanism, and requirement of pre-loading such precise amounts of wadding and powder, this rifle was also given to occasional jamming and other problems, and if struck, had the small potential of exploding. There was the added difficulty that once those eight shots were fired, it took a considerable time to remove the old cylinder and load a new one.

Even so, the possibilities of a repeating rifle occurred to many, and the scientists asked if it might be of use to the army. In testing, it was determined that it was almost useless for men of the line, for after eight shots, it was nearly useless, the gears were frequently ruined by mud and moisture, and the mechanism and its added weight required a man to crouch or otherwise better support the gun to fire it accurately, lest it pull to the left. However, in the hands of a single shooter who could make all eight shots count, would not be closely engaging the enemy with regularity, and had some freedom to lie down or crouch before firing, it was a godsend. As such, it was given to Mr. McBride to field test.

Finally, apparently by his own devising, a tool was made incorporating a pair of protective eye goggles with the lenses of field glasses put on pivoting arms. Similar to the magnifying effect some high end jewelers have begun using for magnifying minute detail, it is said that he has gained a better ability to estimate ranges through determining when an image is most clear using differing combinations of lenses. How a man of so little known education devised such a thing and constructed it, I do not know, though a few men have their theories. Regardless, that he did construct this unique tool and wears it proudly remains a fact. I am now most curious to meet Mr. McBride myself.

March 5th, 1815
---- Base, Scotland

Dear Sir,

I am writing to report our latest success in the venture to which you have assigned us. Because news from Scotland does not so swiftly reach the London club scene as that from elsewhere in England, I thought it best you hear the news from me, though it should come as little surprise, as this was part of your assignment in the early stages. We have made contact with Edward McBride, most recently of the 95th rifles until he was returned to his home region for more standard service until such time as he would be needed in active duty. Your letter was well received by the base commander, and pending his acceptance, we were informed that Mr. McBride would be released into our service for the noble venture you have put forth. I am pleased to report that there was no trouble on this front, and indeed, many of the fellows about the base were most pleased to hear that Mr. McBride might be moving on. By all accounts, he is far happier when he has something active to put his talents and will towards, and all about him are happier when Mr. McBride is happy.

As a figure of national interest, I thought it best that I give some detailing of the heroic figure that is the Ghost of the Moors, amidst the other colorful nicknames assigned him in the media accounts of his exploits. For all of his reputation for stealth, I would have thought the size of the man exaggerated by his accounts, and perhaps it was a little, but he is, indeed, only some small part short of two meters, and as it is reported here, some 17 stone. He has the very look to him of a wildcat, all lean muscle and sinew, and quick of motion and reflex.

For all this size, I received some demonstration of the skills for which he is so well regarded. It is the habit of the local sentries to announce the approach of men returning and visitors aloud. Two of the soldiers near me had a bet placed on whether the man would call Mr. McBride's name, or if he was in such humor as to bypass the guard station entirely. Considering it is well secured here and there is little area with the slightest cover, I was sure this was some local inside joke or the men having some fun with the Englishmen.

Surely enough though, near the time in which he was scheduled to return, I felt a tap upon my shoulder. I will acknowledge that, expecting no such thing and quite tense in anticipation of gaining another voyager among our company, and one of such note, I was quite unready for such a thing, and startled in such a manner as to greatly amuse everyone about, and sending my chair tumbling backwards – with myself, sadly, still in residence. As I was barely aware of anything more than a ringing in my skull on account of its sudden meeting with the floor, a powerfully muscled hand was presented to me, against a field of plaid.

The man who stood over me at that moment looked like nothing so much as one of the bears in the London zoo. His voice was just as deep in timbre as you might imagine from my description so far, and the thick accent of our neighbors accompanied by his own tone seemed to render some words almost a throaty growl. At first, I was unsure if I should take the hand and the spoken offer to help me up after such a fright. When I did offer my own hand, I was hefted to my feet with such force and speed as to almost overbalance once again and go pitching forward. I can only imagine I'd have done so had I not crashed into the Scotsman the helping hand was attached to, moving him not an inch. This amused him no end, prompting the question, as I recall, "Drunk, son, or just learning to walk?" The other men about took up this same humor at my expense. I believe I muttered something akin to "Not every day a man sees a ghost, sir." the last spoken with as much respect as I and my growing headache could muster. This drew more laughter from the man, and soon all about.

He seemed to take a new estimation of me at this response, and answered, "I don't like the sound of sir, today." Even as he spoke he did me the favor of righting my chair for me and kicking it back in my direction. "Call me Eddy."

Past this seemingly inauspicious first meeting, we talked

for quite some time. I must say that Mr. McBride has quite the robust, if entirely gallows sense of humor. It was little time before he had questioned us as to all the manners in which we might horribly die or suffer on our long trip, when he heard account of what has been proposed. Per your instructions, Mr. Toomes made every attempt to answer the questions posed to us. Though I am not certain what you will glean from Mr. Toomes's reports, I feel I should have it noted for the record that I meant your aide no disrespect, but Mr. McBride has clearly taken some dislike to Mr. Toomes. To this end, Mr. McBride was most specific that in asking his questions, he was addressing me, not Mr. Toomes, and insisted that the requested information, in as graphic a detail as was possible should, come from me, if he was to remain interested. I do not think any of the difficulties of this meeting were because of any fault on Mr. Toomes's part. Mr. McBride, simply, is an unusual individual, and I do not think their personalities and styles meshed particularly well.

All supposition aside, trying not to put imagination to work adding color to the visions in my head as I answered every way in which I might imagine our trip could meet with disaster, and certain that he was at this point out to refuse and simply make me look the fool, Mr. McBride acknowledged that those risks sounded dangerous enough to pass a day or two. He agreed that if I would join him and the officers for dinner that evening, that he would make all needed arrangements, and leave with us the following morning. I am uncertain precisely where Mr. Toomes dined that evening, for Mr. McBride made it quite clear the invitation was not for both of us, but I knew that the first priority for the both of us was success at the task put before us, even if we suffered some discomfort along the way.

As a note of sure interest to the men of military experience who will be reading the letters sent to you, I have also seen the fabled gun Mr. McBride uses in preference to all others, though he has quite the personal armament. It is as beautiful and precise as has been described in reports of it, a perfect condition Baker rifle, despite all the campaigns it has seen, kept far more clean and precise than the man himself, who did not bother to shave before dinner. The gears and handle for the complex reloading system used are akin to clockworks, and clearly require extensive and regular care. Among the gear packed by our new traveling companion, indeed, are all manner of clean rags and oil.

I will tell you as well that throughout dinner, he and his fellows shared tales of the war with me, passing on information primarily from the Scots regiments, information which I had largely missed, and that they felt might be of interest to my reading audience, even though my employment as a war reporter had passed. Mr. McBride shared a tale or two of his own, but primarily insisted that I would have time enough to write down the tales of his affairs in wartime, and restricted himself to speaking only of his time with the Black Watch. Instead, dinner time extended quite long into the night, moving directly from meal time to thick beer, upon which they were most insistent that I write down all of these accounts.

While friendly enough, sir, I can but imagine that they feel that their own impressive and heroic exploits during the war have been overlooked by the English media, and some resent this. I am certain that in including such a man as Mr. McBride on your list of people to recruit for this mission, you are well aware of the situations and problems facing the soldiers of the Scotsmen. Nevertheless I have sworn to officially request that if you have some ears still within our government, they be bent in the direction of our Scottish neighbors for their service. Doubtless you have already been doing so in thanks for such meritorious service, and surely it is simply the slow wheels of bureaucracy limiting England's response and expression of gratitude for their service. In any case, I am pleased to report that their patrols do continue, and they have seen to caring for their returning wounded as best they are able.

Now, having made the entreaties I have promised these brave men, I can now report that in exchange for this service, noting down their tales to be passed on (you will find these accounts enclosed with this letter, for distribution as you see them meriting) we have successfully recruited Mr. McBride to our company in addition to Sir James Coltrane. We will be returning with Mr. McBride to the Coltrane estate at the first light of morning, and from there we will begin the longest and most perilous stretch of this first piece of the journey before us, though I will be staying a short time with the Coltranes while Mr. Toomes reports to you and makes certain that the information he was last given remains accurate, for news travels slowly from the Americas.

Yours,
Gregory Conan Watts

P.S. I ask that you forgive my informality in the future, sir. For as of this morning, when discovering me preparing the letters, both a copy for my own records, and the originals to send to you, Eddy discovered that while I had honored his request when speaking, I had been penning his name as Mr. McBride. He grew quite upset with me, and from now on, I am strictly to refer to him as Eddy and nothing else. He will let me know if this situation changes. While I am unaccustomed to such odd and familiar requests, I think it wisest to honor this one. He was most specific.

From the journals of Gregory Conan Watts
March 9th, 1815
Coltrane Estate

During our return trip, Eddy received a great deal of attention, of course. Many people on our route back from Scotland recognized him, and even for those who didn't, he cuts an impressive figure. He bore it well enough, gracious, if a bit distant most of the time. Despite this, I get the impression that he hasn't adapted as well as Sir James to the effects of his fame. He is easygoing enough still, but keeps most people at arm's length, and does not soften his demeanor, nor humor, when in the presence of women and children. I get the impression that while he is interested in the voyage, he is already looking forward to being away.

Before meeting Eddy, I had gotten somewhat used to traveling with a degree of anonymity. During the trip, at least Eddy received most of the attention. Upon our return there was enough to go around. Apparently the Coltranes had been busy in the short time we were away, and do few things in a small way. Imagine my surprise to not only find a very enthusiastic crowd awaiting our return, but invitations to a ball in our honor, which will be attended by no less than the King and Queen.

I am most thankful that Sir James is seeing to helping me prepare for the occasion, for though I've attended a few banquets full of distinguished military men since the end of the war, this is a fancier thing by far. Much as I hate to admit it, it also may help some small amount that Harriet seems just as nervous as I am about an event of such state.

March 18th, 1815
London, England

My Dearest Cordelia,

I am certain that you have read the news of the event held last night. I am very sorry your health prevented you from attending, though I was most thankful for the well wishes from your good father and yourself. His acknowledgment of our impending deeds is, hopefully, a promising sign.

I thought of you often last night amidst the socializing and merriment. Though I was invited to dance a number of times, owing to being one of the guests of honor, I could not bring myself to dance with another. I am certain that you would not only have forgiven me, but chided me for so keeping to myself at a party, but you need not have worried. Each time I refused a dance, upon informing the women of the event that I was very much spoken for, they always asked more about you. I spent much of the evening when I was not quietly people-watching retelling tales of our youth together and enumerating your many charms and virtues. Apparently my tellings were romantic enough that I developed quite a significant crowd of listeners. Even absent, apparently you're quite good at causing a scene.

I also had occasion to take a few pictures at the ball. I could not pass up the opportunity, and our hosts were only too glad to allow me to enter with the camera. Some people were uncertain at first about allowing their picture to be taken, but for the most part it went very well. I had to give a few of the resulting pictures to our hosts, of course, but I was able to keep several, including one of the King and Queen. You should find prints of a few of these, including one of the royal couple and a handful of prints of my companions, enclosed with this letter.

The others of our small company seemed to mostly have an easier time of it than I. Mr. Toomes quickly found a small knot of older military men, mostly retired officers, and stuck with them throughout the event. I am certain such men would have many tales to tell, but even more certain they all left the party knowing something more about tobacco and calabashes than when they arrived.

Eddy took a short time to grow used to the atmosphere, though I am uncertain if it was more a matter that he was unsure of London's social elite, or that they were unsure of him. He stood out even more here than previous, both with his physical stature, rough manner, and the fact he had insisted on Scottish formal wear, kilt and all. Still, once people warmed up to him he fell in readily enough. More than a few of the women tried to catch his eye, though no few of those also found themselves retreating, politely, of course. He has manners enough to get by in such situations, but his manner remains rough enough that he isn't for everyone. I'm just grateful no one fainted.

If Eddy got by, Sir James reveled in the attention. From the moment we entered he had the ear of anyone he wished, and a large knot of admirers. There seemed to be no one he could not dazzle. Military officers, scholars, diplomats... to say nothing of the women. He did not spend overlong talking with any one person or even group, instead handling a great deal of the duties of the guests of honor for the rest of us, seamlessly moving from one group to another to give our regards and accept wishes of luck. No matter to whom he spoke, he seemed to be having a great time of it.

The real marvel, and real horror, however, I must give to Miss Coltrane and Miss Wright. Jillian Coltrane was more reserved than her brother, befitting a young lady of means, but handled those who spoke with her no less ably. Even in times of such chaos, I noticed the siblings looking one another's way more than once. They never said a word to one another, often widely separated, but I don't think they needed to say much to communicate quite well. What truly impressed me in this, however, was quite similar to the statements about skilled dancers. The woman must not only do the same dance, but backwards and in formal shoes. In this case, Miss Coltrane was as impressive as her sibling in dealing with the men and women of wealth and station, but did so while dealing with poor Harriet.

It's not that Miss Wright didn't try. Indeed, she was quite

enthusiastic to be attending such an event. From the beginning it became clear she wanted to speak with everyone, though most especially the young gentlemen present. It just as clearly vexed her that she was nearly invisible next to her cousin, who was getting all of the attention from the rich and handsome young men of England that Miss Wright coveted. Despite many of these young men being of impressive pedigrees, Jillian did not ever linger long in talks with any of them. A few were persistent enough that Sir James excused himself from conversation a time or two when Jillian's fan moved just so, effecting a rescue when potential suitors just did not get the hint.

At least one of these, meanwhile, then had to be rescued from Harriet. I had noticed him a few times, trying to catch Miss Coltrane's eye. I have seen enough military men to judge him an officer, though a very young one. Dark haired and dashing, he had quite a lot of attention of his own, but kept dismissing it to try to speak with Jillian. She was, as ever, polite, but no more, and rebuffed his repeated efforts. Miss Wright was only too eager to step into the void, trying in her turn to catch the young man's eye. I know only what you taught me about fan language, love, but knew enough that she was sending as clear a signal of interest as she could. I am not certain he even saw her, trying to pursue her cousin still. Eventually, her efforts grew frantic enough that Harriet somehow ended up launching her fan at him, striking him squarely in the forehead. Thankfully it did no harm, aside from the embarrassment and sinking her reputation further. For Jillian, at least, it served its purpose. After rescuing Miss Wright's fan for her, the young officer retreated from both of them, and for the rest of the night I saw him only from a distance – usually when following Miss Wright's gaze.

Other than this event, the ball went without incident. The royals were present only for a short time, but even that left quite an impression. Before, I had thought of this something like another military venture. A mission to be undertaken for a greater good. After hearing the King praising us and speaking of our efforts in the boldest of terms I can no longer doubt that all of England is watching us.

I was curious, however, to find that there was barely mention of the rival mission hired by Lord Donovan's fellow. I could not learn the names of anyone involved. Though they technically have the same goals and destinations we do, they also admittedly don't have Sir James Coltrane along, which seems to so far make all the difference.

I only wish you could have been there, my love. I know you would have loved to witness the grandeur of a royal ball, and to have seen the King and Queen up close. Despite all of the splendor already there, having you there by my side would have made it truly perfect. Perhaps there will be another opportunity on our return.

My love, always,
Gregory Conan Watts

From the journals of Gregory Conan Watts,
March 21st, 1815
----shire, Southern England

I could not possibly have imagined how truly exciting my first venture into the skies would be. Stationed in France, I saw many of the military's dirigibles overhead, bringing the troops trained and equipped for such rapid deployment, as well as the runs used to scout out enemy movements. I marveled at the bravery of the men aboard, particularly the captains of those vessels. To fly amidst the enemy's makeshift rockets, I had always imagined, must take a heart of stone and nerves of steel. I had long envisioned what such men must look like, and what that experience must have been like. There were no rockets firing today, but either way, I find myself rather perplexed at what I have found.

Our return to the Coltrane estate was met with a warmer welcome this time, perhaps now that Sir James had taken our measure. There was also his greeting for Eddy, which was friendly in the manner of two soldiers who have faced the horrors of battle together, seen the worst an enemy could throw at them, and survived. I have seen it many times, and it is a bond of friendship like perhaps no other in this world. Clearly the pair knew each other well. They began to speak in clipped sentences and references without providing full detail, to be met with agreements and grins. I could scarce follow any idea of where they may have met and encountered one another so, but quite apparently, these two heroes were well acquainted.

The pair of them, after these pleasantries, invited me for a round of cards. It was just the same as I had previously learned of Sir James. Cards may, in most places, be a diversion for the wealthy and a way to gain some bragging rights over their fellows or find a way to lighten their pockets when they find them too full of coin. For Sir James, they are a prop to aid in talking when not drinking. Mr. Toomes even sat in on several rounds of this game, listening acutely to what was said. It seems that even my dour-faced companion, who seems less and less threatening the longer I have lived with his disapproval – and in the company of heroes – sat in and played some hands with the three of us.

I have no idea who won or lost, and not a coin was exchanged, but it was enthralling to vicariously live, for even a few hours, through the exploits of such heroes as these men have made themselves. Two men with a military style less alike you will not find, but each shows a keen respect for the other's effectiveness, and both seem to hold firmly in mind that half of winning a battle is convincing the enemy he has lost. I have heard similar sentiments, but these, if any can be said to be so, are the masters of this brand of warfare, each in the manner to which he is best suited, and when Sir James has donned that metal monster, I cannot imagine an army that would wish to stand against even the pair.

We played well into the night, pausing only when Sir James excused himself a time to speak with his sister. He was gone for some significant time, but we played on. Without Sir James's presence, Eddy's tone changed significantly, back to the near growl he so often adopts, and his humor, while pleasant, was more barbed. He has at least taken to trying to fish some reaction out of Mr. Toomes more often than he has tried to draw some blush from me any longer. I will tell you that our travel back from Scotland was a good deal more colorful than our trip there. Despite the fact he has not gotten much more than several of Mr. Toomes's long stares, he continues his efforts.

In time, James would return to tell us that news had come that the airship would be ready for boarding shortly after breakfast, and we would be airborne by lunch. I could barely contain my excitement even at that moment, and sleep was nearly out of the question – even had the workshop not been steaming and roaring so fiercely as to rattle the back windows of the house from shortly after we had turned in for the evening until only perhaps an hour before dawn. Just as well, for at least it gave me something to wonder at, imagining what new device or capability might be being added in preparation for the journey, or how Sir James might be laboring at his metal beast to prepare it for the travails to come and shine away any sign of past conflict.

Sleep did come at last, out of sheer exhaustion, but it seemed but moments before a servant awakened me for breakfast. It seemed I was not alone in this, for there were only three people at breakfast who did not seem bleary or discomfited in the least. Sir James himself was as spry and vibrant as ever, speaking excitedly about the adventures that lay ahead. His sister was quite alert, all the more contrasted by her cousin's weary attempts to copy her every motion and gesture (though at one point, this resulted, due to positioning of dishes, in Harriet depositing her hand firmly in the butter. I can only imagine that poor Harriet had only awareness enough to mind the table or her cousin, and chose the latter, to her dismay).

Then there was Eddy, of course, who looked as if he was about to head out for a hike, save that, as usual, he did not appear to have shaved. Indeed, in the time I have known him, I have yet to see him without the same customary scruff to him, and yet his beard never grows any further than that, almost as if he intentionally trims it that way. Simply an oddity which I am sure will continue to puzzle me for some time to come. Eddy, as he would announce to our company in response to Sir James's questioning had "slept like a baby." Tired as I was, and musing upon such odd observances, I had to wonder if perhaps he had emerged into the world with that very half a day's beard. The lady of the house caught me appearing wearily amused and asked after it. The more awake and aware of the company seemed to take some amusement from my mumbling excuse to try to cover for my expression, while Harriet looked relieved that she was no longer any kind of center of attention and the butter seemed forgotten. Mr. Toomes, as is his wont, just scowled over his lone biscuit and jam.

It was certainly a more interesting breakfast than most in recent memory, if only for the company in front of whom I seemed to make quite the fool of myself. I seem to have gained Harriet's sympathy in return for that which I offered her with small glances and shrugs (at least I can hope such things are universal enough to be clear to a Virginian). Breakfast was not, however, the highlight of even the morning.

Before that, however, I should note my observations of our Captain and the company of *The Dame Fortuna* for sake of having a record to reference for my later writings, and to check myself against my first opinions. The Captain himself is a fellow by the name of William Fisher. I understand that he was one of those rare individuals who had the honor of piloting the first dirigibles. This much Sir James himself verified for me before we left. He apparently has the absolute trust of the Coltranes and was handpicked to handle the piloting of their personal craft through wartime. He looks every year of his age. I imagine he may have been quite the dashing, if slender, figure back in his youth during the Colonial engagement of last century, but now he is more akin to a particularly reedy scarecrow, though a scarecrow who has somehow discovered the wonders of beard growth, if finding it an inexact science.

I am unsure how I can accurately describe this most prominent feature of the man beyond simply bushy, uneven, and disheveled. Long and sharpish whiskers grow from the right side of his face above what seems to be some kind of burn wound along his throat and jawline, and only a few prickly hairs grow from this region, yet that side bears the most impressive mutton chop. The left side of his face features a full and curly beard, obscuring his face somewhat, and making his words hard to follow if you try to follow any kind of facial clue for context, and a lip reader would be sorely out of luck. His hair, meanwhile, is worn short, perhaps to indicate that he does have some decorum after all, or perhaps that someone else tends his hair, while the shaving is left to the captain and his mirror. I can only guess.

In any case, despite the fact I am unsure if I'd trust him to cross the street, Sir James swears by him, and I find myself hard pressed to doubt him. Perhaps it is simply that our Captain is quite at home in his native element of the skies, and a bit more divorced from the sensibilities of the more literally down to earth.

The captain is dressed in a hodgepodge of both archaic and modern dress, which does nothing to further encourage my thoughts as to his competence and focus. His jacket is Colonial War period, kept in nigh immaculate condition, as if he was prepared to be pressed to service once more, though it is quite out of date for the modern military, of course. Even so, it certainly does give the man a certain dusty sense of history. The rest of his attire is civilian, and of simple and comfortable stock such as workers in the city wear by preference. Contrasting both is his pocket watch, in the style of those pieces of Swiss make, worn on a long silvered chain. Another chain of the same sort crosses it over his chest like a bandoleer, leading to the opposite pocket, wherein he keeps a compass in very much a similar style to his pocket watch, a top snapping open to reveal the face. My comfort that he keeps such a device is tempered perhaps a slight amount by the fact that while he seems the type to regularly check his watch – a habit I understand and have certainly seen in many other gentlemen – he seems to alternate from checking one device to the other every few minutes. All this while the dirigible is loaded, as if we, unmoving, may have shifted some significant degree away from our current locale. Either that, or he does not trust this most critical of his instruments, or poorly differentiates port and starboard. Neither possibility does wonders to fill me with hope for our success.

As businesslike as the Captain is not, his wife is about and quite focused on the task at hand. She knows where everything goes and how best to achieve every task of organization and preparation for launch, and it is she who receives most questions from crewers and engineers, so as not to disturb her already sufficiently disturbed husband whilst he ensures that we have not shifted one degree east or west for the fourth time since my last trip to help load our supplies. She is a stocky woman, with hands that show she is no stranger to some bit of work when necessity dictates. Life on shipboard, it seems, being akin to accounts from that on a farm where there are simply times where idle hands are not welcome, and anyone who does not pay for their passage must put their worth in, regardless of gender.

Despite this singularly masculine feature, she is otherwise a dignified woman of her advancing age, put together in fashion which was the latest fashion only some few seasons past, rather than her husband's mixture of that which was the height of fashion recently, that which was so two wars past, and that which was never in fashion and with fortune never will be. She is put together such that a gentleman can only imagine the hours put to setting hair just so, dressing just so, and all of the other efforts a lady puts herself to to be presentable, but she clearly feels the effort well worth it even when long since married, and when about to board a ship for a long venture, rather than any social occasion. I cannot call her elegant – Miss Coltrane's presence offers too many unfair comparisons – but she is nonetheless a woman both handsome for her time, and efficient. That she should be attending this voyage with us gives me somewhat more confidence that we might reach American shores yet. Or at least in the process of going where the wind takes us, we should at least have a most gracious hostess and polite surrounds in which to get hopelessly lost.

Speaking of Miss Coltrane, she has written to a number of people of import, both for their well wishes, and to ensure that we will have hospitality should we need it in our travels. I can now see why Sir James has been as successful after the war as he was in it, with her holding the reins of his affairs in daily life, though she rightly defers to her more learned brother on matters concerning pounds and pence beyond the small matters not needing his attention.

In attendance as well is poor Harriet, who made some effort to put herself to work until such time as the Captain's wife learned of her efforts and scolded her most roundly. Mrs. Fisher made considerable effort to try to keep her diatribe below the hearing of most of the workmen, lest she embarrass herself as much as Harriet had already embarrassed her. Apparently it continued for some time, though I did not hear of all of the details. The error of what a lady does and does not do when presented with physical labor such as loading the ship, the errors in her wardrobe, the fact her hair had come somewhat too loose beneath her hat, which, incidentally, was apparently worn at an unacceptable angle – and so on. Undeterred in her own way, Harriet indeed seemed quite pleased to have a ready and willing tutor in how a lady of England comports herself and made extensive effort to correct each and every detail as it was brought up, in the process turning one of her buttonholes into a small tear in her eagerness to correct herself, leading to some increase in Mrs. Fisher's volume. I can see that this relationship, such as it is, is going to be a very long and loud one as we venture forth, for Harriet seems to have no lack of problems with her behavior and dress, and Mrs. Fisher showed no signs of a lack of time to correct each and every such error. The workmen, at least, seemed somewhat relieved for the most part to be permitted to do their jobs without further questioning or direction.

There is one other addition worthy of note as part of our company now, along with the Fishers. The Captain's young nephew, and after the war, his ward, Matthew Fisher-Swift, only just ten years old, flits in and out amongst the workmen, currently too shy to approach anyone unknown, but quite curious as to virtually everyone. He shows some familiarity with the men working, calling them by name and with reasonable respect, but constant curiosity. They seem familiar with him as well, for they have considerable patience with his constant stream of questions, and a couple of them seem to have brought sweets for the boy, which seems to shut him up for a time. He is an athletic lad, running about, climbing, and darting from hiding spot to hiding spot, trying to get a better view of the strange new people who have hired his caretakers.

He seems particularly curious, understandably, regarding Sir James and Eddy, for his gaze was quite fixed on them for most of the work period, and whenever they would move, he would as well to make sure he did not miss anything of importance. I can only imagine that he has heard the tales everyone else in England has, and marveled at them with the rest of us, but also with a boy's fascination and imagination. Indeed, later on in the day, when we were near departure, I spotted him a time or two when he thought he was unobserved attempting to hold himself in the manner of those military heroes when relaxed, shoulders back, chest puffed out, holding his breath as long as he was able to help him hold the rigid posture. At least until his attention span failed him, and he ran off to see to some other vital task related to staying out of the way as he had been firmly instructed several times over.

Given my other observations, I surmise that these random tasks may often have been gathering more small rocks, for he has quite the bag of them at his belt, dirty fingers, and a well crafted slingshot of quality enough that it might be imagined if he has the patience and aim it may be used to hunt small rodents. I am uncertain what he plans to do with this on our trip, or if he is simply prepared and armed for whatever eventuality, in the manner of boys of his age with limited enough supervision to be allowed such a tool. This, as well, probably does not bode well.

The ship itself, called by Sir James *The Dame Fortuna*, although that was not its name during its HMS duty, is much the same as nearly every other constructed since the time following the Colonial wars. Most were made to carry as many troops as could be fit into the vehicles for rapid transport to the war, though some small number were created later by the minds at Oxford when the forces were in need of smaller, faster vehicles for scouting high above enemy lines. This is definitely one of the former, once used to pack as many men into the confines as could be managed. In many of the rooms, you can still see the ties and construction designed for rows of hammocks where men would be stacked, given only some small amount more room to each than should they be stacks of firewood. Now it is significantly more roomy, with only two assigned to each room, with a few rooms yet left empty for those we have yet to add to our company.

The ship is sturdily built, designed to navigate even in difficult weather, but unlike a ship of the sea, it has no armament of its own, for ammunition for such things takes up space, and is considerably heavy, and on a conveyance such as this, weight and space are at a premium. Rather, in the days of the war, it would be defended by the men aboard moving to the rails at the outer edge of the ship, exposed to the elements, and armed with rifles or muskets. As the only threat to these vehicles came from enemy rockets, often only a small bit of fire raining down upon the enemy would discourage them from long attending such arms, leaving them exposed and in the open, though more than a few of our dirigibles were lost as Napoleon's forces studied our tactics and became more effective at shooting them down. I understand that when such occasions happened in the field, the first duty of any survivors was first to rescue men trapped within, and second only to salvaging what manpower as could be gained by a quick survey of their part of the ship, the second duty was to set fire to the dirigible and evacuate, then protect it until it had burned beyond salvage that our enemies could not steal understanding of its construction and use.

As it is their airship, Sir James has his own quarters, while Miss Coltrane will be rooming with Harriet, of course. I currently share chambers for this first stretch of the trip with Mr. Toomes, to my regret, but will be rooming with a man of the continent, one Giovanni Franzini, if we should be able to recruit him. I admit to considerable curiosity as to what he has to add to our company that we are recruiting an Italian, but I trust that our employer knows what he's doing, to risk such a man getting aboard an airship and in the company of two of our greatest war heroes. Despite his foreign origins, I can scarce imagine that I will enjoy his company less than that of Mr. Toomes, who has been particularly cross since learning that fires were not to be lit in the upper levels of the ship, so he cannot smoke in our chambers. The gory manner in which the crewman who related this rule reminded him of the Late George III and his celebratory cigar at the battle of Yorktown did not help Mr. Toomes's mood. The crewer hastened to remind us that the hydrogen envelope had been modified for safety since then, but that it still wasn't safe. Apparently it now results in a longer, slower burn, more likely to destroy the whole ship and keep the secrets of its inner working safe. At least George Rex went fast.

The back of the ship has been converted into a workshop, where the Coltrane battle suit is stored, maintained and also deployed. I have had some small explanation from Sir James as to how this works in the time I have been in his company. The springs and steam pipes mounted on the legs that allowed the prodigious leap I previously witnessed allows the suit to make a small number of such jumps, given some small boost and control over its ascent through the sudden venting of steam, but most importantly the actions of giant and powerful springs built into the knee mechanisms. This same technology also allows the suit to be dropped from a great height, whereupon it can land without loss of function, and no harm to the pilot. He has quietly admitted that it is also quite jarring, and that it always requires considerable maintenance shortly thereafter, but it still allowed him many times to drop directly from an airship onto the battlefield to directly engage and surprise the enemy, and to leap over even significant guard walls to bypass enemy defenses and engage their troops. Such ingenuity, and even having seen it in action I can still scarce imagine it.

The ship has a lower floor as well, from which most of us are restricted. This region contains most of the vital components for providing the steam power used to inflate the dirigible and enable it to fly under its own power rather than being at the mercies of the fickle winds. For those times that the winds are more favorable, the ship has numerous sail mechanisms the Captain can control directly, allowing the ship to be driven by the wind to save power and coal. This, I understand, is by far the preferred method of locomotion, even if variable winds make travel speed occasionally unpredictable. The savings in fuel reserves are a more than worthwhile trade-off.

Beyond those lodgings so far detailed, Eddy will be bunking with the ship's first mate, Mr. Taylor, whom I have not yet met. Unsurprisingly, he is another man of military background and a friend of Sir James from the war. So far, however, he has kept to quarters, or spent his time consulting with the captain. The latter is an activity I have not yet worked up the nerve to attempt, and I am entirely uncertain if I wish to know what arcane activities he has gotten himself to in the piloting of the ship. Each time I think of it, I imagine him working on navigating by pocket watch. Sir James seems unworried, however, which does a good deal to reassure me that we are headed more or less in a westerly direction as opposed to, say, in a more or less nine-ish direction.

The flight itself has been an unsteady-seeming and

lurching affair.[6] Those times I have seen airships such as this one flying overhead, I had imagined smooth and comfortable flight, gliding blithely through fair skies, as figuratively far above the chaos and rough surrounds of the battlefield as they were literally. As has occurred so often in recent days, my imaginings have been most harshly shattered by the reality. At one moment we were on the ground and still, though restricted to chambers for the moments before takeoff. Unsurprisingly, both takeoff and landing seem to be considered particularly eventful and chaotic times for the crew and command of the ship, and all others are to be kept out of their way in these times. After that moment, with only the churning excitement in my stomach giving me any sense of motion, there was then a terrible lurching, and the ship seemed to move not so much upwards as rocking unsteadily side to side so hard that I was nearly dislodged from my hammock, even with my feet braced on the floor.

In the process, one of Mr. Toomes's traveling cases, apparently insufficiently secured, clattered to the floor, strewing his collection of pipes all about our cabin. This, of course, has done nothing to ease his mood, for though I aided him in collecting them once we were permitted, two of his prized collectibles were cracked in the impact. In any case, when the rocking ceased at last, there was a groaning noise and the sound of metal scraping stone. The body of the dirigible shifted, sending us leaning back hard in our seats, and sending most of the scattered pipes tumbling underneath the bunks.

Just as I was certain all my misgivings regarding the Captain would be proven true before we had gotten entirely off the ground, we were righted all at once and simply felt the occasional bump. I was, at the time, somewhat certain that this was the mooring ropes being released, or that were were running along the ground, but peering out the porthole style window, I

---

6 The modern Nike-line Coltrane Dirigibles that most readers would be familiar with have fixed the lurching issue by increasing size and stability. The old war dirigibles rode more akin to the modern fashionable two-seat racing airships, which also prioritize speed over stability. – C B-W.

was amazed to find that in what had seemed a brief time, we were now far above the ground and beginning to move. Without this frame of reference, it is oftentimes hard to tell if we are moving, and how quickly. With the gentle winds that have prevailed so far today, the motion of the dirigible is more akin to rocking, swaying, and the occasional slightly jarring bump over any sensation of forward momentum.

On this realization, for the next half of an hour, I grew more and more ill. Perhaps it was simply all of the excitement at the trip and realization that we were now at the mercy of the skies, and so far above the ground, in combination with this most particular of motions. I made my first venture outside not to experience the wonders of flight or admire the view so much as to lose my breakfast on the countryside below. I can only hope that there was no one beneath. My one other point of gratitude in all this was that there was only one witness to my moments of illness, though I am certain that Mr. Toomes was aware of the reasons for my departure.

Matthew Fisher-Swift was already outside, racing along the outside of the ship, only occasionally steadying himself with the rails. I marvel at his balance, his quick transition to gaining his sea legs, and his utter lack of fear of heights. In any case, he assured me that it happens to most people during their first trip in an airship, before he began to question me about all manner of things, though he was at first most curious about my camera and how it worked.

Questions, of course, I could scarce answer, for though I am well aware of how to refill the chemical trays and with what, and how to fix minor and common mishaps, I do not at all understand its inner workings or how it achieves such a marvelous thing. Still, he wanted his picture taken as soon as was convenient, which I assured him would be no problem. When he was done interrogating me as to my war service and the wonders of my device, he was quickly on to questions regarding Eddy, about whom the boy has an insatiable curiosity. Sir James, it seems, he is well familiar with, though still quite admires. So he restricted his questions to wishing to know more of the sniper, who seems not particularly fond of children, or at least this child, and did little more than growl at the boy's pestering, quite thoroughly driving off young Mr. Fisher-Swift. He may have no fear of heights, but at least the lad has some common sense when it comes to poking at the gruff and dark-humored Scot.

The combination of emptying my stomach, and speaking with Matthew left me feeling quite better. Sometimes, it seems, distraction can be a good thing when it pulls one away from the peculiar motions of the ship. I spent some few minutes once Matthew had departed clutching tight to the rail and looking out over the country before a feeling of guilt overwhelmed me so that I returned to our chambers and assisted Mr. Toomes in collecting his pipes from under the bunks. Though this elicited no thanks, of course, he perhaps snarled less at me for that brief time than on the average. I was still quite glad to leave his company and return to observing our progress – and seeing my beloved country from this unusual vantage point – until the urge to put pen to page and document the experience finally pulled me from the rail.

Now, as I near completion with this task and have left myself adequate notes to compare with my later observations, I believe I shall attend Sir James in his sitting room. I understand he has invited the gentlemen of the ship to play cards to pass the time, always a welcome pastime with such engaging company, and I look forward to hearing his recounting of his previous trips through the air. Perhaps if my confidence is boosted enough by his recollections, war stories, and assurances about his previous travels with the Captain, I will have my courage reinforced enough to venture to the front of the ship and observe our Captain and first mate at work.

March 22nd, 1815
The skies of Western England
50°47'N 03°21'W

My Dearest Cordelia,

     You cannot begin to imagine the views afforded by travel aboard these military dirigibles. While the first day was quite difficult in many ways, that time has passed, and now I am finding myself quite at home aboard this wondrous vehicle. I spend what time I can spare holding tight to the rails outside and admiring the grounds below, though we are now quite near the coast and can see the choppy waters in the distance. Until one has had this amazing perspective, it is hard to imagine the true meaning of "as far as the eye can see," for there are times the ground below seems to stretch on forever. Entire villages and even towns seem tiny by comparison to the sheer scope of vision offered by being so high above our beloved home.

     We were not able to travel particularly close to London, to my regret, in part because we have only so much in the way of supplies, but I can only imagine it would be particularly breathtaking seen from above and out of the crowded paths and shops. Even writing of the experience seems insufficient, for words cannot accurately capture the splendor of the greatest nation on Earth seen from Heaven's own view of it. Still, I am striving to do it some justice if only to attempt to share this sense of wonder I feel with you, for I can never be certain that this is an experience I shall ever have when this adventure is done.

     Looking at the world like this, so many things become possible, and for the first time without needing Sir James's bold assurances, I must wonder if Dr. Bowe could possibly have begun to do the things his books say he has, for at this moment, all things seem possible, though remaining quite far-fetched. The detail of his descriptions and how he describes the wonder of encountering something new so perfectly captures these moments that I now imagine the man must once have been some kind of explorer who went so far from home as to get a feel for such adventures before his mind began to fill in the darker corners of the map. What then, I wonder, might be fact, out of the many volumes certain to be works of fiction?

While I would attempt to go on further about the wonders of flight through the mild skies of this time of year, I am uncertain I could add anything to the wonder you must surely already feel at the thought of it. Even when we were children, you always did have such a vibrant imagination.

Instead, I shall tell you some piece of the more mundane details of the trip. I am afraid I had quite misjudged the Captain in my first estimations. I have visited the front of the ship many times since and found the man I had previously thought of as a disheveled and perhaps senile scarecrow quite ably steering the ship to take best advantage of the weather we have been given. He looks far steadier on the occasionally unsteady and shifting deck of his bridge than he ever did on land, and I see much more of the old veteran of two wars in him now than I do the old man. Indeed, one cannot help but meet the old veteran in the man when anywhere in hearing, for as he travels, he tells tales like no other I have ever heard. Where many soldiers recount war stories, those often involve their fellows, and shared experience. Captaining an airship is a lonely activity, it seems, and requires flawless judgment and a perfect eye and hand, at least if you would believe the Captain.

As it is, he reminds me very much of the older fellows who gather about dockside taverns and spin sailor's tales of the sea and its wonders, dangers and mysteries, and their part in these tales of nigh impossible (and occasionally truly impossible) scope. The difficulty in this case is that it is impossible to tell which these are, for the man has been at this wheel since he was a young man in the 1770s, and no doubt he has seen a great deal of adventure in that time. And, of course, as I have noted, when flying over England and seeing the world so far below, nearly anything seems possible. Despite which, the Captain and his endless tales of navigating the skies stretches the definitions of anything, in this regard. Still, if he has done one tenth of the tasks he claims to have behind the wheel of this craft and the other he piloted since late in the Colonial wars, then surely he must be one of the most accomplished pilots in all of England.

In addition to this, another experience is common to the front of the ship. I have, in previous letters, expressed my sympathies for Harriet Wright, a woman only a couple of years your senior, Miss Coltrane's cousin, the virginian. She is a regular visitor to the front quarters, in part because she seems quite curious about the workings of the wheel and the ship's navigational systems, staring at them with a childlike wonder. But she also, it seems, attends to receive long and stern lectures on how a young woman should comport herself from the Captain's wife.

Harriet shows up three and four times a day as if to present herself for inspection, and Mrs. Fisher unfailingly provides just this service, going over all of Harriet's long list of faults and shortcomings in great detail. Undaunted by what seems to me to be scolding, Harriet nonetheless adjusts her skirts, goes to change her shoes, makes mental note to fix her hair, shifts her hat and carefully changes her manner, ceases fidgeting nervously, and otherwise tries to politely acknowledge every bit of chiding advice she receives from her elder. She then proceeds to humbly submit herself for further scolding later, for no matter how many times this scenario repeats itself, and no matter how much poor Harriet attempts to follow her cousin's exemplary lead, gesture for gesture, and attempts to cleave to Mrs. Fisher's advice and honor her scolding, she does not seem to develop a habit of it, and the list of faults grows no shorter with her next visit.

Despite this, each time she shows up, she wears the same simplistically optimistic expression as if she thinks this time she may have gotten it right, even though I am well able to find three or four shortcomings with just cursory glances, and while I have a fair eye for detail, I do not pretend to be any expert in the proper behaviors and dress of young women beyond knowing what well appeals. Mrs. Fisher, on the other hand, has clearly spent much time and practice becoming an expert in just that, and carries herself as such.

More than once, Miss Coltrane has come to the front

seeking her companion. She does not share any curiosity for the workings of the ship, barely glancing about. Perhaps she truly has no curiosity as to the science of it all, or has simply been airborne enough times in this very vessel that it has become common and forgettable experience for her, hard as I find it to imagine this could ever become commonplace for anyone. Each time, Mrs. Fisher looks her over in much the same discerning manner I have seen Mr. Toomes study everyone, as if looking for some fault. Identical to the results of Miss Coltrane's meeting with Mr. Toomes, each time Mrs. Fisher finds herself lacking for anything to say to Miss Coltrane beyond polite exchange, and thus is Harriet Wright usually rescued from the fashionable torment to which she keeps subjecting herself.

For what it is worth, lest you should imagine Mrs. Fisher an exceptionally well tailored ogress of some sort, her manners are also perfect, and she treats the gentlemen of the ship cordially, as if she were the hostess and they her guests. Her fault-finding is quite restricted to the young women of the ship, as if she had taken it upon herself to serve as governess, and to absolutely assure that no untoward behavior occurs aboard *Dame Fortuna* just because it was once a rough military conveyance. I am certain her attitude towards the gentlemen would quite change if she were to suspect any improper behavior might occur because of them.

As it is, while she has been unfailingly polite to him, I am quite certain she does not think a great deal of Eddy and his constant rugged look and insistence upon wearing his kilt at all times to all occasions. Though she treats him with the same smiles and courtesy she gives to all of the other men of the voyage, when she thinks his back is turned and none are looking, she can muster quite the withering, narrow-eyed scowl in his direction. Eddy, you see, is very much used to the company of soldiers, and he sometimes slips into language Mrs. Fisher does not approve of, noticeably, any insult worse then 'dog.' Eddy is now used to freezing at the sound of a snapping fan, and we have only been keeping company for a short time.

The one additional benefit to Mrs. Fisher's disapproval is that she keeps Matthew quite some distance from Eddy whenever her ward is within her sight, and warns him repeatedly not to bother the guests, though none other have seemed to mind his curiosity so much, and for at least the first ten or fifteen questions, I usually find his youthful exuberance refreshing.

I have also at last met the first mate. Mr. Taylor is a strong and strapping lad of England, of excellent manner, and obvious recent naval experience. In many ways, he very much reminds me of a younger version of your honorable father in physical resemblance and comportment. He has a crisp accent and clear voice, common to many of those who have become accustomed to giving orders over battlefields or to carry over the wind aboard a sailing vessel. It serves well here as well. Though not quite so tall as I am, he outweighs me by at least two stone, and even off duty holds himself almost as rigid as does Mr. Toomes. Despite this military bearing, he has been one of the only men of the ship who has so far politely refused to attend Sir James's card games, though he has been invited repeatedly.

The card games continue to be something of a marvel to me, and have given me a good deal more insight into Sir James's character. Though there was no need, he selectively invites the crewers of the ship, of whom there are eight, to attend his games, usually two at a time. He is firm about the manners of those who attend, and has asked more than one man to leave when he grew too upset, usually after a few drinks, and one to leave simply because he'd imbibed perhaps a bit too much and was speaking of subjects unbecoming a gentleman of England. These events are rare, and though of lower classes, it seems the men value this time with their betters enough that they make effort to comport themselves well. Eddy, of course, is always in attendance, and even he watches his tongue to a greater than normal degree when in Sir James's presence, though Sir James's old friend is given considerably more room to speak freely than, I think, anyone else would be. Mr. Toomes occasionally attends, and occasionally politely turns the invitations down. I try to attend whenever I am not about some other business, for the company remains very informative.

More interestingly, while Sir James only plays cards with

no coin or wager involved when playing only with myself and Eddy, when the crewers are about, he seems more willing to gamble, as is their expectation and habit when cards are involved. Though he gives no sign of it, and I have yet to determine precisely how, I suspect that Sir James is not entirely honest in his playing, for he loses to the men of poorer station much more often than when he is playing purely for the pastime of it, and those who show manner enough to last out the game until they are called to their next shift or to sleep have always left with more in their pocket than when they arrived. He seems quite well humored about this fact, and the men love him all the more for it.

While he is legend for the mechanical creation he invented and piloted during the war, the longer I spend with him, the more I realize that even without such genius and fortune, he would be a leader among men. He establishes such friendship and loyalty among men of many stations, and even manages to slowly educate the manual laborers who serve to feed the engines and do the heavy lifting, as it were, in manners and the pursuits of a gentleman of England. Whatever woman he does finally agree to marry from among his many prospects will surely end up the envy of England.

I fear I must end this letter now, my dearest, for it is nearly mealtime, and Sir James wishes to discuss some piece of our plans for recruiting the next members of our traveling group, though we are quite some time away from America as yet. Still, I can understand his desire to be overprepared rather than under.

However far away I get from you, my darling, my heart remains with you, and I go into this bold undertaking that we may have a future together.

With love,
Gregory Conan Watts

From the journals of Gregory Conan Watts,
March 28th, 1815
Skies over the Atlantic Ocean
47°02'N 24°38'W

Editor's Note:

Gregory kept detailed journals, with an entry for almost every day of his travels, however, for the sake of brevity, the majority of those entries have not been included here. Most of the ocean crossings and long boring travel has been cut, as is the main benefit to armchair exploration. This section is included to help introduce his traveling companions and give some idea as to their routines aboard ship, as well as reminding you that these heroes are, in fact, human, and thus can get bored.

– Dr. Cordelia Bentham-Watts

Today saw something of a change in the routine we have been following for the past week. Though the card games and conversation have been a continuing source of entertainment for the gentlemen aboard, apparently it was insufficient for Miss Coltrane's tastes, as she announced that she had made all arrangements to host an afternoon tea party in the sitting area. While we have had our breaks for tea each day, I quickly learned this was to be a much more formal occasion, as well as a chance for some of us who have not spent extensive time with the whole of the crew to better acquaint ourselves with each other. Mrs. Fisher was particularly excited by this turn of events, and quickly set herself to helping with the final preparations as soon as the announcement was passed among the various members of the crew.

The afternoon was to be full of surprises. The first among them was from Eddy, arriving clean shaven and as well scrubbed as I had yet seen him, though his wardrobe had not much changed. Sir James likewise took the occasion quite seriously and dressed in full military finery to set the best of examples for the rest of us at his sister's function. I did my best to put myself suitably together for the occasion, but in truth felt quite plain by comparison. At the very least I was able to take some strange comfort in the presence of Mr. Toomes, who could not find a polite cause to fail to attend. While he dressed up perfectly well, though nothing out of the ordinary, since he is always quite formal, Elliot Toomes and parties go together something like oil and water; they can coexist in the same rough location without ever actually blending. Even in my tendencies towards being a social wallflower, I was still far more social than my longest-term traveling companion.[7]

Miss Jillian, perhaps with a bit of help from Mrs. Fisher, had everything prepared by the time the rest of us arrived. It was made abundantly clear by Mrs. Fisher that the event was all planned out, and all would happen on schedule. There was an opportunity for formal exchanges of pleasantries, and plenty of refreshments. Despite our rough surroundings and limited space, when traveling with the Coltranes, apparently, there is always room for a bit of civilization and comfort.

That civilization also included the ladies of our group. While they often go about in attractive, but somewhat casual garb for ease of movement about the confines of the ship (Miss Coltrane's usually in heathered grays, to hide the lurking coal dust), today they were entirely formally dressed for a social occasion. I might even have to venture to guess that Miss Wright had gotten some aid with her wardrobe, or had already had four or five sessions with Mrs. Fisher in order to make corrections, for she looked almost entirely together, even if in manner she still was fairly clearly making efforts to emulate her cousin.

For some time, all went according to the carefully laid plan. Despite a bit of the ship's occasional slight rolling motions and adjustments, I got the impression that this was not nearly the first time they had done such an event on board this ship, both Miss Jillian and Mrs. Fisher looking quite practiced, while Miss

---

7 Having met Mr. Toomes, I can assure you that while he was a most steady man, a few of the place settings were more social than he was.
– C B-W

Wright appeared to be practicing, at least. We had opportunity to exchange some of the crew's impressions on the voyage so far, and what expectations and plans people had upon visiting New York.

Throughout the pleasant conversation, however, I could not help but watch the siblings. Having realized how they communicated, following a second, silent conversation even in the midst of casual talk, I began to realize how complex and nuanced their ability to speak to one another is. Small gestures of her fan, posture, expressions – all things one could easily miss were one not actively looking.

Following their gazes as subtly as I might, I quickly got the impression they were taking advantage of this gathering to exchange thoughts about the rest of us. I do not know if it was a matter of professional exchange, or more likely, given the setting, some thought on how each of us were conducting ourselves in such a formal setting, perhaps the two of them assessing how we might do as diplomats, or at least at not embarrassing them in finer surrounds. Under the lens, as it were, I paid extra attention to my manners and responses, trying not to be too distracted by being aware I was being observed.

Any tension I might have felt – or any worry that I might end up the embarrassment of the party – subsided when Miss Wright, after doing so well for a significant time, had the misfortune of mishandling one of the biscuits. In the process of trying to take a delicate bite in the manner of her cousin, it crumbled entirely, and both the biscuit and a fair helping of fruit jam ended up falling down the front of her dress. Had she been a slighter woman, perhaps, it might have been a lesser accident, or simply another stain, which she has an abundance of on some of her other dresses.

Sir James had the good grace to look away immediately, of course. I pulled my eyes away fairly soon after, while Eddy took a few seconds longer. Enough that where his eyes fell earned him a stern and disapproving gaze from Mrs. Fisher. Thankfully, before she had to draw additional attention to the matter, Sir James rescued his friend and made my life that much easier by quickly drawing our attention to one of the lovely pieces of artwork upon the wall, an early sketch of the outside of the battle suit.

Eventually, poor Harriet had to be taken from the room, nearly in tears, that they could retrieve the errant biscuit and find her a new dress, as well as assessing any danger to this one. They were gone for a significant time while the gentlemen of the ship gained a new appreciation for the Coltranes' tastes in artwork, daring not to even glance backwards, even so much to see if Mrs. Fisher might still be glaring at us. She is a formidable enough woman, I could only imagine that I did not need to look, almost feeling her gaze instead.

The incident was mostly put behind us by Miss Jillian's return. With a few disarming and polite witticisms, she rescued the mood fairly ably, inviting everyone back to the table. The rest of the primary gathering continued without further interruptions, save for Miss Harriet daring to return, put back together and dressed a little less formally, and once again in her usual pre-Mrs. Fisher-inspection state, but at least willing to make a new effort at convincing us she could be a proper lady. Her manners obviously need work, but I cannot fault her conviction.

Eventually, almost as if Miss Jillian had planned for some interruption, even if she had not predicted precisely its character, the party broke up into smaller conversations precisely on schedule. Well supervised, but in different parts of the room, people had an occasion to speak in more mixed company than typical, and I was able to speak to the ladies a little more than I had before. Speaking with Mrs. Fisher and Miss Harriet went almost precisely as I would have anticipated. Small chatter, talk of anticipation about New York, including some expectation of shopping and the like. This is not to say they were unpleasant at all, and I enjoyed a chance to get to know Mrs. Fisher by more than observation. Likewise, my feeling of some kinship with Miss Harriet continued, amidst several awkward silences that assured the two least formally experienced and adept members of the company that the other was not entirely alone.

Miss Coltrane, in complete contrast, was a continual surprise. She had little patience for small talk on shopping and the like. Rather, she quickly complimented me on my work in such a fashion as to suggest that she had paid significant attention to the reports of the war. While is is not unusual, certainly, for some word of the conflict, when it appeared in the news, to be read to all members of the household, it seemed that either she perused them herself or her brother spared few details. She knew even some of the more obscure reports, never meant for truly public consumption, but released to some officers on various fronts, such as Sir James. Her attention to detail, combined with her memory, stunned me. She kept the conversation polite, of course, but not only had she obviously been aware of my writings, she made numerous comparisons to what they reminded her of, in the process giving me some concept of just how well read our hostess is.

Matters of warfare, even as light as we attempted to keep it, turned eventually to the philosophy of the matter, and its references in the past. I had to apologize a couple of times, for her French was certainly superior to my own, let alone her Latin. That she was as well versed in Latin as she proved shouldn't have surprised me, given how entirely clever she's proven herself. I did my best to keep up, as I had to agree with her in many cases, that translated work often loses something of its meaning. In one of my apologies, I also learned, in her gentle correction, that she hadn't been speaking in Latin on quoting Aristotle, but Greek. I had to wonder just how widely read she truly was. Especially given that in addition to classical sources, she was equally adept at referencing modern works, including mention of conversations via letters with the wives of many of today's most prominent men of politics, science and philosophy.

The party ended all too soon. When away from home, whether in wartime or now in odder ventures, it's the little touches of civility one comes to appreciate. It did leave me with quite a lot to consider. In particular, I have to wonder if Miss Jillian is not entirely as impressive and surprising an individual as her brother, and yet she has still not managed to quite tame Miss Wright, even after all her time and efforts.

American Colonies
The Civilized West

From the journals of Gregory Conan Watts,
April 12th, 1815[8]
New York
40º 47'N 073º 58'W

We have settled in New York temporarily. It has been a pleasure to return to civilization after so much time in the air. Though I did begin to grow used to it, a break in the routine is most welcome now. We will not be staying here for long, I fear. Per our instructions, we leave tomorrow to make contact with an old university friend of our employer.

Lord Donovan has not given us much information on just how much contact he keeps with Dr. Jonathan Allen Mitchell, but at least he apparently maintains some. To my understanding, few others from the Oxford community claim even that. It is my understanding that the doctor was, in his time as a professor at Oxford, one of our nation's leading minds in the field of mechanics. Sir James has confirmed that the doctor amassed quite the impressive collection of writings, many of which helped plant the seeds for Sir James's own mechanical works, while others were of such complexity that even Sir James confesses he is still in awe of them despite his own successes in the field.

However, while the details are not entirely known, the doctor left the university under somewhat contentious circumstances. The limited rumors I am now aware of suggest it had something to do with his marriage. Apparently there was some controversy involved with it, and shortly after he was married, he left the university entirely. Though normally they would be loath to let go of someone with such knowledge of state

---

8 Yes, it did take them nearly 30 days to cross the Atlantic. Remember, my modern readers, that this is 1815. In 1774 dirigibles were used only for battlefield observation, as they were often outpaced by the artillery, particularly if it was windy. You may be so used to 82-hour crossings from Hyde Park to Central Park that you have forgotten that the Daughterland used to be 'wild' and 'far away.' It used to be that a disreputable son could be sent into exile in Boston and never heard from again. Now exacerbated fathers must spring for passage to Western Australia. – C B-W

secrets and technology as Dr. Mitchell, apparently some sort of agreement was struck. He now lives in the New England colonies, though well away from any major settlement. The Coltranes have been quite excited to meet the man after having heard so much about him through the rumors circulated about Oxford during Sir James's time there.

Apparently, Lord Donovan is of the idea that the doctor might be some use to us in helping refit the dirigible to be better suited for long distance travel and otherwise make helpful modifications that will aid us in our journey, since our endeavors and needs are quite different than those for which the dirigibles were originally designed. Lord Donovan hopes that his note of introduction and Sir James's own reputation will be sufficient to get us an audience with the doctor.

From the journals of Gregory Conan Watts,
April 18th, 1815
Location removed
~44N ~68W

    We have now spent a full day in Dr. Mitchell's labs, and
they are quite the marvel of science. Finding the place at all was
extremely difficult, and if we had not had a dirigible, I am not
certain we would have discovered it at all. The doctor's residence
is in a secluded cove. There are no roads to the place, and any
venture here by land would require significant exertion. Aside
from air travel, it would take not only a boat to reach this place
under most circumstances, but also a skilled navigator who is
knowledgeable about the region. There are many treacherous rock
formations out beyond the cove, not all of which are visible at any
time save low tide.

    Supplies are shipped in by one such knowledgeable
navigator, hired by the doctor, once a month. There is another ship
moored to the docks here that I suspect would be for the doctor's
use if he ever needed to travel, but like much else here, it appears
in poor repair. I would not want to trust my life to such a wreck at
sea.

    Once past the obstacles to approach, the place is habitable
enough. The doctor has found some means of drawing the salt
from seawater, and as such, has a large flock of sheep living here
in unusually green pastures for a coastal locale. The creatures are
largely allowed to roam free about the land. They can no more
easily get out of the cove than a man could get in, and as yet, none
seem to have shown any interest in leaving green fields and flat
ground for difficult rocks or rocky sand.

    Aside from the hostility of the location, the simple docks
and their sole resident, and the vast herds of sheep, the only thing
evident upon our approach was a large, two-story home, not
dissimilar to those kept by men of some means in the countryside.
Much like the boat on the docks, it appeared in poor condition
indeed, all loose shingles and discolored wood, save for the
weather vane and two lightning rods, all of which appeared new

by comparison. On the sea, there are great paddle wheels placed about at odd angles, spinning one way and another constantly, like a half submerged field of children's pinwheels.

As we neared, a mooring post and platform began to rise from the ground next to the house, lifted on a metal framework. Even from a distance, I was able to hear the grinding of gears and metal on metal as the post rose from what had appeared bare ground. When it was fully extended, we were able to moor the dirigible and descend to the ground. We reached the bottom of the stairs to find the large doorway to the house opened to us by Agnes, a large, middle-aged woman of hefty build and Scottish descent. She bade us enter quickly, then offered us tea. She apparently serves as Dr. Mitchell's housekeeper, shepherd, and cook. She is the sole living resident here, aside from the doctor and his flocks of sheep. She was polite enough, but bade us wait in the front parlor while she checked on the doctor.

The front parlor was a fright. It was filled with all manner of devices, none of which had any purpose I could fathom. Especially true as most of them seemed to be unfinished, half-finished, or simply composed of ill-fitting pieces bolted or welded together in some wild fit of fancy before being discarded. One had to be careful in moving about for the presence of bolts, screws, gears, cogs and scraps of metal about the floor. One area had what passed for a table and chairs, though it was really just a handful of crates of differing sizes pushed together and kept clean of any of the doctor's work, quite possibly at Agnes's insistence, if I had to guess.

We made ourselves as comfortable as we could under the circumstances, and talked over eventual servings of tea. It was almost two hours before the doctor graced us with his presence. At least he was polite enough, and quickly apologetic for keeping us so long. The doctor is a small man, not even the height of Jillian Coltrane, and so thin and pale that I might suspect she outweighs him as well. When he speaks, it is in such a quiet tone that one has to lean forward and strain to hear over even the distant movement of the waves on the beach outside, or any rustling of those in the house. I found this particular trait especially taxing, as the crates did not provide a lot of support or comfort as it was. Though he claimed to be pleased to see us, his sincerity was hard to judge, given that the doctor is not a man given to much expression, with everything he says and does seeming drowned in some terrible melancholy.

We took his welcome for what it was worth, and settled in as best we were able under the circumstances. Agnes dotes upon the doctor, and urges him to eat at every opportunity when she has his attention. Save for the mechanism which raises and lowers the mooring post, we saw nothing here in working order. The doctor himself, while polite enough, seemed somewhat distant, offering only vague greetings. We made a couple of attempts to introduce ourselves and state our purpose, but he seemed uncomprehending. Only when we mentioned Oxford did he show any sign of true animation. In the clearest, and most hopeful words he had yet uttered, in response to this effort at introduction, he asked, finally, "So, are you here to kill me then, at last?"

April 20th, 1815
Dr. Mitchell's Hidden Cove
~44N ~68W

My Dearest Cordelia,

Today I witnessed a most bizarre series of events, and learned a great deal about Harriet Wright. These occurrences brought to mind some of your flights of fancy as a child, so I immediately thought to write you of the day's happenings.

We have been staying with Dr. Jonathan Allen Mitchell, a former Oxford professor of some repute, though I have begun to question whether being sequestered here in America has done his sanity some harm. In any case, by the accounts of those who know him and his history better, he has always been known for his eccentricity.

We had some initial misunderstandings as to our purpose here. I will not trouble your mind with the exact nature of the difficulties. Sir James dispelled his misconceptions, but reassuring him of our good will did not produce the desired effects. Instead, the doctor quickly dismissed us from his presence and informed us we were not welcome in his laboratory, and that we should finish our tea and be gone. He then quit our presence with some haste.

Though we were going to leave, Miss Coltrane, for some reason, bade us stay and wait a time to see if his temper would improve. Mr. Toomes and her brother quickly backed her in this argument, so we posted watch, and went back to the dirigible to wait a while.

While the gentlemen of the ship were in discussion on how to proceed, Miss Wright, without alerting anyone as to her intent, descended back down the mooring post steps to the doctor's home. For the rest, I have only Miss Wright and Dr. Mitchell's accounts of it, but have no reason, having witnessed her works since, to doubt them. Apparently, she attempted to engage the doctor in conversation. Failing that, she took up one of his wrenches and some oil, and set to repairing a grinding noise we had earlier heard when the mooring post was mechanically raised from ground level. In the process, apparently, she stated that some of the bolts seemed loose, leading to it not rising perfectly straight, thus leading to metal grinding across metal.

Even having seen her at work with tools now on the doctor's machines, I can scarce believe this is the same farmer's daughter, brought to England to be a lady's companion. Certainly not the young woman who so fancies courtly life as to try to emulate her cousin's graces at every opportunity. Still, apparently she has quite the gift for artifice.

Sir James offered some explanation for myself and the others wondering after this gift of hers. Miss Wright's parents, well off as Virginia considers such things, had been among the first to see that the new laws of England regarding trade in slaves could well impact their business, and thus they invested heavily in some of the new mechanical devices invented by Oxford scientists, intended to mechanize more parts of farm labor.

Shortly after this time, her eldest brother was admitted to university. Harriet took his place helping out as best she could on the farm. While she is possessed of only limited education for a young American lady, it turned out that she had a phenomenal memory for how mechanical devices are pieced together, and while she is no inventor or innovator herself, once she has seen instructions or seen how a thing functions, she can repair almost any device quite ably.

He went on to explain to me that though she did not invent the suit, her eye for when something needs adjustment or bolts need tightening is so advanced that so long as she has seen his schematics for that section of the suit, she can repair it quite ably. This helps explain some of the activity at night at the Coltrane residence – much of the work taking place on the suit is done by Miss Wright. He remains the primary mechanic, but she is his most capable assistant, so trusted with his work that she is often allowed to venture into the workshop alone and unsupervised. She still does serve as Miss Coltrane's lady's companion, of course, but the real reason for her presence with her cousins is this skill with mechanics.

According to the Coltranes, they discovered her gift when they visited America in the time shortly preceding the war. Sir James is a resourceful man, and when he noticed her gift, he helped out the family considerably that they might be able to spare her, for he needed a skilled assistant to help him realize the machine. Apparently, Miss Wright in turn was most enthused to leave farm life behind, in the hopes that she might learn from Jillian and become a proper lady of England. This, at least, is certainly no act. Whatever her gift, she most assuredly is as devoted as she seems to being able to present herself as a fine lady of society and eventually to marry well.

Her difficulties with this pursuit now no longer surprise me though, for perhaps if she truly had such a gift for the manly pursuit of artifice, certainly well beyond my own understanding, then perhaps some part of her mind is entirely unsuited for womanly pursuits. It still strikes me as quite unnatural, but if Sir James continues to trust her skill, then I trust him well enough to do the same.

Whatever her background, her work and observations moved the formerly obstinate Dr. Mitchell. He enthusiastically welcomed her to his home, and bade the rest of us return straightaway. We were allowed, at last, past the front parlor, filled with clutter and his recently discarded experiments, and shown upstairs. The house is extremely spartan, but they do keep guest beds, at least, and the doctor's housekeeper, Agnes, has made sure we have at least minimal comforts. In addition to the rooms, the upstairs also includes at least three workshops full of all manner of experiments and devices, all in far better repair than the discarded items littering the ground floor. There is, apparently, also an expansive basement workshop, but we have not been shown that as of yet.

In any case Dr. Mitchell now seems extremely fond of Harriet, and his tone has changed entirely. Where before he was quiet and morose, he is now possessed of a manic energy and desire to help, taking in all details of our travels so far and what we might need to go forward. He seems quite taken with the plans for the dirigible, discussing them with the Coltranes at length, doing so even as I write this letter. He was speaking rapidly to Sir James of the inefficiencies of coal power, and how his new water powered theory was much more efficient, and easier to refuel.

Apparently, one can fully outfit a dirigible with only river water, if one has the means to split the water into hydrogen for float ballast, and oxygen for fuel. The idea apparently came to him while he was setting up to power his cove using waves and tide, by means of his pinwheels. Sir James's look of wonder was only surpassed by his look of relief when Dr. Mitchell pointed out his purification system was a valid large-scale test.

He has also shown significant interest, incidentally, in my camera, and though I can scarce understand a word he says, I have come to understand that he believes he can make a device with the same functioning, but lighter and faster to function. I have given him leave to examine my own camera, so long as he did not damage it, while Sir James has assured me that if any harm comes to it, he will make restitution and see it fixed properly.

I marvel at the sudden change in the man, and all that his bouts of genius might mean for easing our way forward. Even more, I marvel at this new discovery of the hidden talents of Miss Wright.

Because of the amount of time that will be required in order to fully refit the dirigible, it has been decided that after a few more days to go over all of the arrangements to be made, Sir James, Eddy, Mr. Toomes and myself will journey onward towards St. Louis to pick up the next member of our intrepid crew, while the Fishers, our engineering crew and the women of our company continue to enjoy Dr. Mitchell's hospitality.

In any case, my love, I thought these curiosities and the revelations concerning Miss Wright might spark your imagination, as well as revealing something new about one of the heretofore most hapless of my companions. I send you all my love and best wishes.

My love, always,
Gregory Conan Watts

From the collected communication of Elliot Toomes
May 5th, 1815
New York

Sir,

We have successfully completed the first of your instructions upon reaching the American colonies. We have made friendly contact with Dr. Mitchell, who is now aiding the Coltranes in making modifications to their dirigible for better travel. I do not know how long this will delay our movements, but for the moment, James Coltrane, Edward McBride, Gregory Watts, and myself will be journeying inland to retrieve the rest of the crew. I apologize that I lost track of Franzini and his companion previously, and assure you it will not happen again. I believe everything is in place to ensure their cooperation this time, however reluctant.

I am including a map to Dr. Mitchell's cove, but urge utmost caution. The way in is as hazardous as previously reported. It can be reached by air readily enough, at least. Do not allow the appearance of the home to deceive you. I am pleased to report that the doctor's mechanical genius is entirely intact, despite some of the rumors which have made their way back to England.

On the other hand, it appears that the rumors regarding his wife are entirely true. He has so far refused to reveal any details of what happened to her, but given the medical supplies we know the doctor had delivered here for quite some time, it can be surmised that some severe illness took her life. I will try to gain more details if I can, but do not believe this is as important as assuring that Franzini and his companion are brought into the fold without too much difficulty. I am still of the opinion that there are better people who could serve much the same role you intend, but I know you feel that the man's international contacts and his companion's unique skills make them vital to your plans for this company.

I believe that the current company, particularly those in

the loop of political gossip, are growing concerned about... something. So far, I have been able to answer every overt question aimed at me. Still, I will be eager to leave their company and see them off on their journey for the good of England.

Your servant,
Elliot Toomes

May 6th, 1815
New York
40º 47'N 073º 58'W

Dear Sir,

I have come across a disturbing rumor, passed on to me through some of those gentlemen of the colony of New York that we met only a few days past. We are now traveling, and quite quickly, by railway. We have met with Dr. Mitchell and passed on your greetings, and while a few of us travel to St. Louis, he is assisting in refitting the dirigible to be better suited for the long distance travel planned for it.

Thankfully, the doctor has his own mooring post, platform, and repair facilities set up to house and work on a dirigible, because otherwise, New York would be the only place such work could be done. As it turned out, as there has been no military action here since the Colonial Wars, there also is nowhere beyond New York that is yet situated to resupply a dirigible, or even properly moor one. We have been assured that this will soon be remedied, as there is construction being made in Boston, Philadelphia and St. Louis to construct suitable supply and repair platforms to allow more military defense dirigibles to be stationed in the colonies. This would both give the colonies a wider range of aerial defenses in case of future problems, and allow these stations to easily move troops and supplies between cities.

Several cities in the southernmost colonies are vying for the rights to construct other such stations and receive recognition as viable air trading ports in anticipation of this change. However, as those colonies are not yet in accordance with English law, most notably the slave trade acts, there is considerable argument over whether they should be included in any sort of trade pact, even with the rest of America, to say nothing of the possibilities of cross-ocean trade.

For the sake of some of the gentlemen who may be reading this in your company who are unaware of the situation in America, I feel I should note that the issue of the slave trade is a hotly debated one here, sir. Many of the farms and plantations of the Southern colonies have recently lost a number of their young men, and many landowners feel they have no other reasonable source of labor. Meanwhile, many former slaves who were committed to aiding the war effort are now returning home as free men as part of their agreement to serve in the American black regiments. These served in some infantry companies, and now are trying to find their place within society without money, education or means to gain either of these things.

Indeed, I have become acutely aware of the debate in part because of the preponderance of such men who now work for the railroad, as it is a quickly expanding employer constantly in need of strong backs with little requirement for rarer skills or a high education. This is part of the reason the rails extend so quickly, and the industry has seen such success while many other companies are seeing some decline for lack of manpower, but this also puts them at the center of the increasingly heated regional debate. With Washington, Philadelphia and New York's houses of government so tied up in this Colonial issue with no end in sight, I can only wonder how long it will be before there are greater hostilities or the mother country needs to step in to arbitrate the dispute. I do understand that it is not as heated as it is certain to grow, as slave ownership is not yet outlawed, though some in the houses of parliament and upper ends of society have begun to suggest new laws to this end, but the end of the legal slave trade in England is now seeing its echoes in its colonies.

As I had stated, regional interest aside, we have become aware of a difficulty. It seems that your opponent in your wager has hired his own adventurers, as you apparently suspected he might, to directly oppose us and prove Dr. Bowe's discoveries a complete work of fiction. While at some times this news might fill me with some excitement – after all, the idea of a race certainly adds some spice to the wager – we have learned that some among their number may be taking the instruction to directly oppose us somewhat more literally than one might expect. We were warned that some men of poor and mercenary reputation had been hired by these individuals upon their arrival to give some trouble to myself, Mr. Toomes, Sir James, and Eddy. We are almost certain that they will follow the conditions of the wager like gentlemen, and not directly threaten women or those who have been hired on only for the purpose of piloting the dirigible.

While unsure of the extent of trouble we should be expecting, we nonetheless felt that it was best, when facing unknown parties, to complete our mission somewhat more discreetly than we had been doing, as well as with significantly more haste. Hence the reason we are riding the rails now, and I find myself with more than ample time to write to inform you both of the state of our mission, and facts of regional interest that may eventually impact the political situation at home. We have not yet learned the identity of any of the people placed in opposition to us by your rival, but as we gain any such information, I will pass it on as directly as I am able.

If you will pardon my humble opinion, I find myself quite motivated now to do whatever is possible to stand in your opponent's way, for the idea of hiring American thugs to attempt to hinder a wager seems to fly in the face of gentlemanly behavior to me, though perhaps your opponent, whatever his station, is not up to your high standards, sir, or perhaps he is simply unaware of the tactics which his hirelings deem appropriate in this circumstance.

Your most loyal servant,
Gregory Conan Watts

From the journals of Gregory Conan Watts,
June 1st, 1815[9]
St. Louis
38°38'N 090°12'W

As I write this, my mind is still reeling over the events of the day. I attempt here to note the details down as factually and directly as I can recall, for the sake of my later reference. We spent some time in pursuit of Mr. Franzini, or as his signboard stated, the Great Giovanni Franzini, following news of the small traveling show with which he had become attached. In the aftermath of the war years, a few of these traveling shows have sprung up, following the example of similar spectacles to be found in the European mainland, and following such practitioners as the illusionist Jacob Philadelphia.

Just as England has flocked to Sarah Siddons, delaying her announcement of retirement some few years amidst the national hunger for entertainment and diversion, the Americans too have sought after diversion and spectacle in various forms. Both transportation and cheap labor – in the form of displaced former soldiers and European immigrants seeking a new start in America after the collapse of the European alliance and all it brought with it – have cooperated. While no American performer of the reputation of Siddons has yet emerged (nor is any likely to), New York has some theaters with some claim to the title of the American Drury Lane. Meanwhile, companies touting their versions of Shakespeare and stage technicians with varying levels of talent and a variety of acts have begun to travel the civilized reaches of the Americas to fill this appetite for distraction.

My further research and new resources as we traveled revealed that Giovanni Franzini was a European performer of some small repute and, by my observations, considerable skill, but

---

9 More attentive readers will notice a large time gap. The daily journals of the trip from New York to St. Louis are of interest to those interested in early American civics and the 'wild days' of the Daughterland. As such, they have been included in several studies, all published via Cambridge press, with Watts listed as a source in the catalog. – C B-W

he also had a reputation for affiliating himself with unsavory elements in the pursuit of wealth and promotion. Likewise, he is reputed to have a considerable appetite for gambling.

While never directly arrested on the Continent, he had more than a few people of some social status accusing him of owing them a considerable sum of money, then skipping town with the debts still owed. He followed much the same pattern in England for a time, and did quite well for himself, with the rapidly growing theater-going population and rising popularity of stage phenomena, as well as the considerable national appetite for gambling. Once again, however, he found himself sought after by people with influence enough to have the backing of legal authorities, so while no firm charges have been placed against the man, I can understand why he was motivated to travel with some haste to the Americas, where his name was unknown.

At long last, we found him and his theater company in a town on the western banks of the Mississippi River. There they performed for a circuit of the towns within a few days' travel of St. Louis, which is growing quite rapidly with the news that the railways are planned to reach that city. This growth is further augmented by the news they have received approval for a mooring station for dirigibles as soon as they prove they have significant enough military resources to properly protect this national resource. Many soldiers from the Napoleonic wars have flocked to the city seeking a post with growing, rather than dwindling, needs, and many entrepreneurs of varying reputations have begun trying to stake their own claim in the considerable trade-route possibilities that exist here in this gateway city between the North and South.

After some difficult overland travel past the last of the ever-growing rails, we did make contact with a so-called Mr. Ian Moon, who was able to direct us to the traveling show's manager, though they were initially quite loath to let us even speak with Mr. Franzini, who had become their premier attraction. Still, when Mr. Toomes pulled him aside briefly for a quiet conversation, Mr. Moon became significantly more helpful, though I remain uncertain precisely what offer our employer has made to so entice

Mr. Franzini or what he has that made certain that those who employ him would have so little difficulty parting with him. On the latter, I might be able to guess, however.

Regardless, we were taken to a dusty little saloon full of women of obvious ill repute and scandalous dress, and men of rough character. In truth, the smell of the place alone almost enticed me to turn about and leave this part of the mission behind, but my fellows took to the task with enough vigor that I was reminded of my commitment to the mission, while being certain this would be far from the worst I would see going forward. It was here that I had occasion to see Mr. Franzini in action, for we had arrived just in time for the show. Despite priding myself on my observational skills, I cannot say how he performed even a single one of his tricks. I am certain that in some part, however, this is owed to the presence of his assistant.

He referred to the woman as Julietta Penn, and perhaps that was her name, but she had a dark and Mediterranean look to her. Indeed, while feeling as though I should very much like to see her dressed with some sensibility, or at least offer her a blanket for modesty, in her own fashion she was utterly captivating. Dark skinned with hair a rich black, she spoke with a hint of an accent I could not quite place, certainly some part Italian, but also some brand of Eastern European. Her dress was covered in sequins, ruffles and feathers, and tight enough about the hip as to give some idea of the motion of her legs as she walked. On the raised stage, one could also see the not insignificant height of her heels, despite which she walked with the grace and elegance of any lady I have ever met, though I am quite certain this was no lady.

I am uncertain if it scandalizes me less or more even now that despite her clingy dress, her eyes remain her most unforgettable feature, bright green and vibrant, locking on the members of the audience such that one would think she was performing directly for them. I have heard rumors of women of somewhat similar dress and manner appearing upon the Parisian stage – and perhaps that nation is as hungry for some distraction from the costs of war as England – but I had scarce believed it until now. Throughout the show, I found myself at least thrice closing my eyes and recalling my sweet Cordelia's face, if only to assure myself that I could.

Giovanni Franzini himself, so aided by some combination of his own skills and his assistant's capable distraction and whatever capabilities at sleight of hand she herself possessed, put on quite the show. Small objects were made to appear and disappear, flowers were produced from thin air, and at the end of his show, he seemed to catch a musket ball in his bare hand. And while I am certain that all of this, most specifically the last, was a trick of quick fingers, tricks to draw the eye of the audience away, and simple plays upon the audience's expectations, as all illusionist acts are, I cannot yet say for certain how a single one of these tricks was done, save for one which I would learn the full solution to later on in the evening. I can say for certain that to that point, Giovanni Franzini had perhaps the fastest hands I had ever seen. But I shall return to that rumination. Beyond admiration for his clearly superior reflexes and stagecraft, the man himself was most in need of a beautiful assistant, for he himself reminded me of nothing so much as a fox: thin, wiry, and shifty, with large eyes that seemed to take in everything and everyone as if they might either be the hen house or the dog guarding it.

If he was indeed the gambler that he was reputed to be, I was quite certain at the time that he was looking for marks, as would later be proven quite true. A short man, to go with the slight physique, his thin and oiled beard served only to make his chin and jaw seem all the more narrow. A wispy and equally well oiled mustache did lend him a certain sort of sinister mystique from time to time, and at other times just served to make him seem the more untrustworthy. His dark brown hair contrasted strongly with a pale complexion, though I am uncertain how someone who travels so much by train and attends wide open towns like these could so obviously avoid the sun, and imagined him immediately to be the type to sleep in the daytime while working late at the gambling hall after his shows were completed.

Once more, with hindsight on the day, I am glad to say that for once my expectations and first impressions were proven quite correct. I was growing somewhat tired of so consistently misjudging people, even if they have been some of the most unusual people I have ever encountered. Giovanni Franzini, in his own way and for his talents and contacts may be an unusual and even exceptional man, but if so, he is exceptional in precisely the way he seems to be.

We watched his show with amazement. Eddy, in particular, seemed quite taken with the entire thing, but most particularly the dancing girls, which did not seem to discomfit him nearly so much as it did myself and Sir James. Mr. Toomes, as is his tendency, managed to sit through the entire spectacle of actors, tumblers, jugglers, dancing girls, and the finale of the magic act without giving any hint that he enjoyed any part of the show, or more to the point, that he disapproved of any piece of it any more than any other.

We were directed to the saloon floor and a particular table when the show had finished, there to wait for Mr. Franzini. Mr. Toomes waited there, while Eddy spoke with one of the showgirls, and more than a few of the working girls attached to the saloon approached both Eddy and especially Sir James, seeming drawn to him like they could smell money. Sir James comported himself like a perfect gentleman, of course, while Eddy did not leave with any of the women, but nor did he seem to discourage their attentions.

I fell somewhere in between the two, somehow. One of the girls approached me with offer of her services, whereupon, of course, I told her that my interest lay elsewhere. Somehow she convinced me to buy her a drink while I told her all about my dear, sweet Cordelia. She seemed to find the entire romance quite endearing, and stated just that often, appearing enraptured by the conversation until such time as her employer told her to get back to work.

It was about this time that a young man appeared in the saloon. I would not have noticed him, save that that section of the saloon which I had learned most often housed its regulars went quiet, as did the piano at his entrance. The latter, more than the former, drew the notice of many others, but not all. A couple of the local toughs gave the boy a wide berth, but the boy sat at one of the tables, ordered a drink, and the quiet chaos that is an American frontier saloon began once more in earnest as if nothing had happened. I put it from my mind quickly, for shortly after that Giovanni Franzini appeared from the back.

He and his assistant were directed straightaway to Mr. Toomes's table. He held up a hand, indicating he did not need my help in this one, and he spent considerable time speaking with the pair of them. Both the woman and Mr. Franzini became quite animated some time into the conversation, and at last, Franzini stood up and quite loudly declared that he did not need that kind of help and he had plenty of money, abruptly dismissing Mr. Toomes, who looked particularly cross at this reaction and rudeness. Franzini excused himself, stating that he was missing a card game, at which point he headed towards a game which had begun already, at which the youth I had mentioned previously was seated.

Unsure if I should at this point attempt to help, or simply be glad that we would not be getting the kind of help Mr. Franzini might be, I just watched while Mr. Toomes stewed. As Mr. Franzini was introducing himself to the dealer and taking a seat at the table, the magician's assistant approached, and shortly after her, one of the large, powerfully muscled and well armed men associated with the show moved that way as well. The assistant, now dressed slightly more practically, but quite akin to one of the saloon's working girls, attempted to rest her hand on the youth's shoulder, in much the manner the local working girls approach those men they think might have money and interest in their services.

I began to see the scheme developing: she was the distraction yet again, just as on stage, and between them, they were going to take advantage of everyone at the tables, including this bare-faced boy who they had targeted as a mark. And should anyone have difficulty with them leaving the table with their pockets freshly filled, then the show's burly laborer would discourage any outcry. I now am quite certain I understand precisely how Mr. Franzini achieved such notoriety, so many who felt he owed them a significant sum, and yet no charges had been officially filed. And with his skills as a magician, who could say how many other means he used to cheat those who saw his coin on the table and thought they might pocket some of it.

Except this time, the plan was met with what they had to regard as an oddity. As soon as the dark woman's hand was laid on the youth's shoulder, it was brushed away. I remember the words, in part for the oddest accent I think I have ever heard. "I have a deep and abiding disregard for whores." It had the pacing of American Southern, slow and distinct, but the rich smoothness of European French or Spanish. And then there were elements to his speech that I could not place. Only a few words, but with a cadence and pronunciation like none I had ever heard.

The woman was as stunned as I, but had a biting response, sounding almost hurt. I can imagine that in a place such as this, her advances were not often brushed off, and certainly not so abruptly. "You don't like boys, do you?" she could almost sound like she was spitting, with the Eastern European sharpness coming out through the fading hints of a more refined Italian tilt to her voice. At the insult, the room around them stilled. I am uncertain if it was my imagination, but I thought some few of the regulars made certain they were not near the table.

Suddenly quite worried, I found myself searching the boy for a gun, for I have heard the tales of Americans and their affinity for firearms, such as their pride in their riflemen, and was sure that some surely had the same pride in their pistols. Some few notable duels have certainly been fought on these shores, after all. To my surprise, I did not find one. Instead, the youth had several knives. One in each boot, one to either hip, and a fifth at the base of his back, such as other men carry pistols. Despite this oddity, Franzini and his companions were too engaged in the perception of easy marks and a lot of money on the table to take any notice.

The young man took no obvious offense, beyond a derisive snort, replying simply, "Only thing appealing about boys is they ain't whores." Julietta, having quite enough, stormed off despite Mr. Franzini's initial attempt to grab for her arm and protest.

Shaking his head in anger, Franzini turned back around to face the table. This much of what happened next I remember.

"Well, that was unfortunate. Shall we get on with the game, gentlemen?" he asked with a practiced showman's charm.

The three other men at the table and the dealer began to settle themselves in for a game, but the boy remained still, both hands on the table. "If we're to have a game, sir, you and your money are welcome to play. But the four cards up your left sleeve aren't invited."

The room went cool at that, and all eyes in hearing turned towards the table. There is nothing quite so chilling when among those who take their gambling quite seriously as an accusation of a cheat. Even Eddy stopped his flirtations and took notice, starting to right himself at his chair, while Sir James, still near me, sat quite forward. When those people who take their gambling quite seriously are also mostly armed men of rough tendency and frontier sensibility, that chill grows all the more severe. Franzini knew it, and was, of course, quick with his denial.

The showman was on his game at that. "I'm afraid you must be thinking of my show. I don't bring my tricks to the table. Are you certain you want to call me a cheater, young man?" For the next moment to make any sense at all, I must reveal one of Mr. Franzini's tricks. Normally, I would say regrettably, as to reveal an illusionist's secrets would seem a dire insult. This one time I will make an exception and not feel bad in the least about it. Secreted within his specially made jacket, Mr. Franzini has a very simple mechanical device with spring technology that, with the proper subtle motion would allow him to suddenly produce a small object. In this case, after his shows, when intending to go out into his more lucrative gambling trade and thus expecting trouble, the object for the show would be replaced with a tiny flintlock pistol of little power, but even so, able to be produced and in hand ready to fire within the barest moment. I am certain this device has seen use many times, allowing Mr. Franzini to get the drop on those less than pleased with the results of their games. I digress, but felt the need, should this record ever reach some sort of public consumption, then this device would be necessary to explain the confusion that would result.

"I am not calling you a cheater yet, sir." his table mate

replied coolly, hands still flat to the table, unworried. "I am saying you have four cards insufficiently hidden in your left jacket sleeve. Remove the jacket, and you may play."

Franzini, of course, would be revealed as a cheat if he did any such thing after so clearly stating he did not bring his tricks to the table, so he could not pretend to have forgotten even, and the saloon would rapidly become a very unpleasant place. Mr. Franzini's hired muscle tensed and began a lunge towards the young man at the table, and Mr. Franzini's arm twitched, going for his pistol. The young man moved. This is where my precise recollection of events ends.

A moment later, the scene had somehow changed entirely. Giovanni Franzini's right hand, now holding the tiny pistol, was pinned to the card table by a knife through the trigger guard, plunged through somehow before the man could get his finger to the trigger, sparing him the abrupt end of his career for lack of a pointer finger. The tip of the blade also caught the end of his sleeve, firmly preventing the man from handling the gun further, or retreating from the table. The young man's right hand was held back, not even looking at the brute who had moved directly behind him, but holding a second knife to the towering man's throat, stopping him midway through his lunge, eyes looking about frantically and all other motion arrested entirely lest the slightest twitch carry him forward onto the knife blade. In that same amount of time, Eddy, with his sniper's nerves and trained reflexes, had precisely enough time to go slack jawed, staring openly. I am unsure if anyone else in the room had reacted in the least. The young man had clearly drawn two knives in time to catch the gun mid-draw, faster than the spring could put it to hand and a finger could reach the trigger, and likewise have another blade in hand in time to stop the assault of Franzini's carnival brute, not an untrained-looking fellow. Even with all the time since to process it, I cannot yet say how. Earlier, I stated Franzini had the fastest hands I had ever seen in my life, and to this evening, that was true, and yet he did not begin to compare.

The boy broke the silence. "I cannot abide a cheater."

Two saloon girls fainted, Eddy swore viciously in such a

manner that Mrs. Fisher would have fainted at. I realized I'd stopped breathing, and forced myself to start again. Sir James swore, albeit under his breath.

"The only reason you are alive, sir, is you are not worth the price of replacing the table." the young man added, before rising from the table, not even looking back, but backing off Franzini's muscle with the motion, very deliberate. The boy picked up Franzini's money from the table, and tossed some part of it to the others sitting with them before pocketing the rest. Then the boy deliberately drew out Franzini's money from his belt, and likewise distributed it. This was all slow and careful enough, and the young man obviously had quite the captive audience such that no one thought to question it, and most did not even move lest they draw more attention than they wanted at that moment. Among those being very, very still was Franzini himself.

"You are not in Europe anymore, showman. I am a kind and forgiving soul, but plenty of folk you'll find out here might hold a grudge. If any such are in the room, I hope you're ready to give fair accounting of yourself to them." the teenager added, before pocketing the share of Franzini's money he'd claimed, pulled his knife from the table, in the process sending Franzini's pistol skittering across the table to end nearer the dealer than Franzini himself, and turned towards the door. Enough time had passed that a third woman had fainted, and Eddy had managed to mostly get to his feet, though he'd not yet closed his mouth entirely. Not a man had his gun drawn.

It was at this time that I must say I finally found something to admire in Mr. Toomes and his unchanging demeanor and truly stiff upper lip. For while I was still working on the complexities of making sure inhaling followed exhaling, he was approaching the young man to meet him near the door. This got him a lot of nervous glances, no one daring say a word yet, and the boy staring at him dubiously.

Whatever they said, it was quiet, but the boy seemed amenable to talking with my traveling companion at the least. I had imagined at the time that it was a matter of trying to settle all of this chaos down, for shortly thereafter Mr. Toomes excused himself to have a pipe at the bar with the young man joining him. With the pair having a drink together and speaking in hushed tones, things returned somewhat to normal as all within seemed to have assumed that this new British benefactor had calmed the situation, as occasionally has been done, by buying the young man a drink or two. The one departure from the normal activity about the place, of course, was that more and more eyes turned to Mr. Franzini, and even his fellows from the show had abandoned him to whatever fate he'd doomed himself to by getting caught.

Speaking of whom, the oily man, suddenly looking to me something more like a drowned rat than a fox, now spoke, hopefully, turning his eyes towards myself and Sir James's table after having briefly taken a look around the room.

"Good sirs," he began, nervously, well knowing how thin a cord his life hung by in a place such as this as soon as anyone had the sense to do anything more than breathe, recover the poor women, and gape in awe, depending on their tendency. "I seem to have found myself short on funds and needing an escort from this place. I believe you had a job opportunity available? I'll work cheap. Grazi."

I did not know all the conditions of the deal which had been offered, but either Eddy was sufficient presence in his own right, Sir James worked his magic with people, or their names carried sufficient weight even here where there might well have been a number of displaced ex-soldiers that things settled to merely dark stares towards the magician. Franzini quickly agreed to whatever terms might still be offered to him if we could get him and his assistant out of this place breathing and whole. Grasping at a straw, I put out the deal that Mr. Toomes had offered, pretending that I might know its terms, but for half the money. He did not even blink now, agreeing and rushing to shake my hand, with his own shaking in such a manner that I imagined it may be some time before he could perform any of his illusions again.

It was some minutes later when Mr. Toomes returned with the young man from their conversation just outside the door. Mr. Toomes would confirm later that though he was not certain, he had some suspicion of who the youth was, and had thus taken the opportunity to confirm his suspicion and offer the last of the contracts he had been given by our employer.

He approached, the young man side by side with him. Though Franzini tensed up, he received not the slightest acknowledgment.

"Mr. Watts, I am pleased to say that our recruitment list, and with it, my role in our mission is complete until our employer gives me some further instructions. Sir James, you are in charge now. Allow me to introduce you to the last member of your company," he said, well aware that we'd added Mr. Franzini to our company already, and his assistant with him.

I am certain I expressed considerable surprise at that, for I well knew the last name on our list. The young man extended his hand in friendly enough fashion, as if nothing else had happened.

"Sam," he introduced himself. "Sam Bowe." Dr. Bowe's son.

Realizing what company he and his desperation had consigned himself to, Giovanni Franzini fainted. Julietta Penn didn't move to catch him, or even blink her eyes away from young Mr. Bowe.

June 2nd, 1815
39°38"N 89°01'W

Dear Sir,

    While yet again not truly at the beginnings of the quest you assigned us, I felt the completion of our traveling group progress enough to be worthy of noting. And already I feel quite well traveled in crossing over the Atlantic by dirigible, and imagining how our boys must have felt near the end of the Colonial War period when these airships were new and unknown to the world.

    Likewise for having seen some good portion of the American expansion, traveling from New York City to St Louis, and from there across the mighty Mississippi River to the current American frontier. We have had quite some adventure while there, I assure you, as Mr. Toomes will no doubt report. For the time being, we have set our path back towards the east to rejoin the airship crew and the women left with Dr. Mitchell with our new companions. I am not yet certain how either Mrs. Fisher or Miss Coltrane will feel about adding such a woman as Miss Penn to our number, though everyone has certainly become well aware of the nature of our journey, and that some fellows of this trip will make for unusual company. For the time being, she has made herself quite useful on the return trip, telling stories of her travels across the mainland, and explaining some bits and pieces of the contract you sent to hire them for this voyage. Now having access to Mr. Toomes's books, which he was kind enough to pass on to me, I also at last understand your reasoning for their inclusion, despite the risks they present with mercenary tendencies and ample debts lined up against them. I imagine upon our return to some lands where you may easily send us information, which shall hopefully come soon, you will let me know when such portion of their debts is paid off in lieu of actual pay as to allow them to travel more freely and access Mr. Franzini's contacts should they be necessary.

    Quite ingenious, if I may say so myself sir, ensuring that they are beholden to us for food, lodging and other comfort while you settle their accounts through your own contacts and resources. This has allowed me to trust them perhaps some small part more. Likewise, in speaking with her further, I see why in your notes to Mr. Toomes you mentioned that Mr. Franzini alone was not worth the risk involved in the hiring, and agree now that had Miss Penn not come along, we should have left him to whatever fate he'd found himself in. For while Mr. Franzini is clearly skilled, connected in ways none of the rest of us can match, and traveled in regions which none other of our company have journeyed, she has proven to be everything you claimed. For while she dresses like an American showgirl and speaks in a manner that has caused both myself and Sir James to blush more than once, she is also quite the expert on occult matters.

While belief in the supernatural is for children and people of no learning, the native populations of some of those regions we will be visiting certainly have beliefs based in savage tales, such as ghosts, voodoo, the fountain of youth, and mermaids, even after the manatee-mermaid link had been established. Even in our own home, there is ample population that yet believes in all manner of haunts and aspects of good and bad luck. I do not trust her, as no good man trusts the gypsies, and her blood is half Romany, but she seems quite content to travel with us and make herself useful as much as she might. Likely she suspects how little rope we are allowing both herself and Mr. Franzini, and that there will be those who hope they hang themselves on what rope is left to them.

Speaking of Mr. Franzini, he has been most difficult to travel with already. You may have been made aware that he became faint near the end of the very day on which we hired him, and while he recovered, he has been quite slow to recover entirely, moving unsteadily, acting hesitantly and only after consideration, and his hands shake something terrible even today. I do not know if it is merely something to soothe his nerves, or if it is his custom on more normal days, but I also have not seen him take in any nourishment, only picking at his breakfast, though he will drink of any alcohol put before him. So far, Miss Penn assures us that when he has had a few days' travel behind him, he will be fine and a fair addition to our group.

I also feel that though it is our trouble to deal with, it is fair to warn you that all is not particularly well in this troupe with all members assembled. In particular, Sir James seems to have taken an especially strong dislike to Mr. Franzini, a portion of which I am certain is national pride, and so recently having had no contact with Italians save as they appeared as enemies in the field. Additionally, I believe a good portion is their shared favored pastime, playing at cards. I would guess that the rumors of Mr. Franzini's questionable conduct while gambling has particularly disturbed the leader of our small company. Fortunately for Mr. Franzini, Sir James remains an even tempered and sociable man, continuing to act the perfect gentleman aside from making quite clear that Mr. Franzini is most unwelcome as concerns participation in the card games going on on the train to help pass the time as we travel.

Much in contrast, young Mr. Bowe has made himself quite at home in our company, though he seems particularly well suited to exchanging tales and jokes suited solely for the gentleman's club behind closed doors. Even so, Mr. Bowe and Eddy seem to have become quite the fast friends, particularly in their shared love for hunting, on which they have spoken at length, and in such technical and occasionally gory detail as to often confuse those less initiated in the activity, and to cause Sir James to excuse himself for a short walk about the train while they spoke.

Similarly, Miss Penn has been quite enthusiastic about trying to make up for her rough start with Mr. Bowe, seeking him out for conversation whenever possible and trying to draw him into discussion of what things they do share in common, or into more general casual talk. For some time, Mr. Bowe resisted this effort entirely, and spoke to her quite harshly, though I cannot imagine that as being too uncommon for a gypsy woman who dresses like a show girl and associates with thieves, though that latter trait is only what is to be expected from a gypsy. It was only when Miss Penn drew out her most strange set of cards and claimed to have some talent for prognostication that Mr. Bowe took some genuine interest. Despite Miss Penn's claims, I am thoroughly convinced that her so-called gift is like every other show person's trick. She has simply learned enough of her art as to make some reasonable reading of people and makes guesses or exploits common fool's dreams and insecurities. This makes her seem prescient enough to charge whatever small coin she normally does when performing this art for whatever show she has joined.

Despite the fact that I am well aware of how these things are done, and Sir James has stated he is quite in agreement, and wishes nothing to do with the arcane cards, Eddy seems somewhat curious, and has considered having his future read, or some such, more than once. Mr. Bowe has been extremely curious as to the nature of the cards and the gypsies, which has finally begun to warm relations, if only slightly, between the two of them.

In the meanwhile, Mr. Bowe shows no animosity towards Mr. Franzini, for which I am most grateful after the experiences of their first meeting. Instead, he just shows him absolute disregard, and the two attempts Mr. Franzini has made to communicate with Mr. Bowe have resulted in the showman struggling to find his tongue amidst stuttering and twitching. It would be most amusing indeed, were it not for the fact that they will sooner or later have to work together. For now, Mr. Bowe either ignores him entirely, or just stares coolly until such time as the Italian leaves to huddle back into his uncomfortable seat.

We are now headed back for New England. Until then, I hope this will satisfy your curiosity as to how those you have put such expenditure into are progressing with the tasks assigned them.

Yours,
Gregory Conan Watts

June 5th, 1815
39°48'N 088°35'W

My Dearest Cordelia,

I write in part to keep you up to date upon our progress, though we have hardly yet begun, and in part to clear my own thoughts on varying matters, for though you are not here, you were always ready with good advice. Indeed, when we were but small children, I was always the doubter, while you told me consistently to believe and wonder. And today is such a day where I find myself very much in doubt.

We have added some most unusual new blood to our company. Firstly, young Mr. Bowe seems to me to be quintessentially an American. His dress is rough, made of thick weaves and leathers for durability. Though these layers do far more to hide his form than display it, he seems very much a straight line in build. A straight brown line, from those odd pointed toe riding boots which he wears at all times, to the dark wide-brimmed hat, such as I have seen men of the local frontier sporting in great numbers, which do a good deal to hide their features. His features, what can be made out easily, are fresh and youthful, with no evidence of his frontier living beyond a deep tan.

Indeed, I wonder at his age, wavering between some fifteen and seventeen summers most often. For this he is reasonably tall, though not so much as myself, let alone Eddy. Despite the hidden features, he has a way of looking a man in the eye when speaking to him. Judging by those eyes, I always waver to my older estimates, for I have never seen so determined and self-sure a youth. When Sir James speaks, you want to believe him for the infectious charisma of the man, and his every word spreads its fervor to the room beyond him, whereas Sam Bowe is very much his own man, and seemingly uncaring of what anyone else does or believes, but it is hard to imagine him failing.

Though I have gotten little idea of his build due to his very frontiersman fashion of dress, he cannot possibly be as slight as he might first appear in his height, for he goes about every physical task put to him with such an ease. While he had very few belongings to pack, he moved right to helping the railway men with our bags, and then on to the rest of its carriage, slightly to our own embarrassment. After all, what are such men for if not to tend to the physical laboring so gentlemen do not need dirty their hands? But when he took up such tasks, he almost seemed to casually toss even full crates well into the cars, and lifted a steamer trunk belonging to some part of the show we had recently attended, and now it seemed had broken up, on his own, hefting the trunk and depositing it into the car at his chest level. Eddy could quite certainly handle such a feat, I am certain, but he is a large and muscular man given to such things, and even he seems somewhat perplexed at our new companion, though the two get on famously, and have done so from the time Sam joined our company.

Even for the frontier, he is an oddity. For I did overhear some part of a conversation between Eddy and Mr. Bowe, in which Eddy inquired after Mr. Bowe's lack of a gun at his hip. A decoration which is nigh unto universal here, every man west of St. Louis and many of those in it go about armed with at least one flintlock pistol, oftentimes two, and there is no law about such things. As I have noted, America is quite the unusual and often savage-seeming place, and we have not even reached those lands they consider untamed. This habit is one Eddy in particular seems quite taken with, for as you are well aware, his love of firearms knows few bounds. In addition to his usual rifle, Eddy has taken to carrying two pistols on his person most of the time. He has also been quite excited over news that some American has invented an advance beyond the flintlock mechanism, making his guns much more efficient as an instrument for bird hunting. Many locals are curious as to how this development works and waiting for the wonder to spread.

In any case, Mr. Bowe, who goes about only with a number of survival knives about his person, simply stated that he does not begrudge men who need their firearms, but he has a personal distaste for them for reasons he has not enumerated upon. Despite which, he seems to know how they work, and has discussed the subject at some length with Eddy. The pair also share a passion for hunting, and discuss the subject at length at every opportunity. Apparently their methods somewhat differ, as I would imagine they would have to, given Mr. Bowe's lack of firearms. Precisely how I am not certain, as I lack enough knowledge of such sport to fully keep up with them.

Sir James, an accomplished rider and hunter himself, has tried to enter these conversations some few times now, but always seems to end up quite at odds with the talk, one of the few times I have ever seen the man at a loss. It seems that the process of hunting from necessity and in preparation for work as a hunter's guide so differs from the gentleman's sport as to be nearly unrecognizable to participants in the latter. I have no experience with either, and so either find other matters to question Sir James about, for he remains quite the conversationalist and wit, or simply listen and try to absorb some kind of detail.

Though we had to go all the way to St. Louis to find them, the other two new members of our party are Europeans. We found the two traveling as show people with a circus. In particular, they put on a magic act as The Great Franzini and his lovely assistant. They also, I will note, supplemented their income somewhat with playing at cards after the show.

Giovanni Franzini is a small, thin, dark-haired man. He has been a part of a traveling carnival show for quite some time, and dressed and acted the part. Now that we have been away from show business for a time he has ceased waxing his beard and mustache, and wears his dark hair more free. In the process, now, he is somewhat more approachable. Certainly he has a showman's charm, quick with a joke, clever, definitely observant. He has dozens of stories of his travels and shares them readily. Despite his name, he claims no loyalty to the European alliance. Admittedly, neither does he claim any loyalty to England, but insists that he will do what he is paid to do. Apparently, Lord Donovan felt that someone so well traveled through many civilized areas and familiar with non-English European colonies about the world might be helpful to us. At the very least, he helps pass the time while we travel by train.

The last is Giovanni's companion, a half-gypsy woman who goes by the name Julietta Penn. Describing her in a way fit for a young woman to read of is quite difficult. To say that she comes across as a woman of low virtues is not quite correct. Indeed, when she wishes to, she has proven she is capable of picture perfect European manners. She can walk and talk like a lady, eat delicately, and is surprisingly well read. However, even her traveling clothes are as revealing as her showgirl outfits, and when she does not feel pressed to be polite, she has a most unladylike sense of humor and a biting wit.

So far, Sir James and myself are most often at a loss for dealing with her. Sam Bowe and Eddy, on the other hand, have shared more than a few drinks with her. She and Sam had a difficult first meeting, but at least they seem to be warming to one another somewhat. In contrast, having had a similarly difficult beginning, Sam and Giovanni do not seem to have warmed to one another at all, with Sam now primarily ignoring Mr. Franzini, who makes ignoring him easy by avoiding Sam whenever reasonably possible. Indeed, I suspect that part of Miss Penn's pleasure in Sam's company is the discomfort it brings to her traveling companion.

I likewise know you have an appetite for details of romance and intrigue, dear Cordelia, so at the risk of sounding scandalous, I shall finish this letter with an observation that Miss Penn seems extremely taken with young Mr. Bowe, no matter how much her employer, Mr. Franzini, tries to steer them as far apart as possible. I will report, lest I give the wrong impression, that there are no flirtations involved, and no fans waving nor events for dancing and talk between the sexes. Indeed, the interest is most certainly not shared, for Mr. Bowe has only engaged her in conversation over the aforementioned drinks in company, and seems to have almost as much distaste for her manner of carrying herself as a loose woman as do I, though Mr. Bowe so often departs from civilized ways that I cannot imagine our motivations are the same.

Rather, it is simply that she speaks to him as she speaks to none of the rest of us, both in tone, and how often she tries to engage his interest. More to the point, there is the way she looks at him, with such intensity and longing. Though she is a woman of no virtues I can name, beyond being well spoken when she chooses to be and surprisingly well educated for her station, she does not look on him as a prostitute looks at a man with a full purse either, else her attention should settle naturally on Sir James.

No matter how often she is so casually spurned, her gaze does not waver. I am quite positive the woman, who does not have the good grace to hide such a thing, is quite smitten with Mr. Bowe. I am equally certain that Mr. Franzini, whom she treats with the respect due an employer, but no greater fondness, has noticed as well, and is quite jealous of the fact. I can but hope this does not lead to greater trouble, though I am half-certain it will.

Alas, in my meandering, I almost entirely left my original curiosity. While traveling by railway, there is a great deal of time to pass. In this time, I did approach Mr. Bowe with the certainty he could clear up the matter of his father's travels, surely. While I am now absolutely certain that Dr. Bowe did, indeed, travel to America, as some few of his writings suggested, the rest must surely remain works of fancy. This approach seemed to most perturb young Mr. Bowe, however, who assured me with no room for equivocation that his father is precisely the explorer that he claims to be in his writings.

The chance to prove this, in fact, seems to be part of what Mr. Toomes offered him in their negotiations at the bar some few days past. While the money may come in useful, he was truly motivated by the possibility of proving beyond any doubt that Dr. Bowe's works are not fiction. I still privately doubt, of course. The boy claims not to have seen his father in some time. Since Dr. Bowe retired from active exploration, in fact, however long ago that may be. Given Sam Bowe's youth, he cannot have gone far with the man even if they journeyed together. I can now imagine that the stories which have so firmly grasped the imaginations of the civilized world about the places still dark upon the map were the bedtime yarns spun for Sam Bowe as a small child, and surely he is just cleaving to them as truth as a piece of his memories of his father, of whom he is quite fond. I admit I have some trouble believing that anyone could so favor a parent who left them alone at a vulnerable age on so dirty and savage a place as the American frontier, however capable that youth might be, but such seems to be the case.

Nonetheless, Sam, who would seem the best authority we are likely to get on the matter, is entirely insistent that his father's letters are the literal truth. He states this with such conviction that between Mr. Bowe and Sir James, who continues to seem to believe that if our efforts are sufficient, he can make fiction into fact by sheer act of will, I begin, in my weaker moments, to believe our mission might meet with some success yet. Then I catch myself at such idle dreaming and begin to wonder instead if this place is beginning to drive me quite mad to entertain these notions.

One other note of Miss Penn that I feel I should report to you. I know you are familiar with a few stories of gypsies and their purported gift for divination through reading of cards. Miss Penn is quite skilled in this carnival trick, and has been offering to do readings for everyone. So far I have, of course, refused. Sam and Eddy seem quite taken by this brand of trickery though. Though there is nothing but training and an ability to read people behind it, I do have to be fair and report she is one of the better I have seen at such tricks, a very capable dramatist to be sure. Given your love of wild tales and mysterious stories, and as much as I would probably once again get in some trouble with your maids and doctors for encouraging such a fancy, I thought I would be remiss if I did not tell you we had a gypsy fortune teller in our midst now.

Regardless, my love, I am yet optimistic not so much that we will succeed in the manner our employer intends it, but rather with such men as those I travel with, excepting Mr. Franzini, I am certain we will learn a great deal of the unknown parts of the land, and in so doing gain some measure of fame and fortune such that your father will surely agree that I should make him a fine son in law. The next few years cannot pass quickly enough, and you are in my thoughts, always, dear Cordelia.

My love, always,
Gregory Conan Watts

From the journals of Gregory Conan Watts,
June 12th, 1815
Pennsylvania
40°19'N 079°23'W

It seems we have underestimated the depths to which our opposition will sink. My mind is still abuzz with the events of the day, but I endeavor to document them faithfully and accurately. I now regard my experience in the war as fortunate, else I should now have trouble composing myself to write. It is always unnerving to be shot at, and, it seems, far more when out of the context of the battlefield.

Today we reached a small watering station between St Louis and New York. The great steam engines need many of these, for the engines have constant problems with overheating. I am sure the minds at Oxford are working on this very problem, for it would greatly speed the journeys by rail if they did not require so many stops. I have come to understand that this is one of the reasons the military railroads placed down during the Napoleonic wars were so quickly abandoned, the territory deemed too expensive to make even token attempts to hold. Whole trains almost would be needed to supply them with water, and these stations are quite open and vulnerable. Now there are vast stretches of Western Europe with iron bars nailed to the ground, leading to nowhere, and no other sign that scientific progress ever set foot on those battered shores.[10]

Here in the vast reaches of America, these stations have begun to dot the few railways which are growing up with the country, and towns then grow around them to supply the hot and grimy train crews and those passengers that have elected to travel in this way. It is still a long and uncomfortable means of travel,

---

10 The more water-efficient Engine based on the technology of the Coltrane suit was developed in 1829, specifically for adding rail to the vast reaches of Australia, however it also aided in the Americas. There are still vast miles of unused rail lines in Europe. However, oxen-pulled carts are commonplace on those rail lines without engines, most of which are short stretches away from the cities then abandoned when Napoleonic war fronts moved, and England shifted their supply chains. – C B-W

especially as they must crowd people into the cars so that most of the train can remain dedicated to the pursuit of trade or supplying the frontier towns, a more profitable venture than carrying people about. But where there is any coin to be made, you can be certain someone will try to exploit it. This stop was somewhat more grown than many others, with large buildings meant for the storage of railway cargo and crates so people living in the expanse between the cities, or within the large towns without the fortune to be right on the rails, can leave that which they wish sent to destinations along the rails, or pick up their goods. Appropriately enough, in this time of expansion and opportunity, I understand that the vast majority of this cargo right now is building materials, and the rest is primarily those machines meant to accommodate a farmer, and replace some part of his labor force. These machines are mostly still very expensive, but with a shortage of strong young men accustomed to the various specific types of farm labor – and many people's hesitation to hire former slaves – they are sometimes considered worth the expense, as they were for the Wrights of Virginia.

This place also had a trio of large saloons and a single large, hopeful church, in addition to less noticeable trappings of the growth of civilization. It also had quite a lot of places where a man can hide, as it turns out. We were not there long, with the crewers about filling the train's water supplies so they could retire a few hours and water themselves, when suddenly there was a flurry of motion to my left. Mr. Bowe shouted a warning and, in a diving motion, tackled both myself and Sir James to the ground next to the train.

Before we could react, a shot rang out, then another, with the sound of impact against the very train car we were just departing in order to head for a saloon for a drink of our own. I rolled under the train car for cover out of wartime instinct, and Sir James did likewise. Eddy, not yet fully out of the car, raced back inside. I would learn that his soldierly instinct was not so much to flee to cover, but he headed directly for his beloved rifle, and from there would climb onto the top of the car by kicking out one of the windows on the opposite side. For the moment, we were left without him and to our own devices. In the meanwhile, nearly a dozen men appeared about the area brandishing weapons, all of them looking in our direction.

Though I am certain that Mr. Bowe's actions and sharp senses likely saved Sir James and myself from injury, sheer fortune saved Mr. Franzini from the same. He was a few seconds behind us in crawling under the train, though once he got it in his head to seek cover, he did so with great haste. Miss Penn was, thankfully, still aboard the train car, and thus quite safe until such time as our attackers disposed of us, so long as she kept her head low.

By instinct I kept my head down through the first round of shots, then glanced up to see how best I could try to avoid the men and get out of the line of fire, for I was unarmed. Upon looking up, I saw quite the most insane act of bravery I think I have ever witnessed, for Mr. Bowe did not join us in cover, but rather had followed his tackle by racing directly towards one knot of our attackers as they frantically reloaded, a knife in his right hand, but nothing to stand up to a gun. To assure me that I was not seeing some imagined vision, this glance, as well as a brief cessation of firing while the attackers tried to track us down – or reloaded their weapons, or drew second pistols – allowed me to overhear Mr. Bowe stating, quite flatly, "Stupid bringing guns to a knife fight."

My attention was pulled then to Sir James, rolling back the other way out from under the car and demanding I do likewise. Eddy had kicked out the window by this point, and as we stood, he passed his pistols on to us, already loaded, while he clutched his rifle in one hand and climbed the remaining distance to the roof of the car. No small feat, fitting a man of his size through a window, but he managed. We headed for opposite ends of the car, while only steps behind us, Mr. Franzini took off running further down the car. Using the train as cover, and with only one gun each, we knew we were in some trouble amidst this ambush, but were determined to sell our lives dearly.

As I peeked around the train car, I found Mr. Bowe once again. He had reached the men, though I am quite certain I had heard at least two more shots coming from that direction. He appeared unwounded, and as I watched, he weaved directly into their midst, making firing quite difficult lest they hit one another. He stabbed the closest man, tearing the knife free quite violently and dropping his target instantly. A moment later, a second man fell with his throat cut. Just as on that first meeting, I am quite certain I have never seen a man move so fast as young Mr. Bowe, encouraging my thoughts that perhaps somehow his father is truly simply so extraordinary a man as to somehow defy the laws of what is probable or even possible for a man to accomplish in a lifetime, if he is anything like his son. And then I consider, and reassure myself that the works must be the imaginings of someone with so wild a mind as to have offspring who does not retreat from large numbers of men with guns, but rather charges them with a skinning knife.

With no further attention to allow for Mr. Bowe, I located some of our attackers, who began to advance upon our location, unaware that we had so armed ourselves. The first of them fell a moment later as I heard the crack of a rifle above me. When the target landed, there was neither struggle nor cry, dead before he hit the ground with a rifle ball to the head. A second man fell before they could get any sense of what was happening as Eddy fired again, putting the man down in much the same fashion. Sir James was not long out of the action, as my attention was grabbed by his sudden motion, turning about from his cover behind the train, straightening, extending his arm, and firing. He made his single shot count, for another of the men fell with a shot to the chest, even as the others finally had some idea that Eddy had gotten the drop on them, and they were the ones now in need of cover.

Three raced back towards the storefronts, while the remaining three rushed forward towards the train instead. Sir James dealt most effectively with the first of these, for as the man darted forward, he was met with a blow to the head from the butt of Sir James's pistol. I dealt with a second, accomplished enough a soldier to at least not embarrass myself with missing at point blank range, dropping the man nearest me before he could quite reach greater cover. The third, however, disappeared into the train car. Those running for cover split up, two rushing one way for a pile of crates while one made the unfortunate choice of rushing at a storefront, to be met by Mr. Bowe before he could find a safe place to settle in. To his credit, in desperation, he threw a punch, but Bowe ducked it easily and gutted the man before he could take another step. The other two found cover.

As we hit standoff, I heard a shouting from further on up the train, somewhat nearer the crates. It seems Franzini had recognized one of our attackers. Though I am uncertain if the others could hear them or not, I was able to pick out most of the details of the shouting back and forth.

"Mick? Is that you?"

"Gio? What're you doing here?"

"Does it matter? You have yourself quite the fix here, Mick."

"What's it to you?"

"As it happens, I know these men. I'll convince them to spare you if you'll do me the favor of shooting your fellow there."

There was a moment of hesitation, but Mick clearly thought better of his situation, with Eddy likely having drawn a bead on their position by now, and Mr. Bowe already having proven himself quite insane enough to charge fellows with guns. There was a gunshot, and a lanky, red-haired man stood from cover, dropping his gun. A shot rang out from the direction of Mr. Franzini. At once I appreciated his vicious instinct in matters such as this, while despising the Italian that much more. Perhaps he simply owed Mick some amount of money, and was uncertain that negotiating a settlement would sufficiently balance the account. Truly, there is no honor among thieves

It is testament to the state of America – beyond the civility of New York and the tales of gentleman farmers in the Southern colonies – that once the shooting had stopped, and people had made certain of it, there was quickly a buzz of activity, including people taking it upon themselves to begin dragging the bodies out of the street. It was then that it occurred to me that one had escaped us into our train car. Though I am not especially fond of Miss Penn for any number of reasons, she was still a part of our company. I raced into the car, to find the last of our enemies quite dead, while Miss Penn was about tucking a small blade into her bodice once more. I am uncertain whether she somehow surprised him there, or used some wile to get him to drop his guard, and she has not been particularly forthcoming, but she is casual enough about it that I can only imagine that it is not the first man she's seen killed, or perhaps even killed herself. The reputation of her people as murderers and thieves gains more credence by the day.

Likewise no strangers to killing, we three soldiers were ready to fortify ourselves with a bit of drink after the ordeal, and Mr. Bowe was more than enthused to join us. He and Eddy found their own table, where they animatedly discussed these most recent events as if it had served to do little more than get their blood moving a bit. Sir James was somewhat more reserved, preferring to speak with me and harken back to quiet war stories, where an ambush by armed men makes some degree more sense to a soldier's mind. Miss Penn elected to remain with the car to rest, while Mr. Franzini sat with Sir James and me, but kept his counsel to himself, glancing occasionally at me as if to question whether I had overheard some part of his exchange with Mick. I can only hope I did not give too much away, but regardless, he seemed to take whatever he read from me as assurance that if he dared say a word, he might no longer be welcome at our table.

Nerves reinforced by conversation and drink, and now the exercise in calm that is putting chaotic events into words, I believe I have noted today's events with reasonable accuracy, but now I am especially grateful that the rest of our company is safe at Dr. Mitchell's secluded abode, under the watchful eye of Mr. Taylor, and not left to their own devices and without sufficient protection in New York.

From the letters of Giovanni Franzini,
June 20th, 1815

Sirs,

Despite our best efforts, it seems your lapdogs are hunting hounds. When we earlier refused your offer of employment, I thought we had made ourselves quite clear, but it seems we find ourselves in a position of no choice. I will do what you had asked of me in regards to your hand-picked company, but be certain that this employment is under duress, and the money had best be there, else we shall have further problems.

Likewise, if we continue to come under assault from outside help, my price will increase commensurate to the risk, particularly if former associates of mine continue to be pointed in the direction of our company. I have difficulty enough with my previous dealings without finding they're being paid to put a noose or stray bullet to me.

I cannot speak to Miss Penn's loyalties. She has come along, per your request, as an adviser. So far, she is either suitably frightened of consequence of failure, or is suitably loyal to your coin to keep her mouth shut. I will attempt to keep an eye on her to ensure this situation continues, but cannot guarantee anything if she continues her infatuation with the Bowe boy. That one is too sharp by half. Should that association lead to our failure, be assured, sir, I'll be looking for you with some very pointed questions as to why he was deemed necessary to have along.

Your servant, reluctantly,
Giovanni Franzini

P.S. I can see why this group needs another hand, Sir, although I wish it weren't me. Not one of these are willing to get their hands *properly* dirty.

Mad Dr. Mitchell's Laboratory

From the journals of Gregory Conan Watts,
June 29th, 1815
~44N ~68W

We have returned to Dr. Mitchell's hospitality, and I must immediately wonder if our fellows would not have fared better at risk back in New York. It is true that they have been quite physically safe here. In speaking with them since, however, it seems that the doctor's initial bout with melancholy followed by a period of manic activity was no isolated event, but a regular pattern now. At the end of any project, or upon hitting obstacles sufficient to force reconsideration in his approach, he descends into a morose fit. When in such a state, they have gone days without seeing a hint of the doctor. They are permitted free run about the upstairs laboratories, including use of his tools so Miss Wright can continue progress on at least basic repairs and refitting of the ship, with the aid of our engineers. According to those who remained here, after each disappearance by the doctor, he would reemerge some time later, sometimes mere hours later, sometimes days, but always full of new inspirations and energy.

Despite the troubles this situation obviously presents, on reviewing the work done, Sir James has conceded that the Doctor lives up to his reputation. I do not at all understand the precise nature of what's been done to the ship, but apparently it will drastically increase our fuel efficiency and speed, thus enabling greater long distance travel outside of civilization. Given the doctor's weak constitution most of the actual repairs and refittings are put in place by Miss Wright, and now Sir James, directing the engineers when a task requires many hands or heavy lifting while the doctor primarily provides blueprints and inspirations.

His instability and unpredictability is not limited to his moods either. At times, once he has finished the latest designs for fixing the dirigible he moves on to unrelated projects. He has created the revised camera device he claimed he would be able to, and I must admit, it is a vast improvement over my original device in virtually every fashion. Upon our return, when he heard about the rumors of a new pistol with multi-shot capabilities he also grew quite excited, and has thrown himself into a design of his own with similar ends. Some effort was made to try to get him back on task with work on the airship to better speed us on our way, but all such attempts met with failure. After learning of his descent into melancholy when presented with enough trouble, it was decided that his technical brilliance was worth the price of allowing the doctor to work at his own pace on the projects that suited his damaged mind.

Sir James has thrown himself into helping with the work on the dirigible and organizing for the next stage of our journey. Eddy has mostly stayed well out of the way. Mr. Bowe has shown an utter disinterest in all matters of high technology save one device. In our walk-through of the place he discovered an odd winged contraption of metal and wood and fabric. The doctor was quite dismissive of it, claiming that it was a failed experiment. Despite this claim, the device moves on its own, folding the wings back such that it will fit through the hallways and wheeling itself after Mr. Bowe. I have no idea as to how any device could do such a thing without a human hand pushing it about, but I have observed it often enough to assure that somehow the doctor has created such a responsive machine. Mr. Bowe, in turn, seems quite fond of the device, speaking to it openly as if it could perceive and understand the words. The doctor has not commented upon this arrangement, entirely dismissive of the device and eager to get onto other projects.

At this time we have elected to restrict the Europeans from access to most of Dr. Mitchell's work and especially his journals. Despite their claims of loyalty to our trip it would be unseemly to allow Europeans access to Oxford technology beyond the absolute necessity that we take them aboard the dirigible eventually. For now, Franzini has complained, as we have come to expect from him, but no more protest than he's put forward over much smaller matters, while accepting the restriction and making no effort to sneak around it. Miss Penn has taken it in far better graces, mostly resigning to her temporary quarters or the area used at appropriate times for dining where she socializes with those who will speak to her. I remain wary of both of them, and do not at all look forward to being confined to the tighter quarters and familiarity of the airship with them. Despite that particular misgiving, I am very much looking forward to leaving this place and proceeding to New York. I do not at all think I will be sad to see no more of Dr. Mitchell and his laboratory.

From the journals of Gregory Conan Watts,
July 8th, 1815
~44N ~68W

All of my misgivings regarding Dr. Mitchell have been proven more than correct, tragically so. We finally learned what had happened to Dr. Mitchell's wife. Mr. Bowe had taken the winged device outside this morning, and apparently Dr. Mitchell discovered it flying about the skies around the island, sometimes carrying Mr. Bowe short distances. The doctor grew both excited and agitated at this, while Mr. Bowe was now very insistent upon learning more about the device, which led to a great deal more information than I had ever cared to know. Though I should dread anyone else reading this, as the chronicler of this mission, I feel I must record the events as they were told to me. Besides, hopefully they will prove useful should the doctor rightly come up for trial.

The doctor had originally met his wife through a mutual acquaintance – Dr. Erasmus Darwin – whose theories gained him a considerable readership in scientific circles before he became largely shunned by his peers for his theories on the social sciences and his establishment of a small school which attempted to illegally educate young women in the life sciences. He theorized that with a proper education, a young woman's mind would take naturally to pursuits involving the health and nurturing of others at a level equal to any medical doctor's. Darwin gathered several pupils and attempted to teach them as a university might, though in private. Dr. Mitchell's future wife was one of his first and supposedly most successful students.

The courtship was a quick one. The two shared a passion for science, even if they came about it from different directions. Indeed, that aspect would become part of the problem. He left Oxford when others there became concerned foremost for his relationship with a woman with an education in the medical sciences and an eagerness to share her knowledge with those she considered her peers. Worse, they were concerned that their co-research would be discovered, for even if they pursued it, they knew that it would not be well received. The theory was that by combining her knowledge of the human nervous system and brain functioning with his gift for mechanical artifice, they had a chance of being able to create an artificial brain capable of storing human knowledge, such that they would be able to transfer a living human's mind into a purely mechanical device.

Though I cannot at all condone such a horror, I can understand their inspiration in one small degree. Dr. Mitchell's wife was in a poor state of health, and growing worse, due to a degenerative condition of some sort. Medical science had only means to delay the progress of her wasting disease, it would never cure her. Thus they were spurred on by the thought of saving Mrs. Mitchell's life by transferring her conscienceness to a machine. They experimented for some time, raising a large flock of sheep for use as experimental fodder. While they had only Agnes for the purpose of handling the sheep, she was somewhat aided by Mrs. Mitchell's constant companion, a sheep dog named Bub.

Eventually they believed they were far enough along, seeming to think that they had successfully transferred the minds of sheep into mechanical devices. Given the lack of intelligence and distinctive behaviors of sheep I cannot be sure how they confirmed this, save that some of the devices in the basement are still capable of independent movement, milling about aimlessly. I do not believe such a vile experiment possibly could work, but seeing the devices now still makes me shudder at the thought that in some mad imagining they are actually formerly living creatures condemned to live as automatons. The couple also were out of time, nearing the end of Mrs. Mitchell's life. Thus they built a larger version of the transfer device and completed the machine to hold her consciousness.

Somewhere during this unholy experiment something went wrong. Though the doctor acknowledges that the process had never been entirely painless, the reaction from the device was not at all what they had expected. Mrs. Mitchell's screams agitated Bub to the point that her one truly constant and faithful companion (for on hearing what Dr. Mitchell subjected his wife to in his madness, I cannot attribute such a role to him) felt the need to rush to his mistress's rescue. Bub leaped into the machinery, breaking it and ending her pain. Alas, this last was an entirely true statement, for the resulting explosion killed both Mrs. Mitchell and Bub.

Since that time, the ornithopter, for such Dr. Mitchell calls the flying machine, has not responded at all the way it formerly had. They had constructed it as one of the machines containing their so-called neural transfer capabilities, and had it about as one of the more successful experiments, believing it had contained the mind of one of the sheep. He had been able to get it to make short, halting flights before, and to respond to herding. After the explosion it would no longer do even this, avoiding the doctor and refusing to further his later experiments in flight when he tried to bury himself in his work.

On seeing Mr. Bowe with the ornithopter and its responses to him, the doctor has put together a new theory – that it somehow received the mind of the sheep dog. I cannot, for sake of sanity, put any real stock in this wild theory. Despite that, it shows an uncommon intelligence and selectivity for a machine. To wit, it will not, in any fashion, respond to the doctor, avoiding him, even acting in a manner I would describe as somewhat hostile towards him were the ornithopter an animal. However, it will follow Mr. Bowe, and only Mr. Bowe, and respond to numerous commands that Dr. Mitchell has asked the young man to try, including coming when called, lifting its front wheels off the ground and balancing on the rear when told to beg, heeling, herding sheep and following complex series of verbal commands in direction. It will also fly on Sam Bowe's command, whether carrying him or on its own. More disturbingly, it seems to respond, turning about or coming to Mr. Bowe at mention of the word "Bub," or more particularly and enthusiastically to "Bubsy" – the name Mrs. Mitchell most often used.

Even in this private journal I will not recount any details of the theory or how such things were done past these musings for fear that anyone else might ever attempt such a thing again. Thankfully, even the most learned among us have reacted with equal revulsion, save for Mr. Bowe, who remains quite taken with the ornithopter while remaining disinterested in the doctor's other works.

We discussed the possibility for some time of placing Dr. Mitchell under arrest for murder, a thought which I was initially strongly in favor of. The discussion was complicated when Sir James acknowledged that he had similar sentiments, but the issue was complicated in that Mrs. Mitchell was a willing accomplice, but more in that Dr. Mitchell was a significant risk to reveal both these terrible secrets, and also a great deal about Oxford's research works if taken into custody. He has written strongly worded letters to the directors at Oxford to ask that they look into the matter and determine what should be done with Dr. Mitchell.

In any case, we now make great haste to get the dirigible ready to travel. We have offered Agnes a ride away from here, but she insists she is in no danger. She believes what happened was an accident, and the doctor no longer presents any danger to anyone. He has long since destroyed all of the notes related to the experiments in neural transfer, and she has lived with him for years since that time without any further incident or hint that he would ever take such a thing up again, interested only in regularly mourning his wife, and bouts with the purely mechanical. This has eased my concerns for the safety of others some, but done nothing to comfort me as concerns the fate of Mrs. Mitchell or the disposition of her soul.

I will be very glad to be out of this terrible place entirely, and I have moved from the guest rooms to the dirigible for the duration until the final preparations are made so we can leave for New York.

From the journals of Gregory Conan Watts,
July 15th, 1815
Maine Colony skies
43°58'N 69°33'W

We have finally taken our leave of Agnes and Dr. Mitchell, and for that much I am quite grateful. Upon final preparations we did discover that there was at least one further surprise among our company. We were in the midst of making room assignments, since there is very limited space on board the dirigible, and we can no longer afford to give everyone their own space. When the initial plans were revealed, Sam Bowe quickly informed us that the arrangements made would not be possible, as Sam, it seems, is short for Samantha, and she is not Dr. Bowe's son, but his daughter.

At least according to her, there was no truly conscious effort to deceive us, but she had largely been raised in the wilderness as her father would have raised a boy, and on the frontier, with her favored pursuits and work, she had become more comfortable living life as a male. She apologized, without any real feeling of guilt to the confession, for any misconceptions.

This revelation obviously raised many concerns among the crew. Miss Coltrane and Mrs. Fisher were the most agitated, insisting that once we reach New York, Miss Bowe was to be presented as a young woman, and make no other pretense, lest it lead to some embarrassment or problem for our company in those civilized regions. Miss Bowe was at first not terribly flexible in this arrangement, but Miss Wright once again came to everyone's rescue.

She was able to suggest some garments, used for young women who may be subjected to occasional labor around the farm, that her cousin and our chaperone were content with. Miss Bowe will then be permitted to dress as she sees fit when working as our scout outside of civilized regions. Similarly, while Miss Wright will be permitted to help with Miss Bowe's hair and dress and the rest when she must present herself as a young woman, Mrs. Fisher and Miss Coltrane will not be permitted to directly have anything to do with such matters, with the sole exception of readying her to meet any truly formal occasions we might have to attend.

This arrangement remains an uncomfortable one for everyone involved, and no one is truly happy with the final compromise, but for the moment it is keeping a rough peace among the women of our crew. Miss Bowe will also be rooming alone, though she is to be in a room split between sleeping quarters and a root locker full of potatoes for our trip.

Were these revelations not enough of a complication to the trip, Miss Bowe has also insisted upon taking the ornithopter, which she now comfortably refers to as Bubsy, with her. At first this was forbidden, but she had a long talk with Sir James, and in the end it was agreed that she would be permitted to take the device, a gift from Dr. Mitchell (since it still will not interact with or obey him).

Though I was personally reluctant to take any other gifts from Dr. Mitchell's lab, Sir James talked us into bending to practicality. In addition to the refitted airship and the ornithopter, we are taking the altered camera and four pistols of the doctor's design, which he refers to as pepper-boxes. These are handheld pistols which hold four shots, requiring only a slight turning by hand to operate the rotating barrels, moving a loaded barrel into place over the firing mechanism once a shot is spent. They are complex to reload and run considerable risk of jamming or other malfunction, but the capabilities of a four-shot pistol are significant enough that we could not doubt that they would come in handy – especially after our experiences at the train station. He has also helped make some slight modifications to Eddy's rifle, reducing the chances of jamming and making the canisters holding the multiple shots for the rifle more easily interchangeable.

I am now somewhat thankful that everyone is so eager to get well away from Dr. Mitchell and his home. Without that factor, the other social arrangements could prove quite difficult. Eddy seems fairly at ease with Miss Bowe, at the least. He continues to speak with her as one might a male friend, including their usual assortment of topics that most find rather unappealing. He was also the first stalwart in her defense when the contingent of respectable womanhood, with Mrs. Fisher as its rightful vanguard, declared that Miss Bowe must no longer be permitted to attend the card games in the sitting room. For a moment, perhaps for the first time since we met, I was simply glad that I was not Sir James Coltrane. He seemed at quite a loss regarding the entire matter.

Also bewildered by the revelation of Miss Bowe's gender was Miss Penn. It had become quite clear that she was very attracted to Sam Bowe when she thought him young Mr. Bowe, and now she has no idea what to make of her thoughts. She certainly does not make the attempts at familiarity that she did before. Nevertheless, it is possible she still wishes some attempt at cordiality, to compensate for two false starts. What's more, there is the fact that, male or female, Giovanni Franzini remains terrified of Sam Bowe, and avoids her just as readily as before.

I cannot be certain, but it seems, to my observations, that the relationship between Miss Penn and Mr. Franzini is more contentious than I had assumed. It was obvious that she sometimes found him somewhat distasteful, and he tries to keep their discussions private and discreet. Nonetheless, I get the feeling that he intimidates her more than I had thought, and their relationship is somewhat more like people working together out of some shared cause and capability – and perhaps out of their isolation from the rest of us – and less out of any real camaraderie.

At any rate, watching the debate between Eddy and the ladies over whether Miss Bowe should be kept out of gentlemen's activities, Miss Penn frowned slightly, her eyes darting from the spirited discussion to her partner, barred from gentlemen's activities himself. She then cleared her throat.

"Please do excuse me, Sir James," she said quite politely, "But I would think a reasonable solution, in such unusual circumstances as these, would be to simply provide a chaperone." She looked at the ladies with a smile, eyes shining. "Yes, I do know what those are. And I volunteer."

Thus was a compromise reached, which I appreciate, no

matter how odd it may be that Miss Penn would provide a safeguard to propriety. I certainly still do not at all trust her or her partner. The fact that they do not get along with one another well does not make either one any more a true ally to the rest of us beyond what loyalty we've bought.

July 19th, 1815
New York
40° 47'N 073° 58'W

Dear Sir,

I was quite relieved today when we reached New York safely, having completed the tasks you recommended with Dr. Mitchell.

As you are likely aware, the Coltranes have their own holdings here in New York and have been quite at home since our arrival. Under the circumstances, everyone travels with some degree of security and in numbers, save for Eddy and Miss Bowe, both of whom have refused any escort.

It has been a source of great excitement and rumor here that their number of airships in their mooring docks has almost doubled, for it seems our opponents in this endeavor have also procured a military airship of their own from some agency, explaining how they reached the Americas only shortly behind us. Despite their presence here, there has been no contact with them. The city is better secured than the rough lands where we last met their agents on the way back from St. Louis, and the security detail around the city's mooring station, where we have the dirigible, has assured us that there will be no trouble. Despite this we have left a detail of armed men from our own crew on board the airship at all times.

I am still unsure what sort of men our opponents are, for we have not yet been able to get any news of them. Even amongst the soldiers of this base they are quite secretive, though it is clear they have sources of information regarding ourselves, and significant monies and reach to accomplish their goals. I do not know if their presence here is specifically to try to hinder us, or if they are as focused in this time about recruiting as we ourselves are. I am left with the simple gratitude that they seemed to not yet see fit to menace the women of our group about town. They have restricted their aggressions towards those of us best suited to meet them.

We are quite eager to be on our way to the north while there is still summer warmth (though I must say it is an unseasonably cold summer here) but may be delayed in pursuing your goals. News has just reached these shores of the historic agreement made between the motherland and France. I am unsure as to how much of a hand you and your peers had in the agreement, but regardless, I must extend a congratulations on the compact. The city is in quite the festive mood, and a number of celebrations are being scheduled to accompany the diplomatic functions, some of which are happening here for the obvious symbolic reasons.

In addition, it seems that news of our objectives, in addition to Sir James's and Eddy's considerable innate celebrity, has given us a great deal of popularity here. As such, we have been invited to one of these functions where the former French territories will be signed over to colonial hands by the former French governor of New Orleans.[11] We could not pass up such an opportunity, and indeed, Miss Coltrane, Miss Wright, and Mrs. Fisher are quite excited for the opportunities such a grand social occasion will present. When that is finished we will, of course, be away to begin our adventure into the unknown.

Yours,
Gregory Conan Watts

---

11 The treaty of 1815, part of the extensive post-war concessions on behalf of the governments of the European Alliance, signed over all French rights to lands in North America south of the Great Lakes and west of the Mississippi. While this covered almost a third of the continent, Spain's right to disputed French-Spanish lands was not waived, making the handover a complicated one. The French government considered this a Land purchase, via the canceling of war debts in exchange for the land rights. Certain portions of Parliament called this "France's Just Desserts." – C B-W

From the personal journals of Gregory Conan Watts,
July 20th, 1815
New York
40º 47'N 073º 58'W

Though most unexpected, we at last have some information about those people hired to oppose us. Valuable as it may be, I would have much preferred to have avoided the stress and worry that accompanied the discovery. I have nothing but Matthew Fisher-Swift's word that the events I am recording are factually true, but nonetheless I feel that I must record them. If true, then he has taken great risk upon himself, but done us a remarkable service.

He told no one he was leaving the dirigible. After hearing about the difficulties we encountered on our way back from St. Louis, he had grown quite curious about what manner of people were hired opposite us. No one noticed he was missing for some hours, as Matthew is often absent from our company, crawling about the ship. Once his aunt noticed he was not responding to her calls, which usually raise a response of "In a minute, Aunt Ruth," she raised quite the fuss, and the rest of us were quickly about trying to find him with no luck.

According to his account, not thinking a whit on how dangerous such a mission might be, he went forth under cover of pre-dawn darkness to peek in on the other dirigible. He says that they appeared to have been unloading and loading supplies, both delivering a good deal of material for unknown purpose, and loading crates of unknown content onto their dirigible.

He stated that a pair of men directed most of these trips. One was clearly a British gentleman of significant standing, for Matthew called him a 'dark London fake of Sir James, except hard on people.' However hard he may have been, those about him respected him enough to follow, and he seemed to know precisely where everything should go and how everyone should be conducting themselves. 'Second to His Nibs,' in Matthew's belief, was a large and dirty man in stained clothing, most distinctive to a young boy's eyes for the large patch of scarring on both the back of his right hand and to the right side of his face. While this man still had his right eye, Matthew described it as 'squinty' and 'evil looking,' a different color than the left. The burn extended up a good portion of the right side of his scalp, such that he had shaven his head entirely lest he end up looking as patchwork as our captain. His commands were in a gruff voice and an accent helpfully described as 'not London.' The crewers and loading men seemed quite afraid of the scarred man, perhaps with some reason.

Amongst them at times were three others of particular note that he was able to pick out and that seemed to belong in particular to the airship.

There is little question why the first stood out. He was a massive – taller than any other about by almost a head, if Matthew is to be believed – and brightly-dressed man of Negro coloration. Sir James surmises he might be African. The former slaves among the workmen treated this man with some combination of reverence and abject terror, showing him great respect and giving him a wide berth. Each time he had passed, they would cross themselves before returning to their duties, even if doing so required putting down heavy weights, then taking them back up. Matthew did not hear him speak throughout the time he watched.

The second of these extras was 'near as tall as Eddy, but scrawnier ... likes to hear himself talk, but too foreign to hear right. Spanish, I think. Clothes looked it.' This figure was also notable as he kept himself armed, despite New York's restrictions against doing so. Matthew enthusiastically described a bandoleer which was home to a brace of pistols, with one more such gun resting on his right hip, prompting the childish claim that he 'might be a pirate.' The man's left hip bore another weapon, a bullwhip, upon which he regularly rested his left hand as if he might put it to use.

The last is apparently a woman with an Oxfordshire accent to her voice, but so soft a tone as to make her words almost unintelligible from a distance. She wore a reasonably fashionable dress, save that Matthew had the good sense to be somewhat scandalized by the low cut of her bodice, and the poor sense to bring up this feature enough times that his uncle cuffed him about the head in the retelling.

In time, Matthew was given away, and there was significant chaos amongst the men about the mooring area. A cry went up, and quickly, armed men both of the base and our rivals' own private security, as well as some portion of their workforce, were moving Matthew's direction. Only a single man, thankfully, had begun close enough to provide real menace – the one who had seen motion behind a stack of crates.

The next piece of narration I would find difficult to believe were one other piece of information regarding Matthew not made known to me amidst this telling. While he is indeed the Captain's ward, he earns his keep aboard the ship by hunting the rats and mice that occasionally threaten the ship's food stores with his slingshot. Apparently he has developed significant reflex and aim with the device as one might imagine would be necessary to successfully hunt down such small and quick targets. Thus it seems possible beyond the realm of childhood fantasy that when the cry went up, Matthew took up the only weapon that came easily to hand, and fired a stone with precision enough to strike the man down, clutching at his eye.

Matthew does not believe that anyone got a good look at him in turn, but he did not learn anything more, nor pick out any further people of distinction after this, for his nerves and childhood exuberance were spent enough at this point that he simply ran until he was absolutely certain no one was following him. Then, keeping to cover, he returned to us to report. After this story was told, the young man received quite the scolding from both of his guardians first, followed, more quietly, by the first words of praise and support Matthew has yet received from Eddy. I am quite certain that the latter made far more impression upon him than the former, for though he remains wary of his guardians, he has otherwise gone about his business since with a wide smile and a spring to his step when he is not practicing standing or marching in military fashion, a habit I have caught him at frequently.

July 22nd, 1815
New York
40º 47'N 073º 58'W

My Dearest Cordelia,

    Two matters have converged recently to make life particularly interesting. The first was Sam Bowe's revelation that she was, in fact, Samantha Bowe. The second has been our invitation to a large formal event here in New York to celebrate the treaty signing all former French lands over to England here in the colonies. The Governor of New York, along with the Governors of St. Louis and its surrounding territory of Missouri and the new Governors of New Orleans and Louisiana, will be in attendance, as will the former French Governors of several territories. For several members of our crew preparing for a formal event is a welcome change from our recent activities. Miss Coltrane and Miss Wright in particular have thrown themselves enthusiastically into preparations.

    Where these events converge, of course, is that Samantha Bowe has no formal wear, or, indeed, formal graces that anyone can locate. Combine this, apparently, with the trio of Jillian, Harriet and Mrs. Fisher seeming to have taken offense on behalf of their gender that Miss Bowe should so long have passed herself off as male, and it has led to quite the spirited conflict here.

    Even aside from the prospect of the formal gathering, there have been many attempts to push upon her a woman's clothing proper for her age, all of which received a calm "No, thanks," until at last, Miss Wright, of all people, persuaded her into a split skirt, women's riding boots and a men's shirt of style and coloration as to not completely offend the sensibilities. While she remains completely unmoving on the matter of wearing her hat when outdoors, they have convinced her through their relentless efforts to at least wear her hair down. She has permitted Miss Wright, and Miss Wright alone, access enough to her to get her hair properly combed out and tied back in the barest of fashions, though she will not allow word one of having it styled at this point.

Given Miss Wright's own difficulties with matters of fashion and style, this might seem a frightening thought in its own right, it may be precisely that factor Miss Bowe is counting on to prevent too great an alteration in her preferred style. Truly she would be a scandal greater than Miss Penn in England, but we are trying to give her some room and time to come to more proper dress and manner on account of being an American, and thus not to be held to the same standards.

For a formal event, however, these refusals are holding no weight with the trio, and Miss Penn has joined them in working on getting her to make an exception and dress not merely like a female, but like a lady, just this once. She has attempted to refuse to attend the event at all, but in our invitations it was made very clear that our entire company was to be in attendance.

In general, among all of us, only Eddy seems quite certain what to make of her. Which, rather than perhaps what you are thinking, he seems to treat her not at all differently than when he believed her to be a young man of extraordinary skill and training. They continue to talk with more regularity than is proper, though on the absolute insistence of Mrs. Fisher, to which both have happily agreed without hesitation, they do so only publicly and with witnesses, or where witnesses might regularly pass by. It seems she had an upbringing in some of the wilder parts of the world, where she had to learn to hunt, track and all the rest as one might imagine the boys of a savage society might learn. How she survived in this manner with her insistent disregard for firearms is another mystery to me, but then the woman herself is an enigma and a shock to the senses.

Bringing some sanity to the entire affair, at least as I and her brother see it, is Miss Coltrane. While not claiming any position as enforcer of the rules of the airship as Mrs. Fisher has done, Miss Coltrane has taken a deep and personal dislike to all things regarding Samantha Bowe and has confronted her, though quietly and politely, many times over on matters of manner and behavior from the position of a woman of similar age. Though asked not to participate, she has nonetheless hovered about to supervise Miss Wright's attempts on Miss Bowe. Mrs. Fisher meanwhile has gone back to her normal station for the greatest part, watching all of this mostly from afar, chiding Harriet on all of the normal issues whenever she dares venture into the bridge of the ship, and occasionally then questioning after the efforts to tame Miss Bowe. I fear all such ventures are doomed to failure.

I have to wonder if perhaps this is for the best, because while she is entirely unrepresentable amongst any kind of reasonable society, having not even a gentleman's manners, (or even a Scotsman's manners as the local case may be), she has already proven herself a vital asset when presented with danger. Given that her intended contributions are through her skills as a wilderness guide and any knowledge gained from whatever small ventures she might have taken in her father's company – and her knowledge of Bowe himself – I cannot imagine she could serve her function to our company in any kind of petticoats and corset, however much Miss Coltrane clearly wishes to see the wild girl so caged.

Additionally, the matter of how best to deal with the Europeans has become a question of some import, and as seems to be so much the current trend in events, no one seems quite certain how to broach the topic or to tend to it themselves. Since our arrival, Giovanni Franzini has been the perfect gentleman. Perhaps this sudden burst of civility stems from the rather unique experience, amidst all the tales of children running away to join the circus, that he was deemed so loathsome a man that the circus ran away from him. His partner likely still resents their circumstances as well. I am not certain if she is any less a criminal, but even if not, for people of such character, she may well blame him simply for being the one who got caught. In any case, his manners have been almost up to the standard expected from a gentleman of refinement and education. Almost. Even so, he remains under significant suspicion, and with good reason.

Sir James, as seems to be his way, had made the first overtures to him of some degree of acceptance, welcoming him to the ship and the mission, and asking for some exchange of stories, of which Mr. Franzini has no shortage. Sir James, in turn, is always most generous with sharing his experiences as well as being a skilled listener. However, the cheat has remained inauspiciously banned from that most required gateway into Sir James's social circle and acceptance into the confidence of our leader – the card game. It is, perhaps, unfortunate for him that the very means by which he has usually made most of his traveling money, aside from being the Great Franzini on stage, is also the thing that has exiled him from the primary social circle here, due to his attempt to cheat the wrong person.

While Miss Coltrane has taken some exception to Miss Penn since our arrival, apparently an unapologetically loose woman is still more a part of her experience than one with the audacity to pretend to ungender herself, let alone to go about engaging in combat, gambling, drinking, and all the rest. She has taken to advising Miss Penn on traveling dresses in grays and blues when aboard ship, due to the lingering coal dust that still pervades the lower level, and even mentioning weighing one's skirts when promenading the decks, although the last may have been a small and subtle slight on Miss Penn's existence as a light-skirt. If Miss Penn detected this, she showed no recognition of the attack, simply smiling mildly and calling the idea terribly clever.

For her part, the change in status for Miss Bowe has done nothing to change her opinion of either of the others recruited in the same time as she was. She ignores Giovanni Franzini beyond the necessities of interaction in so small a space as this. Her relations with Miss Penn have slowly grown more cordial, though Miss Penn still frequently seems at something of a loss in how to deal with Miss Bowe in light of her previous attempts to seduce her.

This awkward sociability led to a most curious bit of nonsense as I was working on something recently. Miss Bowe approached Miss Penn as the latter sat holding one of her charlatan's cards, apparently upside down, though of course I did not look closely.

"What occasions the lion?" Miss Bowe asked quietly.

"A battle."

"I'm all for it."

Miss Penn's smile was somewhere between awkward and good-natured, though she did not drop her mystic charade. "This one is inside. The struggle with the self. The weights a soul bears." Her green eyes fell on Miss Coltrane, seated with her cousin away from this nonsense. "Sometimes an animal in a cage or trap, unable to get out, will try to pull things in." This strange flummery went generally unobserved. Miss Coltrane glanced over only to frown slightly at Miss Bowe's ill-coordinated farmgirl clothing. Miss Wright looked over only to smile encouragingly about the same.

Speaking of Miss Wright, while I could be mistaken about this, I do believe that Miss Wright has somewhat caught Eddy's eye. It would not much surprise me, for I can only imagine that around his home, child-bearing hips and a sturdy frame are still of high value as womanly virtues. Whether I am correct or not, he seems to have decided to find more occasions to pass the time in paying polite and public visits that he might more often encounter Miss Wright. For her part, unsurprising to me, she seems entirely oblivious to this attention, perhaps simply through her own innate ignorance of social grace and convention. Surely if she realized, she could not help but be somewhat flattered, for he is still a hero of the land and quite near a baronet's cousin in rank. Perhaps it is simply frustration that Samantha Bowe is barely taking whatever little help Miss Wright can offer, as concerns proper behaviors for a young woman, that clouds her from noticing Eddy's glances.

Regardless, it seems we shall have to rely on Miss Wright to somewhat civilize Miss Bowe, for the party is fast approaching and there is nothing for it but to rely upon her efforts. Personally, I would almost prefer the small scandal that might result from her not attending the event at all than risking what our wild woman might do to scandalize us all before such distinguished company.

In any case, I care far more about what is best for our company over any individual's sensibilities, for when we are finished, I will care not at all should Samantha Bowe disappear back to whatever West there still is in America, or whatever other wild place suits her fancy, for I will be returned home. Should we find success by any reasonable definition, you and I will be soon planning our wedding.

With Love and Hope,
Gregory Conan Watts

From the journals of Gregory Conan Watts,
July 23rd, 1815
New York
40º 47'N 073º 58'W

Jillian Coltrane has been a godsend amidst the chaos ahead of being guests of honor at a formal event with some of the most notable figures in the American colonies in attendance, to say nothing of numerous dignitaries from both England and France. She has seen to it that we have suitable clothing for the event. While for the Coltranes such a concern may be a matter of course, others among our number have never owned such fancy garments in our lives. Indeed, without their help, I could scarce afford such things with all my savings. They have spared no expense to make sure we are all suitably outfitted, and have likewise put forth significant effort to ensure that we know the precise manners needed to get through such an event.

I endeavor to be a good student in these matters, both to avoid embarrassing our company and to learn to one day impress the men of Captain Bentham's social circles, representing Cordelia well as her husband. As important as this trip is, that is an even greater motivating factor, and I do not know that I will ever again have an opportunity to learn from so skilled of teachers in social affairs as the Coltranes. For all this eagerness I will admit to being quite nervous. I believe I very much understand now how Harriet feels.

In addition to all of the shopping and education, Jillian has been kind enough to handle most of the communications ahead of the event. Many people wish our attention to congratulate us and wish us well. She has accepted numerous invitations to tea and written countless letters on our group's behalf to give the best impression possible. It seems that the opportunity to interact with her native element has invigorated her, for she seems tireless in her efforts to see that our best possible face is put forward. These efforts were, admittedly, somewhat delayed by a short disappearance after an unfortunate incident with Miss Bowe.

The ornithopter has taken to following Miss Bowe around

at all times now. While it disturbs me to admit it, the terrible thing does behave very much like an exceptionally intelligent animal. It follows numerous commands, reacts to stimuli around it, and, save when specifically told to stay, will attend Miss Bowe's every movement about the ship. On one such occasion while it was doing so, Jillian attempted to pass Samantha and her contraption in the hallways. Owing to the narrowness of the passage, Jillian's skirts somehow became entangled in its front spokes, and with a sudden movement and a snapping of a lace, she was divested of her dress in a most shocking manner. Jillian's outcry alerted everyone else to the problem, and her brother and Miss Wright quickly came to her rescue. Of considerably less help was Samantha Bowe herself, who did little other than whistle in a most unseemly fashion before falling to uproarious laughter, and since then has passed up very few opportunities to tease Miss Coltrane about her lacy underthings. I fear it may be some misguided attempt at revenge for Miss Coltrane's insistence on making sure Miss Bowe is prepared to dress and comport herself like a proper lady for the party. In any case, since this incident, Miss Coltrane has given both Miss Bowe and the ornithopter as wide a berth as possible. After most of a day in seclusion, Jillian regained enough of her dignity to reemerge and throw herself back into her efforts to prepare for the big event.

A bizarre conversational quartet has developed as Miss Penn and Miss Wright have allied to assure Miss Bowe that if she gives in, just this once, to a custom-made dress and properly styled hair, it will truly only be this once. The two of them sit with Miss Bowe and Eddy, talking more about the party than Miss Bowe would prefer. Miss Penn serves as something as a go-between, buffering Miss Wright's enthusiasm for the grand social occasion by listening to it. I grow more certain than ever that Eddy quite favors Miss Wright each time he addresses a question not to Miss Bowe about hunting, but to Miss Wright about her lab maintenance. Julietta Penn seems to agree, for when Miss Wright instead begins going on about the young Englishmen of distinguished breeding and character who may be in attendance at the party in front of Eddy, she rhetorically swoops in with a grace just short of Miss Coltrane's, if much less decent. She steers the conversation around to the dress again, and Miss Bowe's objections to these new sartorial interruptions are met with an insistent flash of green eyes. I certainly cannot say that I particularly care for Miss Penn in any fashion, but I can appreciate her own variety of tact. Her knowledge of formal occasions and how to handle herself – and how to handle both Miss Wright and Miss Bowe – at least frees Miss Coltrane to attend to her important business and eases the social situation among our company.

July 26th, 1815
New York
40º 47'N 073º 58'W

My Dearest Cordelia,

By the time this letter reaches you, I am sure that the events that transpired in New York will have reached your shores, and you, like all of England will be quite absorbed in the scandal that has so hit us coming from the Governor's Ball just last evening. I know you are aware of my companions, so I am certain you have been awaiting some word from me to document the truth of what occurred when assassins attempted to kill the King and Queen of France (and perhaps some of our own colonial dignitaries) before all present.

We were quite surprised to find out that Louis and Queen Marie would be in attendance, but given the momentous nature of the alliance and treaty, perhaps I should not have been so surprised they made the long journey to the colonies for the event. Given how recent the war was (even though Napoleon, not Louis, was responsible, obviously) it is also not surprising that they would have kept their attendance secret until their arrival on American shores. With good reason, as it turns out, but as it turned out the plans were still not secretive enough.

We were certainly prepared to attend. The battle suit was readied, but ultimately it was decided that the dashing young hero should be allowed to mingle and speak, and that many of the ladies present would be terrified by such a monster, and, of course, there would be plenty of security present on behalf of both crowns in a more official capacity, so certainly nothing of the sort would be needed.

As it matters to some degree for this story, Miss Penn and Miss Wright finally convinced Miss Bowe to dress properly for the occasion, and the Coltranes would make arrangements to pay for the tailors. Currently the vogue is inspired by post war fabric excesses, and post war leisure. I'm hereby reporting that stays are now being called corsets in fashionable New York, apparently a product of men returning home from war and women returning to the home from nursing. Skirts seem to have multiplying gores, as buying English wool is the ultimate in fashionable English patriotism. I wanted you to know, should these trends find hold in England.

As Samantha did not know her sizes or any such thing, and is built, so far as I can tell, primarily rectangular, it took very talented tailors to come and do the work on short notice. The other women present in our group were mostly prepared, though Miss Penn needed something fitting for the occasion, but at least knew her sizes and the ins and outs of women's fashion, while Mrs. Fisher had to be outfitted a bit fancier than her usual means allow for. As she is an employee of the Coltranes, this was no difficulty. Eddy was also to be dressed fittingly for the occasion, though he was grateful that at least some of the dignitaries present were of Scottish descent and character, and thus he would be permitted formal dress in the fashion of his home.

Miss Bowe, however, was quite the sight. I daresay that I have seen happier wet cats. Despite the best work of well paid specialists, she is simply not fit to corsetry, and complained often and loudly that she could not breathe, and while of no bust, even when so outfitted, she is of such muscle that the corset often creaked ominously when she moved about. Her hair was another matter of great debate, for it was tied up and perfumed, which she claimed was giving her the sniffles, and the hat looked positively out of place, perched on her head in place of her more traditional and nigh constant frontiersman's hat.

Surprising us all greatly, Mr. Franzini took especially well to the occasion, and when he had the means and tailors available, ended up looking quite rakish, though still oily and distinctively Italian. But perhaps I shall have to soon edit my thoughts, for with France becoming peaceable, perhaps Italy or Spain will be next. Either way, I would not trust him even were his nation to become our closest of friends.

The most bitter bone of contention in all our preparations regards the matter of armaments at the event. The gentlemen, coming in the capacity of famed war heroes, and unofficially a part of the security measures, were permitted light arms. The ladies, however, were to go about entirely unarmed, which was to include Miss Bowe's knives. These she was loudly loath to part with. Likewise, the ornithopter was not permitted. Thankfully in such time as we have had, she has convinced it at times to 'guard,' per its known commands. When given this order it will stand quite still at the door to her chambers and only move again upon her return. It almost seems excited at these times, if I can express the actions of a machine in emotional terms, though nothing else quite describes the reactions of this contraption, beyond bedevilment. Such curses are not something to which I am yet willing to subscribe to belief in, though I am growing closer by the day.

Almost upon arrival, Sir James and Miss Coltrane were quickly the center of the party, for everyone wanted to speak with them. Sir James was almost immediately beset by friends and strangers alike. It should not at all surprise me by now that he should have friends in these distant shores, both among landed men, former Oxford graduates who have come to New York to aid in its growth and industrialization, and among officers from the war years of sufficient rank and means to attend such an event as this. He found himself some space in this after a few rounds partially by introducing Eddy, who I have no doubt is even now cursing him for the added attention when he wished to greet his countrymen as soon as possible and mingle with other Scotsmen.

In any case, Sir James's respite was not to last long, for Sir James was no further than a few steps beyond these military gentlemen then he found himself quite beset by the folk of the social scene, and many women wishing to be sure they had a place upon his dance card. I am not certain he would have had any real time to see to any degree of guard duty. Even so, he seemed to be enjoying all of this attention.

Almost as popular, Miss Coltrane found herself completely surrounded by all manner of people, from ladies of her station wishing gossip to young men wishing conversation and promises of a dance. Some few people sought some comment from her upon the nature of the upcoming mission and what place she felt her brother and family might play in the diplomacy to come. She weathered it all with perfect manners and even made a point of introducing the ladies with her, much to Harriet's pleasure and benefit – and to Miss Bowe's disgust.

They each had their own attention quickly enough, for today they were celebrities of sorts, even if the occasion was about larger matters still, and not everyone could crowd about Miss Coltrane. Miss Wright made some attempt to show her social graces, which is to say while being quite overwhelmed, she tipped over a small table and tripped over a young gentleman with whom she was trying to flirt. He quickly made his way away once she had regained her feet.

Miss Bowe was more graceful by far, and less gracious by an equal margin. She would have no part in flirtation, and it would have been a complete disaster and perhaps even an incident if Miss Penn had not rescued her and come to the fore as a socially capable woman in her own right, far beyond the indignities of her heritage and previous social status. For this, Samantha seemed quite grateful to be rescued again and again in proper manner, though I have no idea how a half blood gypsy could so well know the ways of England, and show such remarkable patience with people when she had so divorced herself from our company for so long. I cannot be certain, of course, but perhaps she wished to somehow make up for her false infatuation with Sam Bowe when she thought him the dashing and handsome, if youthful, man, rather than the square and undignified woman. Either way, it got them through those occasions, and all seemed to be going exceptionally well at the time.

There was some further time to mingle before everyone was invited to supper, that the people of occasion could salute one another and show significant ceremony up to the occasion. By that time, I had excused myself enough times with explanation of my marital status that I was grateful for the break, though still quite enraptured with watching the charm that the Coltranes show at work in their arena. We all sat, and were placed together, giving some respite to those who had been greatly beleaguered by the masses, and especial respite from trying to even pretend some proper sociability for Miss Bowe. We sat through speeches of the occasion, which I am sure will be echoed throughout the land as great words when the scandal dies down.

It was some time during all of this that the assassins struck, having somehow placed themselves among the serving staff. A young man pulled the top off a serving tray to reveal a pistol, and numerous others throughout the place then rose with declarations stating that France should never bow before England, and would be free of our tyranny, along with similar epithets belonging to such radicals. He drew the gun, which no one was prepared for in the least. Indeed, right now, the scandal should be much larger, and France either in mourning or chaos, but for the interference of a serving fork.

As usual, the first person to react had been Miss Bowe, who, upon the first movement of the gunman, had reacted at once, taking advantage of the fork in her hand and throwing it with such accuracy and force that it plunged into the man's arm and caused him to miss his shot, firing harmlessly into the ceiling instead. Unfortunately there was more than one assassin about the plot – quite the company it seems, and I, in hindsight, cannot be surprised. It is the duty of politicians and royalty to mark such occasions as this with revelry, speeches and ceremony, but we had fought a long and bitter war, and there were hard feelings on all sides. That some of those hard feelings should infiltrate the higher levels of society enough to allow a group of saboteurs and killers in a large and hastily thrown-together occasion should not have surprised me.

These were desperate people in the extreme, not out to survive their villainy, but instead to commit their foul act as publicly and loudly as possible. Guns were watched for fairly closely, but some number had managed them. Others took up other weapons, from concealed knives to swords that it turned out had been stolen from the ceremonial statues about the place, or from display racks. It was quite the daunting show, and there was all at once a great deal of screaming and running about such that any kind of evacuation would have been impossible, though the first of the aides and bodyguards were making their way towards the respective delegations. In this time, the primary bodyguard to the Governor of the New York territories was stabbed fatally by one of the assassins, leaving the Governor and his wife defenseless.

It was a horror, to be certain, but at least unlike many of those present, we had means to interfere, for some of our company were armed, and just starting to get into the habit once more of being defenders of their nation. None were so quick about it as Samantha, however, who had leapt to her feet, and from there to the table. Apparently expecting such a thing, and willing to put up with aiding in terrible behavior for a woman, I noticed Miss Penn tugging upon Samantha's dress hem sufficient to catch her attention, and once she had done so, she withdrew a knife from her bodice and handed it to Samantha. It seems that not all of our women were entirely willing to go without any kind of armament. Now equipped with a smaller but still deadly version of her favorite weapon, Samantha leapt from the table, upsetting it thoroughly, and dove towards the nearest man armed with a pistol. She cut him across the arm enough to cause him to drop his weapon, though I believe she intended to do worse. Finding her reach entirely insufficient, her next slash was to her skirts, giving her greater freedom of movement, but not enough. Having presented herself as a threat, if one both rapidly finding herself short on breath and short on the mobility she was used to, she soon found herself pressed back under assault from multiple attackers.

By this time, Eddy had stood and used his drawn gun to take down one of the assailants nearest him with the butt, then fired once, taking down another man who had taken up arms and rushed towards the Governor of New York. Sir James followed into the fray, managing to catch a man by the wrist, causing him to miss his shot. Another would have stabbed him then, but Eddy came to his friend's rescue, bodily knocking the man with the knife down. The two stood back to back then amidst a knot of attackers, for in taking the fight to the attackers, we had ended up between the kitchens, where most of the attackers had been in hiding, and the dignitaries present, including the King and Queen of France and most of the regional governors.

It was an inspiring vision, the pair of them taking all about them, and at such time as they had clear space, they would find a new target, though firing guns was a mostly impractical thing amidst the near riot as people sought some safety, and the staffs tried to get the royalty and other men and women of import out of the room with haste.

Unable to reach my fellows through the chaos, I instead aided that latter effort, drawing my gun and moving to a doorway. I shot one of the would-be assassins as he tried to bar anyone fleeing through one of the doors, then took up a sentry post by the door, hurrying dinner guests through. This afforded me a fine vision of the rest of the room, and brandishing my pistol seemed to discourage any efforts to engage me too closely, though I was unable to draw a good shot without risking the lives of bystanders.

Seeing that the grounds had been compromised, Sir James was the first to realize perhaps there was some threat we were not seeing. He attempted to rush towards the regional governors to aid in the guarding and evacuation, but was pushed back by the mass of the crowd all about. Eddy roared then, enough to draw some attention as he bulled his way through the crowd, knocking aside what men he needed to, with Sir James close behind him. They reached the dignitaries at last, and were recognized enough as heroes of war that the guardsmen allowed them to fall in. With Eddy leading, they sought to evacuate the British governors, and, as Sir James had expected, there they found another ambush. Expecting this instead of stumbling in blind, he fired rapidly, turning the pepper-box pistol between each shot, managing to fell two men and wound a third before they could get a shot off. Though one of the guards was shot dead, another injured, Eddy managed to find his shot by merit of being taller than the men ahead of him, though their jostling threw his aim off, wasting his first shot. His second was true, and he dropped the last of the men who had not yet emptied their guns, and then Sir James and the forefront of the guard were upon the last of them before they could reload. Even flight was denied the assassins, for Eddy's final shot dropped the one man who briefly made it clear of the conflict and tried to flee.

While they were at that, Miss Bowe had found herself having drawn a great deal of attention from our assailants, having ruined the first shot. Somehow she had found a second blade from the table, and thus was fighting at least three men, perhaps more, though I could not be sure, armed with a bodice knife and a steak knife. Despite this poor armament she was holding her own, though her breath was labored and she could barely move and certainly not lunge into her efforts, due to her own dresses and bindings. The table she had knocked over guarded her back, with Julietta Penn remaining behind her and the table for cover. Our gypsy woman meanwhile had leaned herself across the table and was desperately sawing through the threads of Samantha's bodice with another steak knife, that Sam might fight and breathe. It came free at last, and Samantha lunged forward in her far-less-restrictive undershirts, surprising the men who thought they had her pinned down.

I do not know if she dispatched them or simply fought past them, for even as the others were fighting for our representatives here, she headed for the new royals of France, the original targets of the assassination attempt, and there found their guardsmen fighting a desperate battle. I imagine they were quite surprised to find a woman armed with a pair of mismatched knives, in a torn dress and her undershirts, fighting on their behalf. She has even said since that they at first attacked her themselves, but she convinced them of her good will when she felled a gunman coming at them by throwing her steak knife. She then re-armed herself by groping about on the nearest table for further silverware while fighting off another assassin using the bodice knife she'd borrowed from Miss Penn.

Somewhere in the chaos I lost track of Giovanni Franzini and assumed he'd crawled under a table or under some rock to hide. He quite surprised me later when we learned he'd run down two of the assassins who had attempted to flee in the chaos and felled both, albeit from behind as they were running.

I could not see all of it, but by the end as we regathered, I would swear Samantha had gone through at least two table settings, but had held onto Miss Penn's knife. She was bleeding from half a dozen cuts, at least, and looked a wreck, her hat hanging from one side of her head, still held to one now loosed braid by a single hatpin. She was decent only by the simplest definition, but for all of it, she looked quite pleased with herself, unlike anyone else in the room.

Our small group was once more gathering, soon to be helping in a call for order. We would assist in patrolling the grounds all night, trying to make sure that we had all of the assassins, and no one attempted to flee before they might be questioned. First, however, Miss Bowe asked, somewhat too loudly, of Sir James, "That was fun; do all your parties end like this?"[12]

This is what drew the final scandal, which has hit the rumor mills, I understand. Overhearing our American misfit, the Queen of France fainted.

With love, always,
Gregory Conan Watts

---

12 This quote, is, of course, the source of the title of Sir John Goodall's book on modern scandal *That was fun; do all your parties end like this?* 1832, Cambridge press, reprinted in London five times, 1833. Since, other than the public events of the party detailed above, so little was known about Sam Bowe, the book is rather tangential. However, the quote's use in the title has forever linked the Governor's Ball Attack with standard London Season scandal, simply based on one defender's lack of propriety in dress and demeanor. – C B-W

From the journals of Gregory Conan Watts,
July 27th, 1815
New York
40º 47'N 073º 58'W

I suppose it should not at all surprise me that, of all of us, the one most prepared to deal with matters concerning assassins and conspiracies of murder would be Giovanni Franzini, but he has at last proven his worth. He disappeared not long after order was restored and all guests had been accounted for in one fashion or another. My first concerns were that he had absented himself to ensure he was not blamed for having a part in the assassination, or perhaps even that he had, and was fleeing now that it had failed. As such, no one was more surprised than I when he returned the next morning with news of the assassins and their backers.

At first no one believed him whatsoever, of course, but he offered proof of his knowledge and good intent. The rest of us had mostly been on patrol all night – with Samantha glad for an excuse to put herself to a use she was more accustomed to once she had been dragged off to change back into her typical clothing. None of us had found anything, and by this point were willing to grasp at straws in hopes of learning something.

Franzini acknowledged having utilized some of his contacts in the less-than-reputable parts of New York society to trace them. He was able to lead our troop and a handful of New York's patrolmen to the home of a New York politician previously best known for his fervent abolitionist views. Within the man's wine cellar they found a handful of people hidden away who, under some threat, admitted to knowledge of the assassination attempts. Their host claimed no knowledge of their presence, but some among the killers admitted that he'd had a hand in their hiring and had provided them with the key to his cellars to take shelter in until a way out of the city could be gained. A handful of other names were gained from them as well, primarily local, but also a handful of our own politicians as high up as the House of Lords back in England.

The regional governors, as well as the French royals, have been temporarily put under heavy guard, many being taken out of the city during the investigation as guard against further aggression until all of the conspirators are captured. Despite this, we are still in contact with them through representatives and regular messengers, as they apparently have been quick to place a great deal of faith in our company to resolve these matters ever since our part in saving so many lives.

A full confession was eventually achieved, confirmed through getting the same account from nearly all of the captured conspirators. Most of the money for the effort goes back to Spain. With France ceding all of its former colonies to England as part of the peace and surrender agreement, Spain no longer has any official allies here in the colonies and have found their territories in Florida entirely cut off from those in Texas. New Spain, as it is informally called, is split. As some saw it, their only recourse was to disrupt peace proceedings between France and England, then take advantage of the chaos and lack of leadership. Their agents made contact with a number of people in both the colonies and England who were the most displeased by any hint of alliance with France, the aggressor of the Napoleonic Wars. We do not yet know if these men knew they were dealing with Spain or not, but it hardly matters. This offense remains treasonous in light of our new alliance with our old enemy now that Napoleon is dead.

More immediately, we learned that Spain has also made an alliance with some of the white slavers and pirates from the Barbary Coast and, with this additional help, is preparing to launch an attack on New Orleans. The Spainish have forces in waiting in the northwest Florida forts located closest to our borders in Louisiana only awaiting word on whether the attacks here were successful that they can suitably adjust their tactics to a lack of leadership. Spies have been sent to confirm the information provided by these most unreliable witnesses, but their stories were clear and similar enough that we cannot discount it entirely.

In the meanwhile, as we possess the fastest mode of transportation available and have numerous people among our number with officers' training and experience, not to mention widespread recognition, the regional governors sent courtiers to ask us to travel quickly to Louisiana and make sure the defenses there are secure. If the spies confirm the alliance between the pirates and our enemies in New Spain, then the only means to properly defend New Orleans and English holdings in the region may be to take the border fortresses from Spain. We have been assured that we have the authority to do as we deem necessary to make sure the region is secure against our enemies, which seem to be more numerous than we had previously been aware.

We are assured as well that further letters are being written in order to secure more aid from the homeland, particularly in the form of officers. There are many experienced soldiers in the colonies, many of whom saw action in the war against Napoleon's alliance, but due to the nature of our armies and the best schools all being located in England, there are very few officers here. As such, until we are relieved, we are being asked to provide temporary combat leadership in this time of trouble.

Though Sir James has not hesitated in this, there is some concern among our number, for in this effort we are moving the opposite direction we had hoped, and are quickly losing the summer months so badly needed if we would hope to succeed in finding a northern path from the Atlantic to the Pacific. Dr. Bowe's journals claim there is one, a claim which certainly caught the interest of our sponsors. Still, national security must come before all else, and the majority of our company is agreed that we must hurry on to New Orleans. As such, we have given written and signed testimony as to the confessions we heard and the security operations we took part in for the local courts to use in our absence. Miss Coltrane has begun writing letters to people both here and at home in hopes of gaining greater support for our efforts ahead, and otherwise we are preparing to depart more quickly than we had hoped.

As for our opposition, apparently they and their airship left some time before the party began. Given the presence of a Spaniard among their number, their quick departure, and the conspiracy we have found ourselves embroiled in, I must wonder if perhaps they had something to do with the assassination attempt. Perhaps we shall never know, but if they are involved, I shall hope they will be forced to give a full accounting of themselves eventually. At the very least the messages home should be sufficient to limit their funding from their sponsor until such time as more questions have been answered.

From the letters of Giovanni Franzini,
July 28th, 1815

Sir,

I believe that I warned you that the Bowe girl was going to be trouble. Your miscalculation to this end has made both of us notorious. I killed two for your benefit that night, two who will never waggle their tongues to recruit or incite treason again. The rest of them are all telling the same story and are leading your hunting hounds down an interesting trail.

The governors have been sequestered and are quite beyond the reach of anyone but their most trusted accompaniment and guard. They will be paranoid for some time to come. Any notions of another attempt would be foolish. The only sign of the dignitaries currently are their messengers...

Coltrane and his crew are rushing to the defense of the colonies against Spanish aggression, as asked by the governors. I will trust New Orleans will be ready for a group of this caliber.

As I'm sure you're well aware, these complications and my additional service was not what I signed on for. Similarly, Miss Penn has come quite close to nervous breakdown and losing resolve. Between these factors, I believe some additional recompense to ensure I am willing to continually cover for your errors in assessment – and to ensure my companion's lips remain sealed – would be in order.

In any case, war with New Spain is imminent.

Your servant (reluctantly),
Giovanni Franzini

New Orleans
and the Spanish South

From the journals of Gregory Conan Watts,
August 1st, 1815
On route to New Orleans
39°08'N 077°12'W

We have had some debate amongst our number regarding our choices in our course of action. The most common discussion has revolved around Fort San Antonio, a Spanish Fort from which an attack force could launch an assault on New Orleans. There are other potentially vulnerable points, but this is the one most likely to present an immediate threat to New Orleans and England's trade routes through the region. Sir James and Eddy feel that if the news is true that Spain has sufficient allies to prove a threat to our defenses in the region, the best hope is to take the fort to put them on the defensive and give ourselves a fortified position between primary forces of New Spain and New Orleans.

Miss Bowe has soundly disagreed with this course of action, believing that it will aggravate New Spain to a greater degree and perhaps push the conflict to a head faster than otherwise might occur. Only Miss Penn has sided with Miss Bowe in this regard, basing her defense of the position entirely on the predictions of her cards, saying "Stormclouds are gathering..." or some such thing. Mr. Franzini became particularly irate at her for this bit of prognostication, calling her out as a charlatan and demanding that she know her place.

Adding fuel to the fire in this situation, we have seen that not all of our enemies are among the Spanish. There are numerous people with sympathies for England or France that see the peace treaty between our countries as anathema. Many people in New Orleans still believe they owe their loyalties to France, even though their lands were captured during the war, and now have been diplomatically ceded fully to England. As such, many believe that drastic action is needed to dissuade rogue elements from gaining any more foothold than they already have in New Orleans, and to assure any who are already there that England will not become a casual spectator when the colonies are threatened.

Despite the communications from the regional governors asking us to pursue these actions Miss Bowe and Sir James have argued at length about it. She insists that not all aboard are military personnel, and that no war with Spain has been declared, and thus we should arrive quietly and seek more information before taking any action. Despite these misgivings, she insists she is still a member of the crew, and will abide by his decisions, however reluctantly, even if it means fighting the Spanish. In the end, with three of our members being former soldiers of England, and Jillian and Harriet alike backing Sir James, she and Miss Penn were outvoted.

Of some slight comfort amidst all of the dark spirits, we have not been asked to serve as any kind of long-term military presence. Though we would serve if asked, it is generally believed that our other tasks also serve the national interest. As such, we have been asked only to hold the region until support arrives from England, and then we are permitted to be on our way to the American Northeast to try to find the purported passage to the Pacific through northern waters. I had hoped this would spark some optimism from our guide, but Miss Bowe already does not believe we would be able to reach northern waters with enough summer left to have a chance of success. Still, this is the first hint of truly being able to begin our mission, two objectives of which lie quite close at hand here in the colonies, the Northwest Passage, and finding a land route across the American West, charting our progress and all of the vast, unexplored lands that lie between St. Louis and the Pacific.

Having finally had a chance to truly look over these orders, I am also particularly excited by a unique opportunity that Lord Donovan and others are trying to negotiate for us with the Dutch. Should negotiations go well, we will be the first Westerners outside of a small detachment of Dutch merchants permitted to set foot on Japanese soil in ages. Such an agreement is some way off still, but the rumor is that the current leader of that land, called their Shogun, is most curious about English technology. Because of this, he may be willing to allow our small company into the nation as envoys when the Dutch next travel to the Shogun's court, a journey which apparently happens once every four years. Beyond this objective, Lord Donovan has given us our choice of numerous possible points of exploration. It's a comfort to have it acknowledged that this group is still a band of explorers, first and foremost, even if we will have stand as soldiers again, however briefly.

August 3rd, 1815
Over Virginia
38°21'N 078°20'W

Dear Sir,

Spirits are high, with everyone fully recovered from the injuries incurred during the recent conflict, and our being back onto the ship and away from the chaos of the city these past few days. I can only hope that things will soon settle back into something resembling normal, and that the inquiries sparked from the events at the party will find success in rooting out the conspiracy against our leadership.

I admit that it is with some reservation that I acknowledge that a part of our mission abroad shall involve military objectives, but we do understand that some funding and supply for the voyage is provided by the Crown, and recent events have made certain things necessities. Sir James and Eddy are also still soldiers of the British armies, so we will be traveling first to New Orleans, to rally local forces and investigate the rumors that in nearby Florida, Spanish local forces cooperate with pirates and threaten the lands in the Southern American colonies.

Aside from this first duty, we are still mapping the rest of our route, while acknowledging that certain dates are quite fixed, should we be able to meet them at that time, and will attempt to plan accordingly. After we complete our military duties here, we will be proceeding northward, and from New York I should have opportunity to send this and other letters on to document our progress.

It is hoped that the environmental disturbances and strange skies, reportedly caused by the volcanic activity at Tambora and elsewhere this past April will not delay us overmuch, though the captain has occasioned to say that there are areas which are most difficult to navigate, and the skies darken considerably ahead of us. If we learn anything of note from the region when we travel to more southerly routes, I will pass it on, but it is currently the intent of the crew to give Tambora as wide a berth as we may and still complete the rest of our mission. While some navigators of the royal navy who spoke with us before our departure claimed that our voyage was ill omened by such darkened events and the altered appearance of the sunrise, it has not been much different since April, certainly, and the crew is optimistic. Miss Coltrane loaned me her booklet of Benjamin Franklin's works,[13] including his 1783 piece on volcanic ash and weather patterns. We shall hope the cooling is not too significant, but it is hard to judge these things, it may be up to the full two degree average. Professor Franklin's paper detailed the local effects of an earlier explosion, and I now share everyone's healthy fear of going too near Tambora.

I myself have not been long away from my home, and already looking forward to my return. Yet I am proud to serve, and much as I always look forward to seeing my home once more, it will be all the better to return victorious and with much news from the world beyond our shores for the benefit of the crown.

As of yet, we have no definitive sign of the opposition to our voyage, which I know you have asked after. Should I find any verifiable news of them, I shall be sure to report it in my letters when I am able to send these home. Given that once we leave the Colonial East, most of the land before us is unsettled, or settled only by forces not necessarily friendly to England, such opportunities may be few and far between, but I shall report as I have occasion to do so.

Yours,
Gregory Conan Watts

---

13 Benjamin Franklin, Professor Emeritus of Cambridge, who was sent as an envoy from the colony and got distracted by a library. His works were collected in various volumes, all published by both Cambridge and Harvard presses. This particular paper is dated August 27, 1783 and regards the catastrophic eruption of Laki, in Iceland. – C B-W

From the journals of Gregory Conan Watts,
August 4th, 1815
Mississippi
32°10'N 089°26'W

While we have undertaken the mission given us, I find myself growing more and more concerned. The spirit of this adventure was not originally intended to be one of military nature. Despite this, it is understandable in light of recent events that the British crown should be very concerned about the threat from the Spanish colonies bordering our own lands. Likewise that they should be interested in using whatever resources came to hand to first safeguard our own lands, and then to end the threat of the Spanish promoting piracy as a means to aid their claims on English territory.

Napoleon is dead and the French crown beholden to our rulers. Many of the Dutch colonies held for a time by the French are also quite eager now to discuss treaties and compromise. The Dutch have always claimed that they are interested almost solely in trade, and with their militaries decimated by being forced into the war by Napoleon as he grew desperate, they are willing to cede much in the spirit of cooperation. This leaves the Spanish as our primary rivals within the world of the Americas, and I understand that forces are being gathered from among the victorious armies of England, Scotland, and Ireland to move to support the colonies now as they aided us, and we will soon have the forces needed in America to protect English colonial soil. Should Spain's colonies press a military engagement, the locals will have the leadership and forces necessary to not merely defend themselves, but take the conflict to Spanish territories as needed.

There is some concern amidst our efforts to rally the troops in the region. With many of the locals so recently having owed their loyalties to the French, and with New Spain being so close, there is concern there may be spies among the people being recruited. Certainly there will be any number who cannot be guaranteed to have any strong loyalty to England. Still, if we are going to be able to recruit an army capable of succeeding at our task and defending this region, we have little option but to cast a wide net. The rest of the troops here are just as aware of this, making maintaining morale and solidarity among the troops an additional problem.

Regardless of this shift from our original ambition as purely explorers, two among our number made their fame and fortune from military careers. Likewise, the Captain and first mate remain military men to the core, and all these are proud to serve without question for the benefit of the British Empire. I have more than once passed by Eddy's quarters to find him and Mr. Taylor engaged in discussion of strategy, and seen Eddy cleaning and oiling his armaments to be sure they are in best working condition.

Sir James can now be found almost constantly to be going over his maps, the cards put away for most of this voyage. For the moment, we are united by common cause and loyalty to the crown, not by games and diversion, and his speeches and efforts to keep the crew hanging together have focused almost solely on this, to the motivation of most.

There are exceptions, primary among them Miss Bowe. While willing to serve, she continues to have reservations about the actions in Florida in particular, and she continues to try to persuade Sir James that the attack is a poor idea. Regardless of her cause, she has largely kept herself to her quarters, or keeping the company only of the ornithopter. Likewise, she has refused continually to begin working with guns, despite offers of the remaining pepper-box pistol granted to our company. Even Eddy has not been able to get her to budge in this regard.

Mister Franzini claims no loyalty to England in particular, but continues to firmly state that he is quite indebted to our party, and will do his part to support our efforts. Indeed, he seems quite certain that he may be able to help rally some of the locals to the effort that otherwise might not be so willing to quickly go to another war for the British cause. He says that he has significant contacts within that city that may be persuaded to our cause. We are also hopeful that many of the freed slaves and returned soldiers will gladly take up arms again, for a military economy guarantees jobs. Time will tell, but for now, our only engagement is to be with a single Spanish fort, their nearest fortification to New Orleans, after which we shall be sure it is occupied and fortified once more to aid in the protection of northern Florida and passage to New Orleans, and from there we shall continue our voyage north. I am somewhat more heartened by this last, for it seems that once we leave Florida, the whole of the American experience from there should be exploration, beginning with attempting to find the sea route by which one may sail from the Atlantic to the Pacific that we may have other routes by which to trade, to settle the Pacific Northwest should we find the means for eventual expansion from the colonies to the west, and likely for the eventual opposition to Spanish rule of California.

As we travel, the skies grow darker still, and only the experience of our pilot and his skill with his instruments are keeping us on course, although I have heard him muttering at the skies while attempting sextant readings. Sir James has had to turn no small part of his energies and enthusiasm to motivating the crewers, for among those who feed the engines, and help maintain the basic functions of our ship, former sailors for the most part, and uneducated men given to superstition, each morning brings a new ill omen.

While I am not a man given to such wild theories, I would be remiss now if I did not mention that I am most disturbed now by Miss Penn. Shortly after our departure from New York, while Sir James was putting his cards away in favor of studying maps and treatises on tactics, Miss Penn was again taking her cards out. But hers are of a different sort entirely, of the sort that gypsies and hucksters use to claim to glean hints as to the future. Though Sir James and myself have both warned her against stirring up the crew, she has been quite firm in stating that this is a part of the purpose for which she was recruited, in addition to her wide knowledge regarding occult matters and superstitions of the larger world as they are known to Europeans.

Though the Coltranes, Miss Wright, and myself have not given any credence to her wild theories of prognostication, and the less educated members of the crew have been forbidden from visiting her, Miss Bowe and Eddy have both shown great interest in her claims, and have visited her repeatedly, the latter under close supervision of course, both by convention and at Mrs. Fisher's insistence regarding the precise and exacting etiquette of the ship. She has likewise been most firm about Matthew not being permitted to visit the gypsy at all when she is about her false arts, though he has often shown great interest in what she is about.

Of all of us, Giovanni Franzini, unsurprisingly, seems the most comfortable with her practicing her card tricks and weathers her claims of precognition and omens lying ahead casually. I do not believe he gives any more weight to her claims than I do, but he is used to it, and accepts that she should practice her gypsy ways so long as she follows the rules of the ship. I have confirmed that in her time with the traveling company, she acted as a mysterious fortune teller when she was not earning her keep through other means or as assistant to Franzini, so it is no surprise he takes the matter in stride.

And while I certainly give her art no place in my beliefs, I would be remiss in accurately reporting the events of our journey if I did not report that her most common claims for the near future are ones first of disaster and a loss, and a time of great darkness ahead. What rubbish. On a mission such as ours, matters such as these seem easy to predict, for we will certainly encounter many things which can be tied to these claims. I remain certain that we are now writing our part of the path for the future; it is not written for us.

August 10th, 1815
New Orleans
29°57'N 090°04'W

Dear Sir,

I am certain you will be most interested to hear of the events upon our arrival in New Orleans. As there is no proper mooring post or supply station, we had to restock our wares in Philadelphia, which has seen rudimentary development in capacity to support a dirigible, and from there proceeded south, where we had to make even more rudimentary arrangements near New Orleans. Sir James and Miss Bowe, via his suit's ability to deploy from an airship in flight and assistance from the mechanical companion she obtained from Dr. Michell's island, descended to the ground and were able to make reasonable accommodations for the dirigible to descend, though it was a lengthy and difficult process. Still, it should be secure enough that the airship is in no danger, though we have set guard on it at all times even so, and the connection is limited enough that it could launch quickly if needed. Those remaining on board have instructions to do just this should any threat be presented and we will make arrangements to meet them later.

When all was finished, Sir James and Mr. Franzini, each in his own time, journeyed into the city to make appeal for massing of new forces to seize Spanish territory that threatens British holdings. Sir James carried the orders from the English Crown, authorized by the governors, with the expectations that payment from England will be following us in order to maintain the local armies. Along with this payment, it is expected that eventually reinforcements will arrive from England in order to help protect the region from Spanish ambitions in the longer term. Originally, Jillian Coltrane had also planned to visit some friends she had occasional correspondence with to aid in arranging financial and community support for the plans – but the long journey and living with conditions on the airship have fatigued her sufficiently that she felt she needed to spend some additional time at rest instead.

As such, she is contributing via her pen and parchment entreaties to her contacts, rather than making rounds in person at this time.

Significant forces have been gathered from the expected sources. Many are former soldiers who fought recently in the Napoleonic Wars for the defense of England, returned home to find that they were ill suited to return to other work, and are now proud to once again serve. Sir James has taken direct command of these, for they form our most disciplined and experienced body of troops.

The second largest body is that of former slaves, freed for their service in wartime, who have since found no other occupation and have not wished to depart their home regions for service to the railroad and its hard labor, or resettlement to the western reaches. While many of these have wartime experience, they are poorly armed and their morale is questionable at best. Certainly the locals do not have a great deal of trust for them, but Sir James has been most willing to accept them into service, as we need any able men we can gather on short notice if we are to succeed now against a fortified Spanish location.

After those larger groups, the remnants are mostly either local landowners, a few boys who did not serve in the Napoleonic wars but would have done so had they been of age then, and a handful of local mercenaries who typically provide protection for those venturing into Florida to do business. Expansion may not be the aim of the venture, intended to secure our own holdings, but if we have sufficient forces coming, and if the reports of Spanish conspiracy with pirate powers are proven true, it may well be the result. At the very least, it ensures the cooperation of many of the locals of a trade town like New Orleans, where coin is often a more powerful loyalty than country. Many of these hope that should we have the opportunity, England will see fit to take Florida, as it took much of France's territory here during the war, and the railroad might expand there to access many of the port towns currently held by the Spanish, where they see rich trade opportunities.

Miss Coltrane has been especially active on her brother's behalf as well. While at first, it would seem that talking to the wives of men of estate and power and the wives of those few officers to settle here would not have great impact, her brother credits her with rallying much of the support we have gotten from local businessmen and politicians. Her skill at diplomacy – and perhaps her perfect grasp of French – have earned us allies even her brother did not expect to turn, and she continues tirelessly to seek more aid.

She has also sent out countless letters, drafted along the way, to dozens of contacts in the American colonies. It seems in her spare time, she corresponds with a wide variety of people all over the Empire, many of them people of influence, or at least the wives of people of influence. She has now turned all of that longstanding connection and her considerable personal persuasion to the aid of the Empire and New Orleans.

Mr. Franzini has also begun to prove good to his word, stating that we have further resources available to us, including reports on enemy positions by people who still do some business with the Spanish colonies. As I stated, though Spain remains, technically, an enemy from wartime, for many here, coin is a primary motivator. As such, in order to secure such reports from these spies, Mr. Franzini has had to make some promise of coin. Seeing the value in this information, Sir James has reluctantly put forth the money from his own coffers, certain that the Crown will compensate him for his efforts on their behalf.

In Sir James Coltrane, sir, have no doubt that you have employed one of England's most loyal and valorous sons. He has led us well so far, and though the troop we have gathered are a ragtag bunch, with only some few with uniform to speak of, and mismatched arms in various states of repair, he has excited the whole to be quite enthused about the prospects of serving England, and expanding the influence of the colonies within the British Empire. Whatever misgivings I may have expressed in previous communication, I now apologize for. I am, always, a proud citizen of the greatest Empire the world has ever seen, and am once again proud to do my country service, though in this case I have been armed with pen and camera, and have been asked to document our progress, for morale at home will excite more people to action and support of a new war effort in further lands than mere news of a single victory over Spain. With time and luck, and stringing enough such victories together, it is hoped that Spain might come to see the same light as the French have.

Yours,
Gregory Conan Watts

From the journals of Gregory Conan Watts,
August 14th, 1815
Bateria de San Antonio / Royal Navy Redoubt
30°20'N 087°18'W

I have seen many battles in my time, but had never before had the honor of serving under Sir James Coltrane. The Spanish seemed well prepared for us, not at all the surprise attack we had hoped for. At first advance, there was the pop of organized musketfire from the fortress, and the men were forced to fall back to the edge of range and take cover. There would be no organized lines of battle here. The men of New Spain have long since learned to use their forts and fight in the manner of the Americans.

Sir James ably took command, the booming, metallic voice of his machine easily heard over the chaos. While many were obviously unused to it, even uncomfortable around so strange a thing as the mechanical monster, he has engendered enough respect and renown that he had the loyalty and response of everyone on the field. Men took to cover and organized into their divisions. Eddy took command of a unit of rifles, having hand picked men with experience at both battle and hunting, all armed with Browning rifles. Thankfully, while there are few men with any command training here, the one thing the Americans have in abundance, by comparison, is men whose accuracy, stealth, and ownership of one of the Browning weapons feeds their families.

After the first assessment and contact, Sir James and Eddy conferred briefly, then Sir James began his first feint. He led a charge, the suit taking the brunt of the first fire without apparent harm, leading a group of soldiers large enough to convince the Spanish that it was a real attack, small enough to not endanger too many men, and allowing most to keep some degree of cover from Sir James. First appearing as a battering ram, Sir James brought with him an uprooted tree as well, preventing him from firing, but taking some of the shot and keeping the attention of the Spaniards. Instead, he dropped it some way inside, and the first few men with him took cover from it, taking up firing and cover positions inside the area the Spanish had cleared as a kill zone.

Leaving them there with rifles covering the position, Sir James left the men pinned, repeating the process twice more. A few men were lost, injured by random shot, but we had a front and cover. We also managed to move up Eddy and some of the rifles in the last group.

The fourth charge began much like the others, and by now, the Spanish were somewhat more wary. They had moved their cannons to better cover the area we were attacking from. The sound almost blunted the new rush, men hesitating to rush at cannons, but Sir James never faltered, even when shot splintered the section of tree he was hefting in his hands. This was no false rush, but an assault on the gates, and the enemy figured it out quickly enough. With so many fortified troops and limited space to attack from, Sir James might have made it on his own, but I cannot be certain. Instead, this was where the covered troops came in. Eddy and the American hunters peeked up from their cover long enough to find the cannon crews and began picking them off of the walls. I could almost pick Eddy's shots out from the rest, always the person with only the barest window to shoot down. This was particularly true when he was able to fire shot after shot, without the pause others needed to reload. They kept their rifle shot staggered enough to leave nothing predictable. Some of our foe took cover, surprised, while others continued to fire, and to try to replace their losses.

Sir James gestured, dropping the ruined remnants of the tree, and first, men peeled off from the edges of the trees to reinforce the group with him, and I led a second group forward to reinforce them while the rifles afforded them what cover they could. A few men fell, both in the lead group, and mine, but many lives were spared, in part, by the simple fact that the Spaniards put most of their efforts into trying to do something, anything, to halt Sir James himself. While I do not doubt that the suit will need considerable repairs when all of this is done, he did not even slow, crashing forward steadily, seeming to be doing his best to continue to be the focus.

We caught up with the main group as Sir James tore through the first layer of wire and wooden fortification, slowing only slightly. Sir James and his men provided enough distraction to let more and more of our rifles advance to positions closer to the fort, hiding behind the cover Sir James left behind. The more rifles that reached cover, of course, the more dangerous it became for any of the Spanish troops to stick their head up long enough to draw accurate lines of fire. I am also quickly learning one of the primary differences between fighting among Englishmen and the Americans. The Englishmen I have observed have the greater discipline and training, to be certain. They are prepared for a wider variety of circumstance and adapt more quickly to change in them, as well as learning the commands and structure expected by their officers better. But the Americans depend daily upon their rifles, not just in war time, at least in many of these cases. When you find the huntsmen among them, they are a thing to be treasured, because to a greater degree than any unit I have ever seen, and exceeded only by Eddy's marksmanship, they tend to hit what they fire upon.

With less loss than I'd have thought we'd have suffered by now, we reached the gates. They did hold Sir James, at first at least, but even his initial charge rocked them mightily. There was sounds of chaos from inside the fortification as men rushed to reinforce the gates in a bid to hold them. With the commotion, more men advanced in a new rush, and more rifles took up position with Eddy and his sharpshooters. They continued to clear men from the walls, making special note to remove any cannoneers they were able to pick off, leaving musket fire as the primary obstacle for our men to navigate, and the fallen trees remained as points of fortification in the midst of the battlefield, a place troops could mass while others came forward, then move to join the group nearest the walls.

Sir James alone served as battering ram, hammering upon the walls time and again. Eventually, the bar began to splinter and broke enough to begin to push open, and the most vicious part of the battle began. Each side turned their weight towards the gates, the Spanish trying to keep them closed, Sir James and the Americans trying to force them open. All the while, men with bayonets on both sides jabbed them through the opening, trying to force the other side back.

Somewhere amidst the chaos, I became aware of movement from a different section of the walls, Spanish muskets firing elsewhere than into our mass. Letting myself briefly become distracted, I saw a winged form moving towards the walls under light fire from the few Spaniards who had seen what I had. When she came close enough, Miss Bowe dropped from the ornithopter and onto the walls, engaging the men with muskets at close range with her knives. After she dispatched two of them, she disappeared over the wall and out of my sight, and I quickly returned my focus to trying to direct some part of the chaos at the doors.

Who would ultimately win the conflict was never in much doubt. It took some time, but with Sir James on our side of the conflict, we had a decided advantage in strength. The doors opened further and further, despite all efforts by the defenders, and as they did, the fighting at the gap grew worse. As soon as it had opened enough for Sir James to see clearly inside, however, he put a quick end to it. Lifting one arm, he unleashed a rocket into the midst of the opposition, the explosion scattering men and forcing others into panicked retreat. The doors quickly opened, and we began a mad rush to take and hold position in the midst of the Spanish. There was no room for lines or organization now, and bayonets quickly became the tool of most use as everything became about close quarters combat. In this, the Spanish had a greater advantage, with more of their men so armed, but we had Sir James at the front, tossing Spaniards aside like ragdolls. Likewise, we had momentum.

I realized, in time, we seemed to have one other advantage. I could hear Sir James calling out commands, of course, and Eddy was able to make himself heard over the chaos now and then as well, though we were too far from the rifles to glean anything more from this than that he still lived. But I saw no signs of the highest ranking of New Spain's officers. There was no one rallying their men or changing their instructions, no one directing from the walls or fortified outposts. We would eventually find them, their command staffs, and their guards, all with various knife wounds –

Miss Bowe's contribution to the battle, in her own fashion. I do not know how much of this was her own initiative and how much worked out with Sir James ahead of time. She was not welcome at the meetings for determining out strategy, at the insistence of some of our own people. However, once she had committed to help with this effort, despite her reservations, I know I had seen her and Sir James conversing quietly on a number of occasions, usually seeming quite grim in these conversations.

Without this direction, with the Americans in the fort, and Sir James especially showing no sign of slowing, surrender was eventually inevitable. When enough of their men had fled, and someone took enough initiative to take over, a white flag was waved. Confused fighting continued a short time longer, but the Spanish had little fight left to them by then, and Sir James was eager to call an end. The fortress was quickly surrendered to his command.

Even now, he is working on selecting a command staff and making arrangements to have the fortress fully manned and operational again as soon as possible. Eddy has set himself to drilling and training the rifles, while Miss Bowe has returned to the dirigible and chaperoned company now that the fighting is over.

August 14th, 1815
30°20'N 087°18'W

Dear Sir,

We have taken the westernmost fort in Florida, the old Royal Navy Redoubt, now called Bateria de San Antonio, and held the ground against Spanish reprisal. Scouts and spies have also been deployed to try to determine the strength of the Spanish ships and how many pirate vessels are in their waters.

We have also received reinforcement at last from the farms and colonies that surround us, and we have somewhat recovered from the injuries sustained during the primary battle which led to renewed hostilities.

For now, the reports are that Spain is moving less towards attempting to retake that which is lost, and are looking more to their own defense, reinforcing the other forts and borders of their port towns nearest the land we have seized. There is also already talk among some of the locals of their hopes to expand the conflict, and that England might attempt to take Florida as we once did much of the French west and south. If England is to take best advantage of this period of chaos, then we must have reinforcements quickly from the mother country, and more men with military commission and charisma so as to inspire the colonies to fight for their own defense first, and then possible expansion into enemy land.

We have enough men, for now, to be fairly certain to hold what we have taken, and establish our new borders once new leadership arrives, but there is already considerable division among the locals. Some would very much like to see New Spain conquered, at least in Florida, for the opportunities it would create. Others argue that following all the lives lost in the Napoleonic Wars, there is almost unlimited land in America, far more than could be needed, given the toll taken upon America's working population. This division, among many others, is all the more reason that able leadership is needed as soon as possible, for if left to the locals, I fear significant chaos could quickly ensue.

While we have done all we can here, we will have to be away soon if we are to make the next step in our journey before winter hits. Once true winter hits, travel as ambitious as what lies ahead of us in the north will become virtually impossible. I am uncertain if these men would hold their own and retain this territory without aid or new inspiration once Sir James has moved on. I can only hope that new reinforcements arrive before we are delayed too long here. Other than this concern, our own company will soon be entirely healed and ready to move on, but we shall remain until the last possible minute for the good of England.

In any case, I am more and more convinced by the day that when he sets his mind to the task, Sir James can accomplish anything, whether it is socially, mechanically, or in times of war, for he has certainly pulled some farmers, former slaves, and former soldiers together with only a few days of notice, and taken a major hold within Florida with it.

Yours,
Gregory Conan Watts

From the journals of Gregory Conan Watts,
August 16th, 1815
New Orleans
29°57'N 090°04'W

Miss Coltrane's entreaties were not for nothing, and we have been reinforced heavily by men from the North and from the farms of Virginia and the Carolinas. Many others did not send men, or very few, but dedicated significant resources to the effort in other ways. Her brother may have won the first battle of this new conflict, but Miss Coltrane's efforts in particular have made it sustainable. Building materials and money, along with learned workers, are being channeled to the region around New Orleans and the far north of Florida.

Mr. Franzini's contacts have also proven worth the money they were paid, and he has been able to confirm for us the presence of no less than fifteen vessels of the sort most often encountered along the Barbary Coast, most often employed by the pirates there. While the first report seemed far-fetched, the same reports came from multiple sources. When English forces arrive, they will have their own people confirm these reports, no doubt. If accurate, it would be an egregious enough offense to merit significant resources being put towards breaking any alliance between the Spanish and pirate fleets. There has already been considerable talk about funding a naval effort to put an end to the white slave trade and the vicious pirate attacks off the Barbary Coast, but following the war, the resources have not yet been made available. If these pirates and slavers have allied with a national enemy, then surely those resources will be found.

We also received particularly welcome news. While somewhat delayed by a need for repairs in Philadelphia, after making the significant trans-Atlantic flight, a Col. Bartholomew York is leading a military deployment intended to relieve us. We have been passed on official orders through this channel that when we receive news the Colonel is away from Philadelphia, we may leave the city and our command, and he will take over the effort. In the short gap in between, local officers from Virginia with wartime experience can handle the details and keeping people directed. Though we are all reluctant to leave before the Colonel has actually arrived, it is also agreed that we must make haste on our own journey. What we do next will inspire all of England, and our deadlines are understood by those who appreciate the scope of the tasks set before us. As such, we are making preparations to leave, though there is every intent to wait until there is a report of the sighting of Colonel York's dirigible, to make sure that there is no additional problems with his arrival.

Turning about on her own former stance on the issue of the local war, Miss Bowe has once again elected to disagree with the orders we've been given, and has urged Sir James to stay to see the conflict through until some resolution is reached with New Spain. That would almost certainly put us impossibly behind in the tasks we've been set to, which she acknowledges being well aware of. Sir James has assured her that others can handle this task as readily as we can, and from what we have been able to learn, Colonel York is a man of exemplary loyalty and has a distinguished service record. The city will be in good hands under his leadership.

August 22nd, 1815
Louisiana Territory
31º51'N 088º59'W

My Dearest Cordelia,

We are away from the war effort in Florida. Men from the North and the surrounding regions have reinforced our position sufficient that we believe we can be back to our mission. A dirigible containing a full load of troops and an officer of excellent credentials was verified to have landed in New Orleans before we left Florida, and his troops are even now being deployed to take the position we have been holding.

The first days in which men were arriving without having taken part in the previous conflict, it was almost as if they expected a carnival air to the meeting, and many, I suspect, came as much for opportunity to meet Sir James and Eddy as any real fascination currently with the taking of Florida's westernmost fort. Even so, the recent compact between England and France has somewhat eased tempers through some of this land, and the people are not so on edge with one another as in times previous, but some tension remains. Still, Sir James has managed to soothe much of it.

We are now bound for the northernmost reaches of the colonies to try to find the northern passage by which the Atlantic and Pacific oceans are joined past New York. This is a big portion of our current rush. Should we miss the opportunity to explore in the summer months, the waterways will be too icy to give us any hope of finding what we are looking for. Miss Bowe believes, with the current temperatures dropping rapidly, that we are already too late, but assures us the passage does exist. Sir James remains optimistic that even though we waited until Colonel York actually set down in New Orleans, we might still have time to accomplish our goal.

Though it was an impressive campaign, most of my fellows are quite glad to once more be aboard the ship, despite the tensions which remain. The card games have resumed.

Additionally, Mr. Franzini has been now permitted to join the games on some occasions, but he is required to leave his jacket behind, even though they play for no stakes. He seemed somewhat offended by this at first, but has decided to let his offense go for being at least allowed to take part in the only social occasion which draws any group of us. Miss Penn, present as Miss Bowe's chaperone, seemed less than comfortable with her former partner being permitted at all, but Franzini at least sits far from Miss Bowe – and thus from her.

I am preparing the pictures of the conflict to be dropped off in New York, in the hopes that the northern reaches of the colonies can be inspired to aid more quickly with the new war effort than England will be able. I can certainly imagine that with the quick travel of news up the coast, many people will be quite excited to see some images for themselves. In the meanwhile, Miss Coltrane in particular has been most eager to reach New York, for with the compact between England and France, she is particularly eager to see if news of the advances in fashion and the like have yet reached the most civilized city of the Americas. Miss Wright is equally excited by such possibilities, though I am unsure she will be able to put the news to so good a use as her cousin. Still, it is good to have enthusiasm of any sort aboard the ship.

In the meanwhile, it is unseasonably cold as we travel north. The Southern reaches of the colonies are warm places, especially so when surrounded in such tight quarters as war occasions, but having been only this year to New York, I do not at all recall it being so cold. There has even been some suspicion that if this has been the case for a time, there may be some difficulty with feeding the people in the cities this winter. Time shall tell, but for now, we are about other and grander affairs.

I will apologize that I have no more romantic tale to tell this time of our travels, for we have seen few people save for soldiers, and most everyone aboard in their own fashion has been mostly glad to talk quietly, play cards, and sleep when they are able. Still, a great venture lies ahead of us still, though it feels almost like cheating to be performing this surveying aboard one of our airships when most such voyages previous have been done by sailing ship. But then all such attempts have also failed, so perhaps it is for the best. In any case, most of the land we are traveling to is unoccupied, so we should not run into a great deal of difficulty when setting about our explorations, and soon our sailing ships shall know the route we have traveled and what we have seen. While cartography is not my strongest suit, it seems I am to be the mission's mapmaker as well, so I am finding myself quickly trying to learn the art. I shall have to study further when we are in New York. At least my maps will have sextant readings, so others may follow, as I've been studying with the first mate.

Love, always,
Gregory Conan Watts

New York
and the Northwest Notion

From the journals of Gregory Conan Watts,
August 27th, 1815
New York
40º 47'N 073º 58'W

We were hailed as quite the heroes upon our return to New York. Apparently the news of our activities has reached these shores, as has news of the dangers posed by New Spain to the Southern Colonies. Already there is some talk of war with New Spain to eliminate this threat. Florida might be seized so that the Spanish have less port space, and the colonies can guard only the front along the Texas border instead of needing worry so much about assault from multiple directions. While the colonies are far apart still, even here, everyone knows the importance of keeping New Orleans secure as a critical point in the Mississippi River trade route.

If this is to be their course, I do not know how long it would take them to assemble an army, for the state of this nation's armies is quite in disarray. Everywhere has its local militias, and the Americans do have some access to the military advances provided by Oxford's technology. They do also have a number of American veterans who have combat experience from the Napoleonic Wars, but many of their fighting men also lost their lives to that conflict. The North also does not have the slaves and former slaves to draw upon in any great number, as the South does. We can only hope that the presence of numerous men who have at least some experience in battle will hopefully make up for lack of sheer numbers.

Also a significant problem, we do not know how many local men the Spanish can muster, or how much of indigenous tribes they have impressed for this conflict. I have now come to understand that the native peoples of this land were where the Americans learned many of their tactics, making up for inferior arms and sometimes manpower with stealth, ambush, and knowing the territory on which they fight. If the Spaniards have numerous of these tribes collected on their side, then I do not envy the fighting men of the American colonies the times to come. Still, with any fortune the morale of the opposition will soon be crushed, and perhaps the Spanish are having as much trouble with some of the tribal peoples of their lands as has been rumored, and which has hindered westward expansion efforts in places along the frontier lands. Miss Bowe has also had some words to say for native fighting techniques, for she has apparently spent some time among some of the tribesmen. Given her fighting style and training, and capabilities as a scout, this somehow does not surprise me in the least, though it does not excuse her behavior: after all, she is still a woman of European blood, and yet even when returned to the civilized Daughterland, her manners were atrocious, and have not been much better in any territory. One at times would almost think that she was cheering for neither England nor Spain, for but for the savages in between them. I will be that much more glad when we can return her to her frontier, but for the time being, she keeps giving me occasion to be grateful for her presence.

In the meanwhile, Sir James has put all of his time and effort into speaking on behalf of the Crown and working to expand the effort and cause for war for occupation of Spanish territory, facing the question again and again as to why the Americans should need more land than they now hold, but he has convinced them. Eddy is just as much a local hero, asked again and again to tell his stories, for the idea of a rifleman of his skill seems very much to appeal to the American spirit, and many of their men can more empathize with him than a graduate of Oxford, even as much as the technology produced by that university has taken hold here.

If this winter is as harsh as it is beginning to appear to be, however, I do indeed fear for the people out in the wide expanses as needed to work on the rails. This shall be an interesting time for many people, given the conflicts that currently grip America. Though war is always a difficult time, and it has at last come here, it also seems to quite unite the spirit. I think, in the end, this may be a helpful thing for the colonies. A common cause and a common enemy may repair some of the deep divisions between them. No doubt the reconciliation taking place between England

and France, now that the latter's royals have returned to power, will also help.

I do wonder somewhat as to what Giovanni Franzini is up to. Having proven himself twice now, he has used this greater trust and longer leash to spend a great deal of time in the city and perhaps, if the rumors are true, has found himself acknowledged as something of a gentleman war hero such that he has inserted himself into the clubs and gambling halls here. I can only hope that he does nothing to besmirch our reputation in this land, for so far it appears quite sterling.

From the journals of Gregory Conan Watts,
August 28th, 1815
New York
40° 47'N 073° 58'W

We have settled in here only briefly, in order to assess the conditions and determine if any effort to the north is worth the trouble now. Sir James has conversed often with Miss Bowe to this end, seeming to put significant stock in her opinions and claims of knowledge of the area. These efforts have been somewhat slowed by her regular annoyance that we left New Orleans in the hands of Col. York at all. Originally against taking military actions here at all, she seems to feel that it should now be our responsibility to see it through, no matter how often she is assured that it will be handled capably. We have been assured that a decision will be rendered soon, though the current beliefs seem to be trending towards the thought that the cold is coming on too fast, and unseasonably cold temperatures will make any chance of finding the hoped-for Northwest Passage impossible.

Nonetheless, Sir James has expressed some interest in at least surveying the area from the air, and getting some feel for using the dirigible as a mapping and exploration craft before we venture far into the West, far away from any kind of repair facilities. Everyone has been practicing taking to their roles on shipboard in anticipation of spending a lot of time aboard, and needing to be ready to shift from a more military mindset to that of adventurers and cartographers.

Miss Wright has also made some friendly overtures towards Miss Bowe, trying to come to, if not a friendship, at least a working relationship. Miss Wright has not spent a great deal of time otherwise engaged with most of the talk of war and the situation in New Orleans, but she does seem interested in what parts of the journey she can contribute towards. She has so far had the most success in gaining access to the ornithopter, both to study its construction, and to try to show Miss Bowe the necessary steps and materials for making repairs to the construct should it ever become necessary.

Miss Coltrane has also been most busy, and I begin to understand just how wide she casts her net of social influence. Her shopping in New York, apparently, has been confined primarily to more paper and additional ink, as she has prepared dozens of handwritten letters for the wives of men of wealth and influence all over England and the Americas. She has acknowledged she is trying to make sure that if there is to be war, all preparations will be made, and there will be resources enough to equip the soldiers, and enough support from the Motherland to make sure there are sufficient officers and ships to put to the effort. She truly is a remarkable woman, and far more aware of the situation at hand and what, precisely, would be needed, strategically speaking, than I had given her credit for. Her brother, meanwhile, takes her activities enough as a matter of course that I do not doubt that she has done the like before.

September 15th, 1815
Far North
53°19'N 60°25'W

Dear Sir,

I regret to inform you that we have not found the Northwest Passage, and will not be continuing an active search for it at this time. On seeing the waterways in their current conditions, Miss Bowe assured us in no uncertain terms that the waterways would be too frozen over to gain any useful information from. She assures us that we should not doubt that the route does exist, but it requires travel much further to the north than we had hoped, though such was indicated by Dr. Bowe's journals. Sir James initially wanted to press on anyway, hoping we would find something to mark and map that we might have an easier time resuming this type of effort later.

If anything finally convinced him that the effort needed to be abandoned, it was likely the Captain's doing. He complained bitterly about the cold and indicated quite often that the controls were sluggish, and mechanical troubles were likely if we continued on this course.

I am certain that this news will come as disappointing. We have made almost no progress in achieving your goals, I fear. What's more, it will be at least several months before we could resume the effort here. Even then, with some believing the weather will remain unseasonably cold for some time to come, it could be even longer than that.

If it is any solace, sir, Dr. Bowe's notes and our guide, plus the ability to survey the land from the air did allow us one bit of information which could be of great benefit to the colonies, and through them, England. In the process of surveying the area, we did discover a navigable route from the Atlantic to the Great Lakes by water, with the assistance of an easily placed canal, above Montreal. I am including our maps of the region, and pictures from the air of the waterways. I can hope that this will provide enough good news and solace that the setback in our overall mission will not prove too much of a disappointment.

Yours,
Gregory Conan Watts

September 23rd, 1815
New York Colony
40° 47'N 073° 58'W

My Dearest Cordelia,

Tragedy has struck, and while I hate to burden you with such news (although this letter may well never reach you, and likely just as well) I need to share this news with someone lest my heart should burst. And it seems as if five brave souls should be in as many prayers as might be possible.

We were returning to New York yesterday when a terrible storm arose, far worse than anything I have ever seen or encountered in all my life, coming in from the sea. The air had been quite disturbed for some time, but there was no chance for anything but to try to make it back to land, for in trying to make use of the winds for travel, we had ended up some way out, though we were quite close to reaching our destination. A number of us were resting, for our journeys had taken such a great deal out of us that the few days' rest while traveling had not seen us entirely recovered.

We could not help but notice the dirigible being thrown about on the turbulent winds. Most of the crew rushed forward to see if there was something we could aid the captain with, though the walk alone was difficult enough. I cannot imagine that I would be writing you now at all if we had any lesser pilot than William Fisher. Right now, I would believe near any tale he wished to tell me, though it may be some time until he finds his voice once more. He shouted over the howl of the winds that the instruments were not reading properly, and he was having great difficulty finding his heading. Eddy quickly climbed forward to be an extra set of eyes but declared he could not see enough. Securing his goggles firmly to his face, he left the inside of the ship entirely, exposing himself to such a torrent of rain that it had to be like rocks pelting the skin. He lashed himself most securely to that vantage point, and proceeded, ignoring the horrible pain he must have been in, being struck so by wind and rain and chips of ice, to give what he could make out to the Captain through what language on navigation they shared. I marvel still at the strength of the man, for while I tried at one time to reach him to bring him a blanket, I was pushed back before I could get more than a hand out from the ship, and then we rocked so violently that we were briefly almost on our side, and the first flash of lightning lit the skies.

Everything was thrown about, ourselves included, though some few had opportunity to grab for something more permanent. Miss Coltrane had come forward, and most luckily grabbed for a railing, saving herself from the worst of the buffeting about. Miss Wright was able to grab for her cousin, and spent much of the difficulty with a death grip upon Miss Coltrane's dress until she was able to climb to the railing herself, leaving them both in terrible disarray. It is fortunate that Miss Wright is a strong young woman, else she may well have been lost. Sir James may have had opportunity to grab for the rails as well, having been standing near his sister as usual, but instead he noticed that Mrs. Fisher had nothing but open space near her. He grabbed for the woman just as we pitched so harshly, and the pair of them crashed against one of the windows, which cracked, but did not shatter yet.

I had a better vantage on all of this than I ever would have wished, hanging in space by a blanket which had gotten itself quite entangled in a doorway now sealed shut by gravity and force of the elements. In trying to struggle free, I found myself hopelessly entangled, thoroughly tied to the ship. So bound, I found myself pondering, of all things, how in a disaster sometimes everything seems to slow down to such degree as to allow one to see everything flashing before one's eyes, and yet not be able to do anything. I noticed Miss Coltrane and Miss Wright struggling, as they would for some time, and I think Miss Coltrane may have broken a bone somewhere in her hand amidst the struggle. We will know soon. She also has terrible scratches upon her legs, we have been told, but I believe that owes mostly to her ending up saving Miss Wright's life in the scramble. The window cracked sufficiently that Sir James had an arm break through it, though the damage to his arm seems to look far worse than it actually was. Mrs Fisher was able to find another rail and climb to it, freeing Sir James to grab onto the side of the window before it broke away entirely, though he was hanging from the ship for a time, and even such resolute nerves as his own have been quite shaken by the experience.

Miss Penn, thankfully, was in her quarters, and while we would later find her unconscious, the injury to her head does not appear as if it is anything too lasting or serious, though she is abed even so. Mr. Franzini was likewise abed, and the violence of the ship was so great that he was thrown from his bunk and into the path of his trunk. While alive, I do not envy him his bruises or broken leg, which will keep him off of it for quite some time.

The worst of this first wave of turbulence was reserved for Matthew and the first mate, for both were in their rooms when the rest of us rushed forward. As we were turned on our sides, their doors swung open, and both were tossed violently against the far walls. Mr. Taylor appeared stunned, while Matthew was already trying to struggle to his feet, only to tumble again when the ship righted itself. While difficult for many people, that may have saved Sir James's life, for he was able to climb back through the window and dove for a hold within the structure of the bridge before we rocked again.

The next tilt of the ship was the other way, and almost as severe, nearly throwing Sir James the other way out of the ship, but he held on. Captain Fisher, meanwhile, was fighting the wheel as hard as he was able, using it to keep himself at least at his station when we shifted. I cannot imagine Eddy's state at that time, and all I could hear about the ship was screams, both from those I could see ahead of me, and from the still sealed chambers behind me as Miss Penn and Mr. Franzini were tossed about.

Miss Bowe emerged from her room then, swinging from her door frame and managing to advance up the corridor, leaping across floor and wall as we shifted. I think she shouted to me as to where Eddy was, and I attempted to free a hand enough to point to the door, though I was forced after that to grab full hold once again. Unfortunately, Matthew also noticed this gesture, and I still have not forgiven myself. The wind was not calm then, but we briefly ceased being rocked about so wildly, instead rising suddenly so fast that I felt my stomach sink. My nausea and surprise was such that I somehow only ended up staring dumbfounded as Matthew headed for the doorway, managing to find handholds and crawling at one point, calling for Eddy, likely not knowing that the Scotsman had been tied to the ship itself. During this brief lull, it seemed everyone but myself had made some use of themselves, the first mate was shouting something about a rope coming loose and rushing for the same doorway, not noticing Matthew in his path.

The Captain lashed himself to the wheel. I can only imagine how many storms he has piloted through thus, but he had such panic in his voice and on his face that I am unsure even he had seen the like of this storm before. Mrs. Fisher also found herself something to first hold, then tie herself to, and Sir James seemed to be about the same thing when suddenly he was struggling to untie himself instead and shouting. His voice was drowned out with another howl of wind, and I was spun about in time to see Miss Bowe and the first mate both on the walkway and rails trying to get hold of a section of rope securing the main ship to the balloon above. What neither of them seemed to notice – or perhaps could simply not deal with at the time – was that in their rush, Matthew had been pushed out as well, and was grabbing tight to the rails. In all of this, Miss Bowe's companion had also found its way out of her chambers. Tossed about on its wheels, it struck me quite squarely in its attempts to get to her, unable to quite align itself with the door, which was fortunate at the time. Mr. Taylor had only just gotten hold of the rope when we pitched violently again, and he was thrown over the edge. I resumed my struggles to get free to go and help, but remained firmly tangled up in the blankets tying me to the ship. Much as I regret not having been of more use, it is quite likely fortunate I was so thoroughly stuck, else I may have been lost overboard. Miss Bowe found a good hold and was reaching for the first mate while Sir James was struggling back towards them, or must have been, for he ended up quite close in all the confusion. Just as Miss Bowe was drawing Mr. Taylor back aboard, we hit another rise while still turned about on our side, and now I could see the storm behind us, a horrible funnel of wind and violence such as none I have ever encountered. I prayed at that moment as if the devil himself was behind us, for I thought he might well be. A terrible scream that will fill my nightmares came from behind me, even as I was spun about more, and I saw the wind sweep Matthew entirely overboard, and the first mate, who had been clambering towards the door, managed only to grab the hanging rope before he too was swept overboard. Miss Bowe whistled, a piercing sound that somehow carried over the storm, and then leapt fully off of the side of the ship, pushing herself away from it. The ornithopter struggled through the door at last as it had been trying to do, almost dislodging my web in the process, and dove or fell after them. I saw it extend its wings, and Miss Bowe grabbing for it, though I never saw if she caught hold before it was being pulled away by the wind, and the ship shifted again. Sir James found his way to the doorway, helping to pull me in to more secure hold before being pitched back out himself. He found the rail, and grabbed for Mr. Taylor's hand. I am unsure if the mate saw him at all, focused entirely upon his grip on the rope. Had he reached back, perhaps he might be alive still, or perhaps he would have pulled Sir James into the abyss with him. Either way, the rope was torn free, and I saw him disappear into blackness, still clutching to a short length of thick cord as if it might still somehow save him.

I have learned since that one of the engineering crew was also killed, crushed as the ship was tossed about, and all but one of those good men was injured to some degree. There is very little to hold to in their workspace unless a man is near to some stair step with rails or at stations for difficult weather, but in this case, the wind turned from rough to this devil storm so suddenly that there was no chance to respond.

Sir James was able to entangle his arms and legs in the rails so firmly that he was able to hold to the ship, trying to reach for Eddy, but giving up at last lest he be lost entirely. I cannot imagine that he could have seen much beyond a few feet from his face amidst the torrential winds and rain. Though I am certain he was still trying to get to his friend, at one point he reached blindly enough that I was able to grab his hand, and though he pulled hard, I was able to keep my grip enough to pull him in out of the weather. I can take no credit for saving his life, for it is quite possible that his grip may have been enough to survive the storm, but he credits me with it anyway. The people at the front eventually had been able to secure themselves firmly enough to ride out the storm, though I do not think anyone can call themselves unhurt.

I do not know how long the storm lasted, though even with all evidence now suggesting that it is over, I am still sorely tempted to say that it seemed to go on forever. There is no chance that the Captain long had any idea of where we were headed, but he kept the ship from spinning or diving entirely, though I am unsure his hands will ever be the same from his grip upon the wheel, and both hands are heavily bandaged now. Still, it seemed that the first heading he had us on with Eddy's heroic aid was enough to keep us just ahead of that horrible wind tunnel, for eventually, when the storm passed us by, we were inland some way, and drifting with a gentler wind. I am not certain even now who was the first among us to realize that we were no longer being battered so, and it seemed had survived the ordeal, but eventually, those of us still able began to try to find our legs again and move about to rescue the rest and check upon the unconscious. The damage done is extensive, and no one's quarters survived intact, of course. We eventually made our way back to New York City, which is heavily damaged, and the storm had such an effect on the region that a section of the land once attached is now an island off of New York. How any of us escaped alive we are unsure, but most grateful for. It shall be some time before we are able to resume our journey now, and indeed, we must take some stock of the situation now, for we have lost our guide, and most tragically, the Captain and his wife have lost their ward, along with the first mate and an engineer both dead to the storm.

Eddy is also in such condition that it is not yet known if he will live or die, for he was most battered about, has a broken arm where the rope was tied most securely, and nearly drowned. That he lived exposed to the storm is a testament to the fortitude of the man. We are told there is hope if he lives out the day. The rest of us who survived will recover, though I am unsure if the Captain and his wife's spirit will ever be fully recovered, for they loved Matthew as their own son.

I do not know what else to say, dear Cordelia, save that I am sorry for even in theory resting such tragedy as this on your mind, but I must write down these events, and at least pretend to share them with someone else, for my failure to save Matthew's life when I might have rests most heavily upon me, and I think I will never be the same again. Even if the voyage, now seeming ill fated, carries on, I will have to long consider my own path forward. Only the hope that I may yet return to England as your fiancé gives me any motivation in the least to keep going, if it is decided that we continue at all.

Thank you, my love. Today, though you are not here, you have given me more solace than you can know, as you have always eased my mind from the days of our youth.

My love, always,
Gregory Conan Watts

Editor's note:

Gregory would never send this letter to me, of course. Not a thing for a young woman, or any woman of England, to read, especially in that time, but I am glad I was able to give him succor in his time of trouble, of course. I believe the only reason that that letter never found the fire, and instead was buried in his journals, was probably as it gave him some manner of comfort in difficult times to come.

– Dr. Cordelia Bentham-Watts

The Great September Gale of 1815

New York Evening Post, *Special Morning Printing*, September 24th, Free Extra.

The **Press of New York** would like to apologize for failure to print on September 23rd, as is the press's duty to the public. However, even should printing that morning have been possible, distribution would not have been, for most citizens were sensibly *well in shelter.*

At the **Naval Air Post in New York**, sudden action was required to save the Colony's only Airships. Two of our great ships were vented, a process only available due to the age of their design. These were there bound down with as many ropes as possible to ground based buildings. The *third Airship* was severely damaged when it crashed into the *new 10-story building* currently in progress up town on the newly named 4th street. Air Naval officials assure us that the third can be used for parts to repair the other two. The Air Navy's mooring area had *Oxford* wind sensors rated up to **125 miles per hour.** They were ripped off of the roofs.

Outside of New York, the barrier island known as **Rockaway Beach** to the southeast of the main island was overcome. The next day it became clear it is now two islands. Already, there are plans to call the second, further island by a new name, although the only proposed name so far is the uninspiring *'Long Beach.'* The newly organized **Port Of New York** has sent some remaining ships out to view the changed coastline, and are confident that shipping can continue uninterrupted once they have found all the ships.

The Airship of **Sir James Coltrane** and company, *The Dame Fortuna*, limped into New York in the early morning hours of the 24th, having borne the storm on the **open skies**. Tales of a brave Captain *lashed to the wheel* were told in hushed voices, although their damage was great, but not yet enumerated.

In other areas in the region, damage was also severe. **Providence**, capital of our little sister Rhode Island, was flooded by an 11-foot storm wave that funneled up *Narragansett Bay* destroying uncounted houses and ships. They have marked the flood with a line on the **Old Market Building**, hoping to always remember and never see its like again.

This storm also caused damage **throughout the region** in Connecticut, Massachusetts (notably damaging the bridge at *Dorchester)* and up through New Hampshire. Full reports will become available as stunned citizens make reckonings of the damage.

Already a talk has been announced at **Harvard**. Professor John Farrar, the *Cambridge*-trained Hollis professor of Mathematics and Natural Philosophy wishes to share his observations of the storm, and propose a theory of *'moving vortex' storms*.

The last recorded damage of this magnitude was **The Great Colonial Storm of 1635**, which recorded 14 foot tides in Providence. The early settlers feared for the *end of the world*. The Editors of this fine Paper hope we may avoid any further storms of this magnitude for at least another 180 years.

From the journals of Gregory Conan Watts,
September 26th, 1815
New York City
40º 47'N 073º 58'W

My failure is, through circumstance which I will never
forget and remain in awe of, undone, and for it I must rethink my
opinions of Samantha Bowe. While she is most unladylike, she is
also now a heroine to not only the royals of France, but to both
myself and Matthew Fisher-Swift. I do not know how she caught
hold of the ornithopter, how it survived the storm, and least of all
how she found Matthew before he struck the sea, but it seems she
must have done all these things as she claims.

We were trying to assess the condition of the ship at the
mooring post in New York today, for there is no better way to
forget tragedy for a time than setting to hard work. Sir James is
recovering well, and Eddy has regained consciousness but will not
be walking any time soon. Miss Penn and Mr. Franzini will be
under doctor's care for some time longer, and the Fishers were
about mourning, but Sir James, myself, and Harriet Wright were
about assessing the ship, with Miss Coltrane keeping a close eye
on her brother, when we heard a terrible creaking. Though there
were quite a few people gathered about, watching in what cannot
be anything but awe, the crowd parted.

Samantha Bowe came back to the dirigible, torn half to
pieces, bleeding and bruised all over. Over one shoulder was the
limp form of Matthew Fisher-Swift, and at first it seemed as if she
had recovered his body, at least, until I noticed his back rising
even when she was still – though in poor condition, obviously, he
breathed. Partially serving as a crutch and partially being dragged
by Miss Bowe was the frame of the ornithopter. It was still
moving, but with both wings stripped to shreds, one axle broken,
and a handful of areas which should be securely bolted coming
loose.

We rushed forward, of course, and Miss Wright, the closest
of us, was just able to grab Matthew in time to hear Miss Bowe
croak something which Miss Wright was sure was "Fix him,"

before she collapsed forward. I do not know her condition now, nor what her odds of further survival are. I do not know how long she traveled to get here, but what has been revealed to us is that though he will be in bed for some time, Matthew Fisher-Swift will live, and while scratched and bruised quite badly, he has escaped with a broken leg as the worst of his injuries. The doctors believe that when they hit the land or sea, Miss Bowe must have cushioned his fall with her own body, and the ornithopter slowed them enough that the fall was not immediately fatal.

Harriet Wright has since been frantically setting to trying to repair the device, and Sir James has gone to help her. Though I am still certain that it was the product of the worst kind of mad science, I cannot any longer call it a devil machine, and can no longer doubt that it has not only recognition, but some true kind of loyalty. Much as it pains me, I find myself hoping that Sir James and Miss Wright's memory for repair are sufficient to repair it. Miss Coltrane has occasionally followed them to see to their progress and supervise Miss Wright as they work frantically, but just as often has been forced to remain abed to rest and have her own injuries tended. All of them have said that though the workshop is in ruins, and Sir James's device is in terrible repair, Sir James and Harriet Wright will not work on anything else so long as the ornithopter still seems to have animation to it. In the meanwhile, given her state when last I saw her, some doctors are saying much the same of Miss Bowe.

I myself write this from near the front of a church, for while I normally do not perform work such as this documenting while at worship, it seemed somehow only right to note the occurrence of a miracle in these surroundings. I joined Mrs. Fisher, who has been here almost constantly, save for the short time she was permitted to visit Matthew. I can only imagine that she, too, will be much easier on Miss Bowe going forward, unless she sees her attempts to make a lady of her as some kind of favor, in which case she may become more determined. Best I not pass such suppositions on to Miss Bowe should she ever be fit to receive visitors, lest she wish she were dead.

September 26th, 1815
New York City
40° 47'N 073° 58'W

Dear Sir,

I know that communication has been forwarded to you
regarding our state and the tragedy that befell us as we returned
to New York. With Eddy and Miss Bowe somewhat recovered
from their individual injuries, we have had opportunity to discuss
the future of this mission, and you will be pleased to know we
have elected to press on once we are more fully recovered, though
we are making some sacrifices to this end for the sake of haste.
The rescue of Matthew Fisher-Swift was most heartening for all of
the crew, and it was felt that the brave men of the ship who
perished in the monster storm would have wished us to go on.

For the sake of having more time for them to recover, as
they represent most of our ground operations in non-critical, non-
combative situations, Eddy and Miss Bowe will be mostly at rest
for the first portion of our voyage, and aboard the dirigible. They
– and I – will disembark once we reach the furthest edges of
American civilization to the West and travel on the ground from
there. I will supply you and the English public with what pictures
I am able as we travel, along with the written account of our
journey. The dirigible will track our progress as we go, but as the
largest part of our mission is to locate Dr. Bowe's route to the
Pacific ocean following his account, we will not be returning to the
ship at any time save as is required for survival. This may be
considered necessary at times, and will be at the discretion of our
guide and Sir James, as this winter is already suggesting itself to
be exceptionally difficult in these climates, and I can only imagine
that it will be as bad or worse further inland.

The repairs upon the ship proceed almost as quickly as the
injured parties are healing, and the city of New York has been
more than generous in supplying us with everything we might
need in order to speed these repairs along and prepare for our
voyage west, including spare parts from their worst damaged

airship. Dr. Mitchell's drawings on winter-proofing and insulation, which seemed fantastical overkill in April, are now being treated as scripture by the engineering crew. If they have their way, no pipe on this dirigible will be left uninsulated, nor any cable joint left without reinforcement.

While I am certain all of England is quite interested in our progress, we seem to have caught the spirit of this city as well. I have come to understand that there are a number of celebrations here to mark the decision to continue to the west, despite efforts to prepare for a harsh winter time and the efforts that are going towards the war effort to our south.

I have not heard any great news as concerns that conflict, save that the American colonist soldiers under the command of Col. York have so far been able to hold the ground taken, and there may be some plan to attempt to take one further Spanish holding in Florida in the near future. Sir James has tracked that progress and planning to a greater degree than I have and, of course, with a firmer grasp of tactics. I wonder, is there any news as to further reinforcement from England? It would be most welcomed in this conflict should it continue to escalate.

Yours,
Gregory Conan Watts

Letter from Heathsville, Northumberland County, Virginia Colony
Archives, Wright Collection.
September 28, 1815

Mother! (and Daddy too!)

I hope all is well down on the farm. Did you get hit by the
Great Gale last week? I do hope the orchards are doing well.

We were hit by the Gale while in the air. Don't you go
panicking, although I will admit I did so while it was all going on.
Jillian and I entangled ourselves in the railing and clung on.
Cousin James and darling Eddy were braver then brave, and I'm
sure that Captain Fisher (who <u>tied</u> himself to the <u>wheel</u>) saved us
all. Samantha Bowe (Dr. Bowe's daughter, you remember) showed
her family's true grit when she leapt from the ship to fetch back
our ship's boy, the captain's ward. She arrived in New York
looking like a drowned swamp rat, but with a whole Matthew and
herself in a state.

We're in New York for a bit more, doing repairs and
insulating. We had frozen pipes while looking at waterways up
north, and we'll not be able to rely on constant water supplies
inland. The crew is fully capable of wrapping pipes, so I've been
replacing ropes with cables where they connect the envelope to
the carriage. Those ropes were snapping right and left during the
storm. (No panicking, Mother.) That's how we lost our first mate.
(You either, Daddy.)

Jillian is fully in her in town mode, here in New York. Her
fashion dolls for autumn and winter came here to the main post
office and were waiting for us. Of course, not content to be the
most fashionable person in New York, she's gone bigger. She's
hosting a fundraiser tea for the soldiers injured in New Orleans
(you've had that news, right?). She'll share her fashion dolls with
all the best Ladies of New York in return for the sentiments on
behalf of those brave men. The Ladies are glad to pay to be
around Jillian and be seen supporting the cause, and James is
thrilled that she's keeping New Orleans and the cause in people's
minds. I am fixing the ship rather then attending, as the ship is the

priority, and we leave as soon as it's finished. I am still trying to fully reconcile myself to that.

It's odd, I suppose, to be back in the Americas and not have stopped by to say hello. I swear (using only the most lady-like language to do so, Mother) that we flew almost straight over the plantation on the way down to New Orleans, or was it the way back up? Anyway, if you saw a dirigible, it could have been us, but we didn't stop, as we are so behind, and running before the frost. (Speaking of Frosts, Daddy should ask one of the College Professors about Tambora. Scary stuff. Harvest early.)

In response to Mother's letter, yes, I was in the same location as the Queen of France, but no, I do not believe that she remembers me. That was quite the night, before the men hustled us back to the ship. The men went back out again, but Mrs. Fisher was so in shock about the whole thing that she added Port to our tea, not even just brandy. Imagine that!

We go west next. We'll likely beat the post to St. Louis. I have no forwarding address to give you, for you cannot send mail to be held at the Pacific Coast. Perhaps New Orleans, or New York?

Give my love to everyone, and ask the dear Reverend to light a candle in the name of my crew every Sunday.

Your Loving Daughter,
Harriet Wright

The West by Air
Wonders of the West

From the journals of Gregory Conan Watts,
October 4th, 1815
Ohio Territory
40°58'N 076°53'W

We are at last away once more. There was worry for some
time about a number of our people, but their recovery has done
wonders for the spirit of adventure. Young Mister Fisher-Swift has
proven most resilient, and while he remembers almost nothing of
his recent adventure, he has recovered almost entirely. Miss Bowe
likewise has proven to be extremely resilient, can count a healthy
constitution and capacity for rapid healing among her plethora of
gifts, and has resumed full activities. For her recent heroic efforts
she has had a somewhat easier time of it from Miss Coltrane. I
would still not call relations between these women friendly, but
both seem to prefer it that way.

On the note of Miss Coltrane, she seems to be struggling
mightily with her own injuries. Her hand, as it turned out, was not
fully broken, but the injury is nonetheless slow in healing and
useless to her much of the time. She continues to be with her
brother and cousin where she is able, but has been at times
overtaken by dizzy spells or moments of weakness sufficient that
she must return to rest sooner than she'd have liked.

Miss Penn is fully recovered, though she still has
nightmares of the events, causing her to have some difficulty
sleeping. Not having a proper physician aboard, Miss Bowe has
taken a good deal of time to speak with her on such occasions, and
despite the early difficulties, the pair seem to be becoming good
friends. Despite my earlier misgivings about the both of them, I
find myself glad for it, both are good company once one can
forgive the fault that they are not English, and thus cannot be held
to the same standards one might a woman of England or even
Western Europe.

On a related note to Miss Bowe's recovery, the ornithopter
seems entirely repaired, and once again has set itself to following
Miss Bowe about when allowed. While its mannerisms disturb me
at times, and perhaps others as well, more of the crew seem more

at ease with its presence and lifelike behavior since the rescue of young Mr. Fisher-Swift.

Eddy has made a nearly full recovery, though for a time he had quite the scare, for he had at times difficulty getting feeling in his hand, especially on particularly cold mornings. He has not had difficulty with this in some days now, so it is hoped that whatever the problem was, he has fully recovered from it. He still appears quite the sight, I fear, but he has taken his scars with pride. Miss Coltrane, in particular, seemed quite worried for him, and visited him when she was able along with her brother. It was some small blow to his spirits, judging by his expression and glances, as he would have preferred had it been Miss Wright who visited him, but her time was largely spent in first repairing the ornithopter, a task to which she showed immense dedication until the task was done, and then set herself to repairing the workshop, in which, I understand, she is quite at home.

The person who it seems may never recover fully may be the captain, for he now walks with a pronounced limp, though nothing was broken. Such violent jarring when tied to an object like the wheel cannot have been good for a man of his advancing years. The bandages have been removed from his hands, though they are even more heavily scarred than before, and a mark of the voyage will always be just before him, for some parts of the wheel seem to have taken bloodstains from his struggle with it. These have not come out entirely no matter how much work is done at it. Had we more time, I think everyone would have preferred that the entire thing be removed, burned and replaced, for it is a terrible and disturbing reminder one cannot help but notice for our shared experience.[14]

In better news, we can hope, when both are recovered from their injuries, as a reward for his courage in recovering from so difficult an event, Eddy has agreed to allow Matthew to room with him for the next stretch of the voyage, and will begin training Matthew in filling the part of his powder monkey, for it was a

---

14 Gregory would not get his wish on this account. The macabre wheel was removed as far as the Public Exhibition Hall of Air History, in Cambridge. Thankfully for most sensibilities, it is behind glass. – C B-W

most helpful function that the first mate had filled for a time. Young Mister Fisher-Swift has already begun asking almost on the hour when he will be "recovered enough."

Of final note, Mister Franzini appears to have precisely the constitution one would expect from so small and thin a man and has not healed quickly at all. He keeps mostly to his chambers, and complains of pains often, especially when he has to spend any time upon the crutches prepared for him. Still, he has welcomed the opportunity of having no particular responsibilities upon the ship, that he may spend most of his time in Sir James's card room, playing with whoever will game with him, though he remains disappointed that no stakes are to be put up among this fellowship. I would imagine that he was displeased having to be under such close watch while in New York, owing to his injuries, but at least it ensures that we left New York as popular as we arrived.

The station's help, our celebrity status, and the chance to make alterations to the airship out of need has allowed us to do a great deal to refit it from its military purpose to something more suited to our mission, including a few more means to somewhat allow people to board or disembark without a station, though the rope ladders make for a very difficult climb, especially if they are not yet secured on the ground. Should conditions ahead prove especially harsh, as they are looking to, it will come in most useful sooner or later. This is part of the reason for our somewhat southward course as well, for as nice as it would be to winter in New York, we have a great deal ahead of us, and we are already behind quite some distance from our intended time, because of the time spent in the far northern reaches, and then the difficulties resulting from the storm.

This looks to be no winter to be trying to travel, so we are beginning our trip as far to the south as we can without running into some risk from Spanish forces. Eventually we shall have to move into the teeth of winter, however, for Miss Bowe is quite certain that the path eventually requires very specific routes through mountain ranges, and her father's journals seem to bear this out. If it is true that the two of them know some wild territory,

America would seem to be it, given where we first encountered her. Despite the conditions we are expecting to find, she does not seem concerned with navigation amidst the winter weather, though this is also the woman who dove into the worst storm any of us has ever seen for the life of a child, so her lack of concern does nothing to comfort me. Competent and skilled she may be, but while I will be eternally grateful, I must still acknowledge that sanity is not among her strongest traits.

October 8th, 1815
Ohio Territory
40°04'N 080°47'W

My Dearest Cordelia,

I will herein beg your forgiveness, and shall hope this letter is not too disturbing or graphic for a young woman's sensibilities, but we have had quite the adventure today, and it is inspiring enough that I felt you would surely wish to hear of it.

We had been traveling for some few days towards St. Louis, that we could make a final preparation for fuel and supplies. The winds have been entirely uncooperative, and the unseasonable cold just grows worse by the day. I worry that even if there is a route through these mountains Miss Bowe speaks of to the west, they will be entirely impassable for the ice and snow, or at least more treacherous by far than they might be at a better time. We would have been much better off to have skipped the first steps of our exploration and come directly this way.

We have, by chance, been following the path of the railways, heading much the same way as ourselves. On this particular day, we were also enjoying the coming of mid-afternoon, and some hint of warmth, along with the winds finally dying down some amount that at least we were not fighting them. Miss Bowe and Eddy, both more accustomed to cooler climes, were out on the side of the ship watching the grounds below. Even as much as we have now been traveling by dirigible, some views remain wondrous sights that very few eyes have ever seen from such a vantage.

Suddenly, they raised quite the alarm. A group of well armed and horsed bandits were coming up fast upon one of the trains. They were some distance short of one of the water stations, close enough that the train had grown particularly sluggish and much of the crew would be occupied, and yet far enough as well that the armed men of the station would not be able to see the attempt even should the train get quite some distance. It seems to me the height of insanity, since such things are well guarded. With so few trains traveling the American rails, they could be after any number of things: the gold to be stored within westerly fortresses, the wealth of city people traveling towards the frontier, or the railroad's payroll. For a group this size, likely all of the above played some part in their willingness to make targets of themselves over open territory.

Surprise also played some great part in their ability to approach without other alarm being raised. During the early stages of the war, while tracks for troop movement were being laid down in occupied territory, the English learned hard lessons about properly securing stations and posting guards about a train. Ever since the lessons learned from early European raids upon train stations were applied, however, the thought of raiding a moving train was all but unthinkable. I know the riverboats on the Mississippi river have been targets of bandits before, but I had never heard of a postwar effort to take a guarded train.

Watching from above, it seemed like the bandits had a great deal of knowledge of the train. Perhaps some of them had ridden it before, or had paid off an informant from the railroad. In any case, they seemed to know precisely where the guard stations were, shooting down the few people who were in position to oppose them before anyone aboard the train realized what was happening. A number of them were able to clamber aboard the train from there, boarding the middle cars of the train in numbers before splitting into groups. Their speed and organization was obvious, not needing to hesitate to discuss the plan, just as they seemed to know precisely where to hit the train where it would not be in sight of any station.

I was able to watch through one of the porthole windows well enough to see these early stages, and to watch Eddy and Miss Bowe leaping into action. For Eddy, it was a figurative thing. He called for Matthew to prepare his rifles and bring them out, even as Eddy crouched at the railing of the dirigible and lowered his goggles, toying with the lenses until he found his range while Matthew was responding. While he might have gotten off a pistol shot, I do not think he wanted to warn anyone below with anything less accurate than a perfect first shot. Matthew was quick to respond, racing one way up the corridor at all the shouting, having to squeeze past the Coltranes and Miss Wright moving the other way, heading from where they had been on the bridge towards the workshop. There, Sir James would be able to get suited up, and his sister would have a discreet place to watch the battle to come.

For Miss Bowe, the leap was more literal. Apparently not having had her fill of such acrobatics yet, she whistled, and the ornithopter wheeled itself to her side with great haste and somewhat more grace in getting through the door than last time, with me not blocking its way. She leapt onto the rails with perfect balance, then launched herself into the sky while the ornithopter found room to unfold its wings and dive into the open after her. She caught its axle mid-flight, pulling herself up into a position by which she was able to glide down towards the train at great speed, while they had not yet seen her.

The first sign the people had of us from the train below was Eddy, rifle in hand, braced properly in a kneeling position and having found his range, shooting first one, and then a second man as they were trying to pull themselves onto a train car. I briefly lost track of the action in racing for my camera, for this time, I had the room and footing, and at last had a real opportunity to capture some of my companions in action. By the time I had returned with the unwieldy device, Miss Bowe was upon the train and engaged with three fellows, ducking beneath their shots and attacks with pistol butts and knives. She soon dispatched one of them, then weaved between the other pair. While she was at it Eddy was shouting commands to Matthew, who, finally in his first real opportunity to help his chosen hero, was struggling as ably as he could to follow these instructions to the letter and handling with great care the much revered rifles. One man after another fell from horseback or the train as others fought forward, boarding in areas they had cleared of guardsmen and moving along the top of the train towards the engine so they might put a stop to it.

I maneuvered as well as I might for vantage, struggling to keep control of the camera, managing easy pictures of Eddy, as you will see accompanying this note when I have opportunity, and somewhat more difficult pictures of Miss Bowe as she raced after the attackers along the top of the train. Amidst it all, I did hear Eddy quietly cursing, despite the child's presence. Apparently the men were splitting now into groups, and some had gotten behind Miss Bowe. He set about protecting her flank as she raced after the men trying to stop the engine, cutting down some others who got in her way with illusion of even slowing her down. I am already imagining that very soon poor Matthew will get cuffed about the head for repeating some of the new words he learned in this occasion.

By now I have become familiar with the sound of gears grinding and steam venting from the back quarters of our ship, for it means that Sir James has prepared himself, and is ready to join the fight as well. The leap was perfect, moving to cut off the group of men heading for the storage car where the safe is kept. Unfortunately, the top of the train was not at all suited to take the sudden weight, and the suit went crashing through into the safe car. While I lost sight of him then, I did see at least one of the bandits tossed bodily out through the hole in the top of the car, and Sir James's presence quite headed off those already making their way into the car as well as those heading there. By the time the suit clambered out through the hole, those who remained outside were quite ready to surrender themselves.

Those headed to the front made their way into the engine, some three of them, including both a man we would find out had played at least some part in organizing the raid, and a very large and daunting individual. Miss Bowe reached the engine just after they did, for while they had a significant head start on her, she navigated the tricky footing of the coal car far more easily than they had. There were some gunshots from within, and at least once I was able to make out the large man trying to engage her, and would eventually see him thrown from the car. At last our ship came up close enough that I was able to see her dispatch the final man with a thrown knife before he could bring the train to a halt. Some few of them did eventually escape, all those who thought better of continuing their venture upon seeing real opposition, but every man who boarded the train was captured or killed.

It was quite exciting, and I truly hope not too much for your fertile imagination, but I know you well enough that I am sure you would want to hear of such an unusual event in detail.[15]

I also wrote an account for the newspapers in St. Louis and made them copies of some few of the pictures. Our fame spreads as we travel now, and the railroad has named us heroes for the saving of the safe of property deeds and the railroad's payroll.

In the meantime, it seems that Miss Bowe in particular is quite looking forward to getting back to St. Louis, for she considers it far more comfortable territory than those other locales we have visited. Mr. Franzini, meanwhile, has found himself having a new bout of pain from his slowly healing leg (or possibly his reputation), and has decided he will not be leaving the dirigible in St. Louis.

Very soon, we will have to plan very carefully, for we have at last a very long stretch ahead of us with no friendly territory in sight and no means by which we might restock the airship, so almost every area that is not absolutely critical will soon be used to store extra supplies for the times ahead.

I will attempt to write again soon, though I do not imagine that my letters shall be going anywhere for quite some time once we leave St. Louis.

My love, always,
Gregory Conan Watts

---

15 Gregory knew that I had already read all of Dr. Bowe's Journals, even those considered too exciting for a girl in a fragile state. My days spent in active wonder and excitement were aided by a young footman of my father's, who experienced his own armchair adventuring in sneaking me the books. – C B-W

From the journals of Gregory Conan Watts,
October 15th, 1815
St. Louis
38°38'N 090°12'N

Following the excitement of the railway incident, we have
had excitement of quite a different sort. While New York was
quite discreet regarding the other visitors, for whatever reasons
and whatever our status there, our heroism on the railways has
increased our popularity here such that we were able to learn
something, at long last, of a concrete nature regarding those who
oppose us. Another airship came through this region two days
ahead of us, and stocked up for a journey that has to be at least as
long as our own. I am glad that they did not have either the
resources or room to buy out all of the available supplies
necessary for such a trip, though that would have also quite
perturbed the officials of the railroad.

Similarly, while this region has also had the early frost, it is
not so severe as the eastern coastline, and they knew nothing of
the storm which wreaked so much havoc in New York. As such,
resources for food and clothing are more plentiful. They are
expecting winter storms quite soon, so warmer clothing was
available, though we have had to make do with whatever was on
hand. Even so, we are currently grateful for anything we can get,
for the dry chill here is quite unlike that of even the worst winters
in London and its surroundings. It is not so much the seeping cold
that gets into everything, soaking the clothes through – and
making one wish for a warm fire, a pint and a place to get dry – so
much as it is a creeping chill that finds its way into the bones and
settles there, such that you think you might never get warm.
Winter aboard the dirigible, where we cannot set fires, is not a
pleasant prospect, but we have lost too much time already.

I do not know if they have had any part of such difficulties
as we have, but the people aboard the other ship came through
town, all very much matching Matthew's descriptions of them.
They also had a number of gunmen with them that the locals did
not recognize. When we asked after him, the dark-haired man was

reported by a number of local merchants as having spent a great deal of time discussing the best divisions of weight for feeding such a small army of men with the limits of an airship.

They also bought a large amount of oil such as is sometimes used to lubricate gears in more complex devices to keep them running well, which tells me that they have their own man of Oxford or some New York inventor among them. Given what we know, I would be willing to wager that it is the bald and scarred man, for his injuries very much seem to be of the sort one could receive from working with steam power. It is only supposition, all manner of accident can happen to a man, but it is at least something to go on. Sir James in particular has been most interested by this news, and he and his sister have been working diligently ever since that time looking through his terms at Oxford and trying to determine what we might be facing, for he has not yet recognized any of the men described, though of course the scarred man may well look quite different now than he did before his injuries. It is also quite possible that we have not yet seen their scientist, and the scarred man is more a mechanic or operator of something with gears and steam powered systems.

We do also know that they outgun us significantly, either because they are planning some further ambush, or believe they need additional arms.

We also have some small information about others within their group. The woman came through some parts of town, earning no friends here with her insistence upon precise tailoring and being displeased with nearly everything she was presented. While I certainly know enough of proper ladies to understand the drive for looking just so, I cannot imagine she could have expected such things as are available in England or Paris, or even New York when out here. She paid quite well when she finally received something that suited her, somewhat easing tempers, though she had apparently threatened repeatedly to buy nothing after all their troubles, or to refuse to pay for inferior workmanship. Miss Coltrane in particular was most interested to hear this, and believes that in the future, she might now be able to somewhat track this mysterious woman, should we reach more civilized regions, through what she knows of her fashion tastes. It seems an odd way to trail someone, but I do not doubt that she knows enough of what she talks about to do just that. A shame we were not able to get more information in New York, for it is most uncomfortable going into an already risky venture knowing that so many well armed gunmen are preparing some resistance to our movements.

Lastly, the large Negro man received a great deal of attention while about town, for though they have seen plenty of black men working for the railways, he did not dress like any slave or freedman. Instead he stood out to most here as much for his brightly colored clothing as for the coloration of his skin. His purchases were also most odd, primarily candles and a prolonged search for a skinning knife that suited him, rejecting many perfectly usable blades along the way. Apparently he was most specific, and the shopkeeper was not entirely helpful, for he had stayed behind the counter out of fright of the man. The shopkeeper was not the only one that the man had that effect on. We have also learned something of his manner of speech, which locals know enough of to have identified as quite similar to some of the slaves who have not been that long out of Africa, though he speaks English confidently and well, simply with a very heavy accent.

It may, in the end, not be a great deal of information beyond what we might have supposed from the information Matthew was able to bring us, but it has almost entirely confirmed his account, which is valuable in its own right. So far he has always seemed quite honest, but one never knows about boys of his age. Wild imaginations are often common, and may even fill in details in their minds they did not see without them entirely willing it. And in such a time as things may be life and death, even a small amount of information is far better than nothing. Most importantly of all, we know that we must expect an ambush in the coming few days, for while a dirigible may sustain a large group of men for a considerable time, as was proven in the past, it quickly grows crowded if not all of the men are of military training and sensibilities and well used to one another, and provisioning is not exact. In almost any other circumstance, so many men in so small a space as a dirigible would lead to trouble quite quickly, and not all of those described by the locals as having boarded seem to be well trained and drilled soldiers. Even if not, they can easily be dangerous men, and the locals are very certain every one of them was armed.

Editor's note:

Lest you think every day was exciting on the journey, I have included the following sample day out of Gregory's journal. While it does not add directly to the narrative, some knowledge of the day-to-day affairs of exploration is useful.

– Dr. Cordelia Bentham-Watts

From the Journals of Gregory Conan Watt,
October 19th, 1815
39°15'N 094°25'W

Today we mapped from the Dame Fortuna, although I'm not sure the bitter cold of the airship railing is any less chilling than the ground. The gently rolling hills of this morning gave way to flatter plains. The presence of a mere four buffalo, apparently separated from their herd by some means, both piqued our curiosity and gave us some small measure by which to judge our speed over this otherwise mostly featureless terrain.

A small hamlet on a bend in the river offered opportunity to exchange information. The name of the town, Liberty, has proven useful for our map. Sir James also took the opportunity to ask after our competition. I am not certain whether I was comforted that they had seen no other airship but our own, or worried that we still have no news of them.

I bought a bit of excess paper from the local schoolmaster. He asked if the news from the east included unusual cold, as this weather is beyond what is normally experienced in these parts, which is apparently good for keeping his students in their seats, but poor for the late-harvested crops. I mentioned Harvard's suspicion that it is volcanic, related to Tambora. This reassured him, especially as it would explain the red snow that had fallen recently.

Red snow was, admittedly, a fascinating phenomena of which to hear. I'd have said it was impossible or superstition, but nature continues to prove herself more powerful than man's comprehension.

Aside from my need to replace paper – and the wish that I had more for my camera – our provisions continue to serve quite well. Bison roast is still superior to mutton, although it remains to be seen if I will maintain the same opinion at month's end. The cold really is most inhuman. I have been forced to begin carrying my ink inside my vest, under my arm. If I don't, when it freezes, the glass bottle sometimes breaks.

From the diary of Julietta Penn
October 19th, 1815

Cold.

Dreams of the storm. Dreams that I'm cast into the ocean during it, treading water with pockets full of coin. Other times, dreams of dying of thirst, but not from heat.

So cold. It won't stop soon. The darkness folding its shroud around the world.

The World. I hold that card again and again. Inverted Fortitude around Miss Perfection. The Devil for the job. But so many times, the World. I'd like to say I've never been afraid of it. Not even at its most serious. All things must turn.

But I am afraid now. Nearly every time I look at him. It doesn't make sense. There's more to fear out there than the soul of a weasel. How did I get myself into this?

I don't even know the scope of 'this.' These others. I almost feel the tugs along the net where this African has just been. Need to know more. Yoruba? Igbo? Haratin? Am I dealing with Vodoun or with Juju? Mildly vexing that few here will take the threat of such things seriously. Sam might, if she can take threats seriously.

Samantha Bowe, whose disregard did not abide entirely as circumstances changed. My shield from Giovanni. Fair trade for my embarrassments? Can I call her a friend? I fear not enough basis for comparison. Can't tell her everything, of course. Still, it helps. Were there indeed a man around like her, maybe even I could fall in love.

October 25th, 1815
Missouri Territory
40º49N 098º36

Dear Sir,

We have begun our journey with promising results, for we were not long past sight of the towns dotting the colonial frontier when Miss Bowe set on a very certain route. She seems quite knowledgeable about this region, which is no surprise. The tribes native to these lands have not given us any trouble yet, and Miss Bowe doubts that will change, though she says some of the tribes to the south of here are much more aggressive. She's assured us that so long as we follow this route, we should have little trouble for some time. She is also quite insistent that in no way are we exploring on this venture, for she and her father have passed this way numerous times on the path he first discovered before her birth. Her certainty about the perils of the region and the comfort we have been able to manage despite the early beginning to winter assure me there is some truth to this, so at least we can be certain Dr. Bowe came this far.

The land is plains for as far as the eye can see. Were it not for the snow, this would make travel by ground easy. This also comforts us that no ambush is coming today, for lying in ambush would be a most uncomfortable thing indeed, and it would be almost impossible to hide in the white of the surroundings. Likewise, we could easily see any natives coming, should Miss Bowe be wrong about their peaceable nature. For now, the only living things we have come upon are the herds of buffalo, for these monstrous beasts, a larger version of Europe's wisent, are everywhere here. I am including a few pictures of these, for certainly sights common to the American frontier will still much excite the people back home with our progress and the wonder of the unknown, or at least, seemingly unknown to all of us save our guide.

So long as she keeps track of the land, and while we are in such easy territory, we have had no trouble agreeing to spend our nights traveling slowly in the dirigible, for we cover more ground, but should we need to retrace our steps, we could easily find the markers we left the day before. This territory is so easily navigable that I cannot imagine that anyone should have trouble finding their way through here, with only the threats of the native inhabitants and what predators hunt the buffalo herds, perhaps, though I would not wish to get too close to those beasts myself. Miss Bowe states that more difficult travel lies ahead, for depending on how far we choose to travel by air, we are likely not far from reaching ground with more hills, and eventually we will come to mountainous regions. She remains unworried for this, saying she knows routes through the mountains which should not trouble us too much, but then she is not carrying the camera. Were it not for the airship, we should certainly be traveling by horseback, but the occasion to journey through the air much speeds us upon our way, allows us some time off of the frozen Earth, and allows us to survey and mark our route accurately at the end of the day before light has gone entirely.

Thankfully, the skies here do not seem to be suffering the early darkness of the more eastern lands, but it is growing late enough in the year that our traveling time is growing less and less. In a way, I do not mind, for travel by air is far easier, though it lacks a great deal of the trailblazing feel. When my feet feel frozen solid, however, I am more than glad to leave the blazing to people like Boone and Miss Bowe while I read by candlelight in greater comfort. When we reach these mountains, of course, we shall have to spend more time camping, for our trails must be better marked, and there will not always be occasion for the ship to get close enough to us to lower ladders. I can assure you, sir, that climbing an unsteady rope ladder at the end of a day when my fingers have gone so numb that I can no longer work the camera is no great pleasure, but certainly gets the blood moving. Miss Bowe always ascends last, for despite how unchivalrous this would seem, she also is the least affected of all of us by this climate, having lived in regions quite similar, and has no difficulty in waiting and steadying the ladders before scrambling up herself. She says the only difficulty with this end of each day for her is the skirts get in the way of climbing efficiently, and she shall insist, whatever Mrs. Fisher and Miss Coltrane say, upon men's pants when we are about navigating the mountains. I know it is unseemly, and I shall hope this letter is not widely circulated at home, save what parts of it are more of adventure and less of controversy, but so long as we have no great difficulties, the services of the guide you led us to are well worth the trouble.

Yours,
Gregory Conan Watts

November 2nd, 1815
Northwest of St. Louis
42°52'N 105°52'W

Dear Sir,

It seems that the contents of my last letter were somewhat prophetic, for we have had quite the fright today. I shall endeavor to describe in it in detail enough to be helpful now, but I will hope you will forgive me if I am at times somewhat vague.

We had made good progress, and just as our guide predicted, we are now in territory with more hills, and can see mountains looming in the far distance. While we approached the foothills by air initially, to test our equipment, most specifically my camera, and our ability to get about in the snow, Miss Bowe, Eddy, and myself had descended to the ground. These hills have no particularly distinctive features, which made them somewhat hard to navigate, and as we travel, we are still making a map of the land we pass over that others might follow.

While traveling through snow which had to be over half a meter in depth, we heard a great noise from behind the cover of a hill some distance off, with a herd of buffalo between it and us. I was in the midst of photography already, so you have the good fortune of having some few images of what transpired next before I was of wit enough to take up the camera and run. Emerging from this cover was a mechanical monstrosity, not at all like Sir James's man-like creation, but more like a single railroad car, though there is no track in this territory. It emitted such noise and clouds of steam that it seemed very much the draconic thing then, spitting sparks and smoke as it roared along. This trackless rail engine must have seemed at least as monstrous to the herds of buffalo, for they startled horribly, as you might well imagine.

I missed the first sounds of gunfire entirely, but Eddy and Miss Bowe both agree that seconds past the emergence of the trackless engine, men came up from the hills in ambush, firing upon us, thankfully at such range that no one was hit, or likely in great danger from musket fire, but also into the buffalo, not as hunters might, but to further spook and herd the massive beasts in our direction. Eddy grabbed for my arm then, and I quickly took up the camera, for though he said it should be left, as I have previously stated, it is worth more than my own life, and even amidst panic, I had not taken so great a leave of my senses. He swore then in such a fashion that I am glad I cannot rightly classify Miss Bowe to be any proper sort of lady of society, and the other ladies had stayed safely aboard the ship. He took up the tripod for my camera, while I grabbed the rest, and then we ran for our lives, seeking hills or other impediment to the herd that did not have gunmen behind it. We must be thankful that they were just guided in our rough direction, and not seeking our end by evil intent, for, despite such ponderous appearance, when frightened they move rapidly, and the ground shook beneath us even then when we had but turned to run, making it all the harder to keep our feet.

Miss Bowe has proven herself the fastest of us over ground repeatedly, in addition to the reflexes you have heard of at the Governor's ball, but she did not flee past us. Instead she moved first towards the stampede, waving her arms and moving like the tales told of Spanish bullfighters, trying to catch the eye of the frightened and angry bulls at the head of the stampede that they might move her way in some effort to alleviate the threat, even though the monster was behind them. She then split away from us, heading not for hills, but more open and easier ground. Insane and again unchivalrous as this was, we were in no state to argue, and made for the hills.

As we ran, though some greater part of the herd had moved on Miss Bowe's path, there were bison enough to spread wide over the ground, and I could feel them getting quite close behind us. Though the hills might have deterred them, I am both uncertain if we would have reached them, and even if we had, I am not positive under such a rush that it would have done enough. Some short distance ahead of us, a brass and iron miracle descended from the ship, though for once, I could barely hear his mechanical monster as it landed heavily upon the ground before us for the thunderous sound on our heels. He recovered from the great leap, then braced himself, arms crossed, leaning slightly forward into the oncoming rush, and down to one knee, as steady as he could hope to become for the approaching onslaught. We managed to reach his position, somewhat closer than the less certain cover of the hills, and ducked behind him and prayed. Some part of the herd split about so daunting an obstacle, closing ranks again only shortly behind him, but numerous times I heard the crash of horn and skull on metal as not everything quite entirely avoided him, and as I was leaned against one metal leg, I could feel him jarred side to side. Once I was showered with scrap metal and bolts, and for the first time, feared that not only we, but Sir James might not survive the encounter. In time the herd passed us by, racing on into the plains. The armored suit looked worse than after any armed conflict, but one arm still moved, and he was able to stand, if unsteadily. Eddy and myself were quite unhurt, save that Eddy has since had more than a few unkind words to say for my camera.

We had entirely lost sight of Miss Bowe, but my tone would be entirely different had we lost someone. The fool woman had not only escaped the herd, but as we were recovering some part of our nerve, she came to us to ask if we wanted to help dress the bison she had killed, and more importantly, to report that the trackless rail engine and all of the gunmen had disappeared amidst the chaotic events. She asked if we wished her to track them that we could deal with this threat then and there, but after only brief discussion, common sense prevailed over our not insignificant rage. Sir James's suit was quite damaged in the event, and we did not know what kind of armament the engine might have. That they outnumbered us by a wide margin did not come up at all, I do not think, for we have by now gotten quite used to being greatly outgunned.

What this new monster of industry was – and confirming that it is related to the company set out to oppose us – shall remain a thing for another day. Still, we are quite certain that it was definitely no accident, as certain as we are that their actions are those of cowardly men. Should we encounter them again, I can only imagine that we will take Miss Bowe up on her offer of tracking them or avail ourselves of Eddy's tracking skills, for common sentiment aboard ship is that the world would be a better place for their absence.

Repairs to the suit have begun while the rest of us recuperate. Sir James, in particular, while not badly hurt so far as anyone can tell, is badly shaken. As such, he has taken to bedrest for an uncertain amount of time. In this, he joins his sister, who continues to struggle with occasional spells of weakness and fatigue since the storm. Knowing the Coltranes, I am certain we will see both about again as soon as they are able.

Yours,
Gregory Conan Watts

The West by Land
Push to the Pacific

November 6th, 1815
44°36'N 110°47'W

My Dearest Cordelia,

    It has been a grand day. The past few days of travel had been mostly consumed with plans and discussions of readying ourselves to deal with ground travel and the terrible cold of this winter. Much as I would prefer to do everything from the dirigible, it was agreed that we could hardly claim a passable land route without documentation from the ground. Likewise, while a summer passage would be infinitely preferable, we work with what we have. Miss Bowe assures us that a number of possible routes exist, and has led us towards one of the more manageable in her estimation.

    She also gave me some confidence in her knowledge of the area, as well as giving us all a break from the repeated planning sessions. As we approached a region in the foothills she grew quite excited, insisting we all needed to anchor for a time and come down to the ground. She assured us that it was quite safe, and the cold would not be a problem for long. Though puzzled, we dressed as best we could for the weather and most of our number made their way to the ground.

    Immediately I was struck with a strange, sulfurous odor which seemed to hang over everything. It was not overwhelmingly powerful, but all-pervading. Miss Bowe eventually led us to the source of the smell, coming from all about us. There were a number of strange pools of scalding water throughout the region. She said that they were perpetually heated by magma underground, closer to the surface than normal. The pools were amazing enough, and a few of them even openly boiled and shifted on their own, despite the still day. More impressive still were great geysers of water, which erupted violently from beneath the ground in places. Miss Bowe knew them all well enough and kept us clear, thankfully. I was able to take a few pictures to send along, but have to wonder if they are nearly as impressive with little to give them scale. In any case the presence of all of the pools kept the area much warmer than a lot of the surroundings, which I was grateful for.

Still, the greatest wonder of the day, at least to those who had become accustomed to being half frozen, was still ahead. We had to return to the ship and travel a short distance off our route, but Miss Bowe again insisted it would be well worth our while. When we set down again there were more pools, still smelling of sulfur, but these were merely pleasantly hot, rather than boiling. She insisted they were entirely safe, but heated naturally. Some of the natives, she said, attributed healing powers to these springs. I do not give any credence to any mystical healing, but in such cold climes I can only imagine a chance to get the chill out of your bones would do anyone some good. We separated into the appropriate groups. Eddy and Miss Penn quietly exchanged a couple of ribald quips after it was decided we would bathe in the pools, but any such talk was quickly quashed by more sensible members of the group, and the women went their way, the gentlemen another.

The scent was still difficult to deal with, but I eventually became used to it. In any case, it was a small price to pay for the chance to literally wash away the chill. I am certain that even in warmer times the water would be refreshing, like a bath that never cools.

The presence of such a natural wonder also confirms Dr. Bowe's accounts of this part of the near west. He described much of it perfectly. Still, far harder journeys lie ahead. For the moment, after such a day as today, I cannot help but be optimistic. The task ahead is daunting, but it seems a little less so now that I'm warm at last.

My love, always,
Gregory Conan Watts

November 7th, 1815
45°21'N 111°44'W

Dear Sir,

We have had another day of some occasion as we traveled
into the beginnings of these great and Rocky Mountains. Maps to
this region are included among my notes and pictures. Eddy and
Miss Bowe have begun preparing for this leg of our venture, for
which time four of us will be quite alone. Miss Wright has
temporarily given up most of her trappings of civilization for as
warm of clothes as she could manage, for since we need our
guide, she still felt that under no circumstances should Miss Bowe
travel unattended with two gentlemen of England. I will be
documenting our progress here, while Eddy is the last of our
company.

For the first time, we shall have no support from the
dirigible no matter how much we may wish it, for they are
seeking a trail by which they may easily travel through the
mountains. Miss Bowe has provided some information, and
according to her, one could eventually travel around them far to
the south, but that would put the one in range of sighting by
Spanish rockets. For now, it is daunting, but I am certain they will
find a route which is passable by air at least as simply as we shall
find a way traversable by foot. Miss Bowe assures me that it
should be no great difficulty, for she knows a path that leads to the
lands to the west. The terrible cold, the deeper snow here, and the
weight of the packs of supplies and my camera all make this hard
to believe, even if the route is known to her. We have split the
weight as reasonably as we can, and the two hunters among us
have not doubted they could restock our food supplies. There is
plenty of wooded land here for firewood. Water, in the form of
these snows, is more plentiful than any of us could ever wish for.

While on the first of these hunts today, Eddy believes he
has found sign of human passage here, though thankfully no sign
of the trackless engine. I could not imagine that such a thing could
ever navigate ground like this in any case, but I am nonetheless

grateful, and do not look at all forward to coming across that terrible piece of artifice again. Once she was shown the sign Eddy came across, Miss Bowe was in agreement. We have set camp in as protected a place as we may, trying to find reasonable compromise between ability to see people coming and protection from hostile gunfire. I fear that despite my military experience, I have been little help, for ever since we put down camp, Miss Bowe and Eddy have been about discussing tactics in a manner very unlike military talk. Here, the lay of the land very much influences their decisions not only of travel, but how we may protect ourselves as we go. There is much about not giving away our position and keeping to locales where we may move around an ambush. There has also been talk of trying to take the fight to them, in the hopes they have not seen us.

To this end, conditions are even more miserable than previously described. We cannot light more of a fire than a small bed, and even then in heavy cover, just enough to warm our hands and lay a pot within to melt snow. Even then, our experts watch the surrounding region closely to ensure we have not given away our position. I am certain in the future I shall remember this as a most exciting and adventurous time in my life, but for the moment, it is all I can do to not worry about freezing to death.

Yours,
Gregory Conan Watts

From the journals of Gregory Conan Watts,
November 12th, 1815
45°13'N 112°38'W

We have made better progress than I ever might have
hoped. Whatever my employer is paying Miss Bowe, it cannot be
nearly enough, for she moves through this land as easily as a man
moves through his home. The ground is difficult, the snow is
deceptively deep, and freezing remains a constant risk. Miss
Wright in particular has looked constantly most troubled by the
journey and the terrible cold, but she has not yet complained for
it.

We also have some bit of help from now being able to light
a fire. After the discussion of two nights past now, it was decided
that we would not be able to survive the deeper mountains
without being able to build a fire, so our only options were to deal
with the men sharing the valley with us or to outpace them. While
this set of choices was discussed for a time, it was finally decided
that while were it either Eddy or Miss Bowe alone, they would
prefer to outpace their pursuers than take the risk of fighting, but
with the camera and two inexperienced people with them, they
would have to take the chance.

This was a mission on which stealth and position would
have greater meaning than number of guns, if they were to have a
chance of success, so they found a place where Miss Wright and
myself could take cover, with only one easy avenue of approach
that I could defend us for a time at least. Miss Wright had one of
the pepper-boxes as well, but had barely ever handled a gun
before.

They left an hour before dawn, cautioning us once more to
start no fire, no matter how cold we became, and listen for any
suspicious sound. They gave us a word by which we might
recognize their return. I will say here that nothing so makes one
aware of every slightest sound of a wooded area as being told to
be aware of suspicious sounds. I cannot estimate how many times
myself and Miss Wright startled, and she nearly screamed some
few times at what we eventually deemed to be nothing. It is

fortunate that we did not have to use our guns, for I am certain my fingers were too cold then to find the trigger, but I know I reached for my pistol a number of times.

I do not know how long we huddled nervously amidst our blankets and thick clothing, jumping at the sounds of the woods and trying not to imagine the worst of scenarios, but the sun was not too far up in the sky when the sound of shooting began. I believe the first thing I heard was the sharp crack of Eddy's prized rifle, but cannot be absolutely certain. Though our woodsmen have not spoken much of what occurred, I would like to think they found the men trying to locate us and whatever location they'd chosen for an attempt at ambush before they were sighted themselves. They have confirmed that they were not native men, and they are certain that it was to be an ambush. Soon after that first shot, many more followed. There must have been a dozen men at least, or they were armed with variations upon repeating pistols as we have been. I was able to distinguish the difference between the thunder of musket fire apart from the sharp snaps of Eddy's rifle, picking out his shots from theirs, and at least confirming he was still alive. Only some few shots into the exchange, the screaming began, with shouts of commands mixing with shouts of pain, both from many sources. It seemed the enemy was quite confused to have been found and confronted as they were, and perhaps they had thought we would not find sign of them.

The two returned together, giving the password that we should know it was them and let them approach. Even so, I almost attempted to fire out of nervous reflex, fumbling for the gun, for I had not at all heard either of them until they shouted out the password. It is possible that even for all the precautions we have taken, they could have gotten back into camp without our notice. Miss Bowe was a terrible sight, bloody, though I saw no wound on her, and as dark and intense as I have ever seen her. I know it had to be done lest they ambush us with greater numbers, advantageous ground, and firepower, but it currently still seems a terrible thing to me, to see her in this state. I had quite worried she might seem to enjoy it as much as she had the assassins' fight in

England, but this has nothing of the same feel to it. Pure and simple, this was work for snipers and assassins, putting men in the ground with little opportunity for them to even see death coming. Certainly they knew the risks when they took payment to come after us, but there was no cheer in our companions, just a workmanlike resoluteness to their mood, doing what they had to do in a fight for survival with greater numbers of determined rivals.

It was not nearly so many as in the group reported to be aboard the other dirigible, of that they were certain, so we suspect that the other airship has outpaced us and scattered gunmen throughout the entrance to every apparent valley they could find in a reasonable range. Had we taken another route, we likely would have found a similar ambush. I am becoming quite worried for our companions as they seek a point where the peaks are low enough or there are sufficient valleys to move the airship through. Should our opponents have found these same spaces in advance, the *Dame Fortuna* will be in danger of being targeted by rockets.

They are loath to speak of details, much as Eddy often has a dark humor, and they have spoken of similar campaigns in times past. Perhaps they will do so again over this when it is a recollection, and not our current situation. Eventually, I am fairly certain I will be grateful that they are not sharing much information, even if my reporter's mind is curious, in some dark way. They have shared at least one detail for certain, as it is information we did need for peace of mind, of a sort. Despite that assurance, the news and the look of them when delivering it chilled me almost as much as it comforted me: they left not a man alive.

November 15th, 1815
45°30'N 113°55'W

Dear Sir,

It has been a terrible struggle against the elements, and even Miss Bowe, though not seeming inconvenienced, has stated that this winter is exceptionally cold and the snowfall heavy here. Had she any less certainty in her course, we would likely have turned back some time ago, for the walk is often most difficult. Some hours we must spend in what caves (some made solely of snow) or cover we can to avoid the wind. Still, she has not wavered or turned back even once, absolutely positive of her route through the mountains. Were it not for this, I am certain we could have spent several weeks surveying this territory and not found a sure way through, and even more likely, we could easily have gotten lost here to never be seen again.

Hunting, at least, has not been difficult, for game here is plentiful, and we have two very skilled woodsmen providing for only four people. I do, however, worry for Miss Wright. She showed great courage in coming to attend to Miss Bowe, and she is a strong and hardy woman, but this is clearly beyond her experience, and not at all like English or Virginia winters, even at their most difficult. We have twice had to stop for a longer period than we might have hoped in order to allow her to rest and warm herself when she nearly collapsed. Should she take ill, we would have a much greater difficulty on our hands, for there is no medicine and no place of any warmth to go to, and we even lack the supplies for tanning hides and furs that Miss Bowe or Eddy could make replacements or additions for clothing, though they are considering working out what they can so that Miss Wright might have more and warmer blankets. She does not often complain of the cold or fatigue, but she struggles and lags behind, even when Eddy has forged just ahead of her and I with a lumbering gait to better break up the snow and create a trail we can more easily follow.

Miss Bowe states that we still have some days to travel at

this rate in order to emerge from the mountains, and even there, we can only hope we will soon locate the airship soon once there. In the time in between, we are trying to find the best compromise between making haste and giving us enough rest that Miss Wright's condition does not deteriorate. We passed the highest point yesterday, but it is not straight downhill from here.

Yours,
Gregory Conan Watts

November 18th, 1815
45°23'N 114°17'W

My Dearest Cordelia,

I can only imagine that you would sympathize greatly with poor Miss Wright. I know your health has in some times been quite delicate, and you have spent much time abed. Miss Wright, though she still faces her difficulties courageously when she has her wits about her, grew ill two days past. We had attempted to avoid this by taking frequent stops for her to rest – for which I here quietly admit to being grateful myself. While I wished I could be of more help to our trailblazers, I was exhausted.

Initially, she collapsed while we walked and could not find her feet again, let alone continue. We set up camp and built the warmest fire we have had yet, and tried to let her rest and recover her energies. Her fever only grew. We cared for her throughout the night, and Miss Bowe has managed to create her a weak broth that she has been able to keep down, which has been something, but along with tea, is all she is able to handle. Though it is warm, and we make sure to feed her regularly to help ward off the chill, it cannot be enough to help fortify her long against the cold.

After that first day, when it was determined her condition was not improving, it was decided we had best press on as quickly as we can. Miss Bowe has ladened herself with most of Miss Wright's supplies in addition to her own, and some part of Eddy's. I have taken the rest of Eddy's gear, while he carries Miss Wright, bundled in as many blankets as we can manage. We stop often to let him rest, to fill her with warmed broth and place her by a fire, and to look after her condition. Miss Bowe has shown some talent for backwoods medicine, and while it is hardly a physician's care, she is still among us. Eddy has been able to do little but rest on our frequent stops, for the exertion of carrying a person's weight over this terrain strains even so large and strong a man. Even so, when recovered, he goes about gathering wood and tending the fire so that Miss Bowe can hunt when needed, scout about us for danger, and work on preparing the broths and making new blankets and shoes for Miss Wright. It is messy work, but we are hopeful it will be done in time to do her some good.

Out of necessity and desperation, Miss Bowe has begun to instruct me in how to handle the hides, for they take a good deal of attention and regular maintenance in the progress towards becoming clothing. I have a great deal more respect than I had previously for the furrier's trade.

Eddy himself is almost inconsolable. Had I not observed it before, I now would be most absolutely certain that he is quite in love with Miss Wright, and his spirit would be crushed if he failed her now after permitting her to come along out of some highly developed sense of propriety. He looks after her with such care, and though we can tell easily how much it is exhausting him bit by bit, he has not yet said a word as to the difficulty of carrying her such a distance.

Miss Wright, for her part in this, seems less and less aware of us and our efforts by the hour, but at least she does not fight our efforts to feed her, and she is sleeping when we stop to rest, and even sometimes while Eddy carries her through the mountains.

I do not know that this letter, either, will ever see you, but as always, you are my comfort and solace, my love, and when I have such troubles weighing my mind, I know that I am in your thoughts and prayers, and have hope that we shall survive this experience after all.

My love, always,
Gregory Conan Watts

From the journals of Gregory Conan Watts,
November 22nd, 1815
River fork 45°17'N 114°37'W

We have at last found some help and hope in these
mountains, though I do not know if it will be enough, or if we
found it in time.

The valley has led us to a native village of a tribe Miss
Bowe calls Apsáalooke. That she has been here before is obvious,
for she speaks the language fluently, and after what seemed some
enthusiastic debate, we were eventually welcomed among them.
The people of the tribe know her, and treat her almost as one of
their own. She hunts with their men freely, though Eddy has been
forbidden in their hunts. They are, however, most interested in his
rifle, as they have only a few firearms among their number, mostly
received from fur trappers who had come into this territory. We
have seen no trappers' camps, but it is known that some
Frenchmen had been into this land before us.

I cannot make out a word of the language, and while Miss
Bowe has spoken some few names in introduction, I have
difficulty managing even that much of their words. Still, they have
given us shelter, warmth, and eventually welcome when we were
in most desperate need, so I have attempted to be polite. For the
greatest part, my efforts seem to amuse them more than anything.
At one time I might have been offended, for their ways are strange
to me as well, but when a people have helped to save my life, and
possibly those of a traveling companion, it becomes much harder
to take offense with them. If this was a society which Miss Bowe
knew as well as she seems to before coming into our company
then I can also see where she gets much of her habit. They are a
savage people, certainly, but also quite at home on this land, and
most generous with strangers who have come out of the
mountains. I cannot make much of what I see here mesh with the
tales of wild and vicious Indians from the most popular stories of
them. They place a great deal of emphasis on family, and caring
for both their children and their elderly. The latter receive great
reverence from the rest, and their wisdom and experience seems

to guide much of the tribe's decision making, and certainly that of individual families from what I have been able to observe.

With some explanation from Miss Bowe, a couple of the younger men have permitted me to photograph them, but the older members of the tribe are firm in refusing that I be permitted to do so, and I will respect their wishes. I am almost out of pictures as well until I can get more paper, so I am trying to save these last few pictures for the truly unusual.

A topic of especial debate related to Miss Wright. Miss Bowe has affirmed that they were at first most reluctant to allow any of us entry to their camp when they learned we had an ill person among us, for it is oftentimes seen as a terrible omen. For this reason, there was some discussion, but they are people of strong sympathies, and certainly seem to understand the bond we have with Miss Wright. That sympathy and good character would ultimately win out, and since that time they have seen to her care. Eddy and myself are forbidden to see her, but Miss Bowe has assured us that she could not find a better chance of survival anywhere west of New York. Though I have my doubts of that, I am certain that I could certainly do no better, and her caretakers have been very determined and attentive. In our last days of travel, Eddy carrying Miss Wright the entire way, I was growing quite discouraged for her chances. Now, at least, we have hope.

Despite all the courtesy and care they have shown us, and despite Miss Bowe seeming at home here, the rest of us could not be more of outsiders, and I think the Apsáalooke will be quite pleased to see the backs of us. Miss Bowe and their scouts are both watching the skies for our airship. In almost any other circumstance, I know myself enough to say that I should very much share the sentiment, and be quite unhappy to be among ungodly savages. But these are good people who have taken in three strangers and a woman who, much as they speak to her as one of their own daughters, is still a white woman. They have given us food and cared for our sick, and for the first time that I can rightly remember, I am finally warm again.

December 1st, 1815
45°17'N 114°37'W

My Dearest Cordelia,

On most accounts, today is one of the happier days I have had in this journey. Despite that, and having a great deal of good news to share, I cannot help but feel for my friend Eddy.

Miss Wright awoke this morning with her fever broken and in good spirits, most eager to be on her feet and moving again, though it is agreed she needs to rest for some time before she will be prepared to travel again. At this time, I cannot much complain about spending more time among the Apsáalooke, for my early concerns for savage ways and unholy ritual has been replaced with a writer's curiosity. I still cannot make my tongue find its way around their words, but at least they still find it amusing that I try, and some few have agreed to respond to nicknames that come somewhere close. Miss Bowe is also a patient translator back and forth, though they have little time to give interviews.

For as generous as they have been, this winter is apparently most difficult for this region, and their old men and women have spoken of a time of great difficulty ahead, as they read the signs and skies. They are careful with their food and preparations, and may have to move completely, though it may bring them into some conflict with other tribes. The only reason they allowed us here was the respect they hold for Miss Bowe and her father, a detail about which she was hesitant and embarrassed enough to translate that I am fairly certain she speaks the truth, even had she ever seemed given to idle boasting. She has done everything she is able to make sure she leaves them with more than we consume, and after much discussion with Eddy and myself, we have agreed to give them one of the pepper-box pistols once we have shown them how to load it. While it is a rare prize to be certain, they are most certainly responsible for saving Miss Wright's life.

She is a difficult patient, apparently, not able to get up and do a great deal yet, but not wanting to sleep either. We have allowed her to occupy her hands with checking my camera for any damage due to the cold, and cleaning the pistols, keeping her reasonably happy.

During this time, she also learned fully what Eddy had done for her, and somewhere along the way, he expressed some deeper feeling for her. This was a difficult conversation to be near, and I feel terrible on behalf of my friend. I do not believe he meant to say anything of the sort, for when he is not darkly amused by his own black humor, Eddy is most often shifting between grimly determined and stoic. She was most grateful for his efforts, certainly, and cannot thank him enough, but she reverted somewhat to a Virginian's practicality and forthrightness in admitting she did not share his feelings, or have anything in her heart for him but great admiration and friendship. It seems she has her heart quite set upon never returning to the rural life, and being married to one of the young gentlemen of London and becoming a woman of the city.

He was a good gentleman about it, of course, but he has not been the same since. It is difficult to gain a real sense of privacy here, as we know no one save each other, and it is most bitter cold without the windbreak from these tents they have provided us, but he has been as isolated as he might be under the circumstance ever since, though whenever she happens to come about, he does ask Miss Bowe after Miss Wright's condition, and when we might resume our travels.

I now fear that two of my companions shall have a great trouble ahead with matters of the heart. I feel for them, certainly, but must also be grateful that I have the love and inspiration of a finer young woman than I could ever hope for, and she awaits our success back in England.

With Miss Wright recovering rapidly and the progress we have made so far, I am more hopeful by the day that our return will come quickly, though it cannot possibly arrive soon enough.

My love, always,
Gregory Conan Watts

December 3rd, 1815
West of 45°17'N 114°37'W, Cloudy.

Dear Sir,

We have at last left the hospitality of the Apsáalooke, and while it makes me long for sight of civilization again, I will always appreciate having had this experience to see the natives in their own homes. To see them as they truly live rather than how they are portrayed in the wild tales that reach England. Miss Bowe has cautioned me that there are tribes more violent than the Apsáalooke, but we shall be avoiding most of those by a wide margin in the path she has laid for us. For the moment, I have quickly been reminded just how cold this winter has become. I can only venture that if we were seeking a way through these mountains blindly, we should have long since been dead of cold or starvation. We now have better boots for the climes, and blankets as well, but the greater weight of winter packs has slowed our progress as well. Still, in those times that we pause to rest or set camp for the night, I believe it well worth it.

I would strongly caution every man who will follow us to follow the route we are mapping exactly, for this region teems with wild things, and even more dangerous, any number of places where a man not being very precise with his step could plunge to his death, wander down some false trail to never be seen again, or any number of other perils. I would also suggest that this is a far better trip during the spring and summer months, though I am told that much of the region has snow early in Autumn and late into the Spring.

I would also recommend including some frontiersman or trapper who might know some piece of the tongue of the Apsáalooke, for in speaking with Miss Bowe, I have learned that this tribe is very spread throughout the surrounding territories. They could be great allies in learning the lay of the land and finding the way around if they can be befriended, while such numbers, if there is any true alliance between those who identify themselves as a part of this people, would make terrible enemies if provoked to violence. Though it is true that they have few guns, save those they have traded for, they have skilled warriors among them, mastery of their own simpler weapons, and hunters who share Miss Bowe's gift for moving unheard.

Though their entire village is capable of being packed and moved, should their food supply shift enough to merit it, and they likely will, once they no longer wish so much shelter from the winds and snow as they have found in this place, I have still marked it on the map, for if given reasonable gifts and offer of friendship, this people and this village have proven helpful to at least this one group of travelers.

I am not including so many pictures as I had before, as I am almost out of supplies for the camera. Much as I would wish to include far more of the Apsáalooke and the area we have recently traveled through, many of them refused to have their pictures taken, and I am saving my last pictures for more unusual events. I have tried to make up for this by giving some written detail upon the included map, and individual descriptions of some of the things we have seen here. Rest assured that should anything truly uncommon turn up, I will attempt to include a photograph, but for the moment, one of the greatest dangers of this area is that so much of it looks very much alike, with many of the same sounds and similar life and flora. If we did not have the guide we have – and had our path not been clearly marked by passage through the village – I could not tell at all if we had traveled this ground already or not.

Yours,
Gregory Conan Watts

From the journals of Gregory Conan Watts,
December 5th, 1815
45°33'N 115°28'W

Disaster almost struck us today. We have not yet entirely emerged from the mountain region but are out of the thickest part of them and reaching the foothills. Travel is somewhat easier now, but still far from easy. Much of yesterday was spent having to forge our way through blowing, deep snow, and I do not know entirely how we managed to make any kind of time at all, or at many times, even keep moving forward, as the wind would tug our snowshoes in all directions. Miss Bowe tried to keep us sheltered as often as possible, and with some success, though often paths were very specific, and required her moving well ahead of us to scout the way. This did give us some opportunity to rest. At other times, there was simply no help for it, and Miss Wright and I followed in Eddy's path. Such travel as this is best left to a Finn or Norwegian, not men of England. The warmth of a good fire or even the Apsáalooke village now seems a distant memory.

We can confirm that there is a way, likely not far from here, where an airship can make it through the mountains, however, for we saw a ship that we took for our own.

Moving out into the open, we tried to signal them until Eddy managed to clear the glass of his lenses and got a closer look at it before we could put up a signal rocket, and warned that it was not our own. We found cover again quickly amidst the hills, but either they saw us, or were already trying to find us. Some hours later, Eddy was perceptive enough to notice some motion he felt was odd higher up the rocky hills through which we are traveling. Miss Bowe separated from us then to try to gain a better idea of who or what might be up there, for she has figured out how to better move over the top of the snow and ice than those of us less used to these environs. I believed I heard a deep voice then, with a Irish accent if I do not miss my guess. I do not know the language, but Eddy knows some small piece of it, and has agreed that he heard the same thing.

Just after this, we came under fire from somewhere above. We ran then, finding some cover amidst trees and hills where we believed we would not likely be seen from the shooters' apparent position. Eddy said he counted at least five, unless they had repeating guns like our own, though I do not imagine the pepper-boxes would do more than fire one shot currently, the mechanisms must certainly be frozen. Eddy listened to their shots and eventually put his head up, only to quickly shout a warning and duck back down as a crashing and rumbling noise came from above.

Either someone had prepared a trap, or the gunfire had brought down some part of the snow from the mountains and larger hills in a great, sweeping wave. It washed over us, our eternal burial prevented only by our shelter, which left us with a small pocket of air and darkness, surrounded by snow of an unknown depth. Miss Wright panicked at first, but we calmed her nerves as quickly as we could, reassuring her that there was nothing to worry about. For a short time, while Eddy and I dug and did not at first find daylight, I was worried as well but did not voice my worries. Eddy struck daylight first, just as I was growing somewhat concerned about how much air we might have. The shooters must have been gone by then, for Eddy was not fired upon. There is faint hope that they may have been lost amidst the avalanche as well, but no one takes that possibility seriously. We are not so fortunate.

As we were emerging, we found Miss Bowe searching for us. She had found a way up to where the shooters had been, but by then they had left, and much of their track was obscured under the new wave of snow, that she could not tell what had become of them. We have been much more alert since that time, and have returned to keeping only tiny cooking fires when we must light a fire at all.

By the time all of this had passed, we had lost all sign of the dirigible, likely among the mountains. We are certain now that they found a path through or around the mountains, or perhaps have friends among the Spaniards, and they then traveled ahead of us and left mercenaries both ahead and behind us. No one has passed us, and Miss Bowe is certain there is not another easy way through the mountains near here. I worry most for the possibility that they may have in some way tied themselves to the Spanish to our south, for that would mean much of the far west coast could easily be forewarned and quite hostile to us, and there may be many more men looking for us here, some of whom may be trained soldiers or else natives aligned with Spanish forces. Thinking we had left our pursuit far behind, we have made no real effort to cover our tracks. Our best hope now is to make haste and trust that our guide has superior knowledge of these lands to anyone that might be set against us currently.

From the journals of Gregory Conan Watts,
December 8th, 1815
46°01'N 115°54'W

   We encountered some part of our pursuit today, and have
seen their airship again. While we were resting, there was some
noise from the higher grounds around us. Though we have been
told to keep as quiet as we are able when at rest, some noise
startled Miss Wright, and she screamed. This brought a flurry of
motion higher up, and forced us to react quickly.

   Though we were certain we had not been seen, the sound
was enough to catch someone's attention, and soon there was a
round of musket fire all about us, one shot striking a tree within
my line of sight. We scrambled for greater cover. Miss Wright and
I traveled deeper into a wooded area while Eddy and Miss Bowe
split to either direction, seeking some vantage point from which to
bring the fight to our enemies. We soon lost sight of them. Some
time passed before anyone fired again, each side not wishing to
give away their position. When I did at last hear a new round of
gunfire, it was Eddy's rifle, followed by a man's scream, a
different man shouting, a second shot, and silence. I almost
shouted to him for a report, but remembered that we have not
seen these people traveling in any group smaller than five yet.

   There was a shout in another direction, and then the sound
of footsteps coming our way. The steps turned into a run, and a
shot struck a tree only just to my side. Close enough, in fact, I was
struck in the face with wood splintering from the impact of the
musket ball, and it was something of a small miracle that I was not
made half blind. I was quite startled, of course, reacting slowly as
three men emerged from the woods near us. One stopped to
reload his musket while the others, coming from behind us, tried
to move to where they could get a clear shot. I managed to be
faster, some part of my old training coming to the fore, and lifted
my gun, shooting one man in the center of his chest as he was
lifting his gun. I attempted to turn the pepper-box to bring around
another chamber, only to find, as I had suspected in less hurried
times, that the mechanism was quite frozen solid and would not

turn.

I thought I was a dead man, but before he could fire, a knife buried itself in the side of his neck. He dropped to his knees in the snow without firing a shot, as the first was still struggling to load his gun with gloved hands. Miss Bowe was upon him, and had cut his throat a second later, as he was turning to face the way the knife had come from. He fell, and then she made certain the other two were dead before approaching us. Eddy came a few minutes after while we collected ourselves, once we had gone a bit deeper into wooded areas. Miss Bowe reported that she had seen a larger company, but most had gone another way while the group of three had been sent directly towards us. I am just grateful she came back.

Eddy had a similar report, having found a scouting group of three. He was able to shoot down two of them before the third had disappeared. Eddy had followed for a time, but heard more voices than he had bullets, and ventured back to locate us once more. He has been able to confirm that there was a deep Irish voice among those he overheard. In time, they elected that we should track them a way, and when we come close enough, Miss Wright and I should stay back. They do not wish the inexperienced among us moving alone or straying too far from the other pair. We found their tracks easily enough, enough men that I could not have missed them. We followed for a long time, before we came around a bend to see the dirigible in the distance. Eddy, with his lenses, was able to make out men climbing a rope ladder to it.

Not wishing to see too many reinforcements, and believing the group that had gone away from us was likely going back to their ship to report, we changed course, and began once more to try to get out of the foothills entirely before they could catch up with us again. We are covering our tracks more now so that they cannot track us so easily, though it slows us down. Still, it seemed a wise suggestion.

Now that we have seen areas where a dirigible may leave and pick up its troops, we can only hope to find some sign of our own soon. I should be glad to leave these murderers and the terrible cold behind for my quarters and easy travel once again, and I know Miss Wright feels much the same. At least we can be fairly certain that once we travel only a short distance further we should be able to keep track of the other dirigible if it pursues us, and should be able to see it before it could see us. There is also the risk, of course, that they may be able to see our company. I am trying not to consider that they might already have found them.

December 11th, 1815
46°25'N 117°01'W

Dear Sir,

We have at last emerged from the hills and found ourselves in more level territory once again. Despite the change in terrain, it is no warmer here, and now we are more exposed to the wind. We have sighted the opposition's vehicle three times now, but it seems to be keeping to the mountains, probably believing that there is no means by which we could have evaded their notice without doubling back into that greater cover. Eddy has been able to determine, with his goggles, that they occasionally pause to bring men up or down their rope ladder. If it has been combing the mountains so long as it seems to have in search of us, then it must have some kind of source of fuel here. Dr. Mitchell's work on our dirigible has made it much more efficient for this, but all others still should have similar range, unless it is turning back soon – or they have some similar developments.

The other possibility is that they have some sort of agreement with the Spanish. After all, they did seem to once number a Spaniard among their company. While the Spanish have no dirigibles of their own, what fuels we use to power them might not be entirely a secret. I cannot imagine that any Englishman would risk our national secrets in such a fashion, but it is possible that the Europeans among their number may have mutinied, or your opponent does not know what the opportunists he has hired have done.

This is a matter of emergency enough that I will be attempting to get this report back to you as soon as is at all possible. We have evidence enough, certainly, of our travels that we can confirm that Dr. Bowe has come this way in the past, and his daughter, no doubt, knows this land well, so if we must turn back, then we shall do so that English forces might be aware of the risks, unless some greater information presents itself.

For the time, we still wonder what has happened to our own company, for we have seen no sign of them. While we wait, I have not been entirely idle, or forgetful in the attempt to watch our own backs. I have continued to map our progress, now a complete route through the mountains from east to west. I can only imagine that in a warmer time, the land ahead of us would be well suited to settlement and some manner of farming, though Miss Bowe has stated that there are a number of tribes of varying temperament and society in this region, depending on which way one travels.

We are currently paused to try to wait for our ship, to keep track of the other, and to determine how best to proceed in the current situation. If we are to reach the west coast north of Spanish land, we must make our way westward, without turning south at all, but if we do not meet our dirigible sometime soon, and leave it too far behind, it could be some time before we could possibly chance to find one another again, and we dare not send up a signal rocket until we are certain our enemy would not see it and our own people would. Currently we are sure of neither.

Yours,
Gregory Conan Watts

From the journals of Gregory Conan Watts,
December 14th, 1815
46°15'N 117°25'W

Christmas approaches, but today I am simply grateful for
the gift of our lives. We emerged from most cover into flatter land
yesterday, and while we had hoped we were far enough ahead of
pursuit to avoid notice – and were focused at last on making good
time – they must have both a sharp-eyed scout and a telescope, for
we saw the opposing dirigible coming in our direction. Though
we disappeared again into wooded ground, going well out of the
way of the path we had hoped to take, it did not break off its
pursuit. Eddy was able to sight it deploying more men some miles
behind us after it had made up a great deal of ground. It then
moved beyond us to drop others. We traveled into deep country,
where we would be hard to follow, and worked for a time on
carefully making certain both my pistol and Eddy's rifle were in as
best of operating condition as we could want. Then Miss Bowe
decided that we were unlikely to do well with too large a group
trapping us here. She and Eddy argued briefly, but at last it was
agreed she would lead one of the groups away. She disappeared
into the wood, heading for the people behind us to cut them off
before they found our trail.

Though I do not know for certain what occurred while she
was away, I have her account of it. She came upon a group of men,
sighting them before they spotted her. Had she a company of men
with guns, she might have killed them then, but alone, would not
engage so many. She crossed their path ahead of where they
would travel, leaving a path they might easily follow to lead them
off. Moving back in her own footsteps, she found a place she
might watch them from. She reported that their company had
easily found the trail, and there a fierce argument erupted. A man
with a Spanish accent arguing that it was some trap or trick, for
there was only one set of tracks, and they were clearer than those
he had found nearer the mountains, while the other fellow,
seeming in charge of the company, an American by his voice, she
has reported, argued that it was the best sign they had, and they

should follow it. In the end, their number was divided, with four or five men traveling with each of them. The American followed her false trail into the wood, while the Spaniard tracked it back the other way until the point she had covered her tracks.

She followed the Spaniard, for she was more concerned for someone showing his skills than the other, to overhear him confirming to those men who had proven loyal to him that it was a trick, and to keep close, lest they be picked off one by one. Showing more sense than I've come to expect of her, she elected not to challenge five men with guns at once. They began to circle in the snow, intentionally leaving themselves a wide path to make passage back through the area easier. They spent considerable time seeking new tracks from Miss Bowe, in hopes of either tracking her down or driving her towards their other group.

While she evaded him, she reported it was a close thing, and throughout the experience, he was taunting her in English and Spanish alike – it seems she also knows something of the Spanish tongue, though I do not know yet how much. Though he attempted to get some reaction out of her, obviously, and kept his men quite on alert, she was at last able to get behind him by leaving a trail to direct them, and moving back by going through the trees in a wide circle. Some few times they paused, perhaps believing they had heard something, but it was not enough for them to change course. Still, she seems to have some respect for the tracking skills of this Spaniard, which is high praise indeed coming from our guide.

After delaying and misdirecting them, she came back to our location, and we moved throughout the rest of the day to put as much ground between us and them as we were able without moving toward the area in which the other dirigible dropped troops off. It circled for much of the day, but we made certain it would not see us. Still, it was a nervous day for all of us indeed.

Late in the evening, by climbing a tree, Eddy was able to see two campfires in opposite directions, one closer to us than we might have liked. Built high, these were used for signals, and the other airship picked up most of its men and moved further to the south, where it will likely drop these scouting parties off again tomorrow. Unless we can find some way to throw them off our trail entirely, the next days will be long ones indeed. Miss Bowe is talking of spending a portion of the night leaving another false trail leading south, since though they have one tracker among them who has seen through her ruse once, it divided their number before. While I am still making a map of our journey, I fear that it shall not be nearly so efficient a route as it might be were we not being pursued. I hope I can be forgiven this necessity when our final route is turned in as proof of Dr. Bowe's previous travel through this region. For that matter, I am even more concerned right now with having the opportunity to turn this in at all. Civilization seems further away each day.

From the journals of Gregory Conan Watts,
December 15th, 1815
46°19'N 117°34'W

Miss Bowe returned after her trip last night with report that they had left scouts behind to continue tracking us while the airship continued south. She had managed to hear them before they found her, and was able to separate the group. She stated that she was able to dispatch the men, one by one, and one time surprising three of them. I still have no reason to doubt her account, and she was in one of her deadly serious moods, with her hands and clothes alike stained with blood, when she returned to us. She believes there are others out there but made certain that they would track a false trail south by leaving those footprints directly away from a group of bodies.

She is concerned that the Spaniard or his equal is among their woodsmen, however, and no matter how determined they are to avenge their scouts, they will sooner or later see through the deception. As such, when she returned, she bade us move, even in the middle of the night, and keep to her footprints so we did not leave the path she forged for us, for we had to put all the ground we could between their men on the ground and ourselves while the airship was not searching for us as well.

We traveled through the night and well into the day with no concern now for cover, just haste and making up ground moving north and west. For now, while they are about, we cannot hope to meet our own company again, so we will travel to where Miss Bowe believes we might avoid them or have a more defensible position. There is some concern for the local tribes, and Miss Bowe has many times checked the trees about cleared areas.

We have also taken a terrible risk, especially recalling our encounter with the buffalo in the great plains. Finding a massive herd of elk, she led us between some of their number, though we kept as far away from any single one of them as we could. She cautioned us especially to avoid those which looked smaller than the rest, for while the calves would not be terribly obvious, some of the herd might still be defensive of the youngest. Though it seemed crazy at first, not only would our trail be covered over by the herd for quite some way should someone follow us back north, but she was challenging any of their trackers, whether her newest nemesis or any natives with whom they might have made a compact, to dare follow us through the middle of a herd of elk. By keeping quiet and following her advice, somehow we were able to navigate across the land without incident, and only a few nervous glances from some parts of the herd.

We have since found regions with greater protection from being sighted, and not having seen any sign of their ship or people, we have resumed covering our trail after us as we move. As I write this, Miss Bowe has agreed that we should spend four or five hours at rest, but no more than that, and she and Eddy are trading watches that Miss Wright and I may sleep the entire time, at least once I finish this account. I am exhausted after the best part of two days awake and walking, occasionally running, but I found I could not sleep until this account was completed, lest I forget some detail.

From the journals of Gregory Conan Watts,
December 18th, 1815
46°14'N 117°53'W

We are no longer being pursued. We have reached new
cover and higher ground from which we have been able to
observe the way behind us. Eventually, pursuit reached the herd,
of that much we are certain, for eventually we sighted a rocket
fired from near that region, and the airship traveled to their
location. With his lenses, Eddy was able to determine more men
were being picked up, and from there, the ship would travel north
a time before heading south once again. We have supposed that
there were simply too many possible routes we could have taken
for them to adequately trail us over open country once they lost
our trail and did not pick it up again quickly.

Though this is a relief, we still have seen no sign of our
company. There is some thought that they may either have seen
the other ship, and made no effort to cross the mountains in the
regions we were in, or they missed whatever areas the other ship
traveled through and they may have headed northward. We are
moving that way now, cautious for any sign that we may still be
being followed. Given the past evidence, it is hoped those who
were previously following us are either giving up, and going back
to some other plan, or have decided we traveled south instead for
more easily crossed and warmer lands once we hid our trail. In
any case, we are certain the enemy have lost enough men that they
will not spread their numbers too thin in trailing us. Additionally,
from our current vantage point, we should be able to notice their
dirigible anywhere in the region. For now, for the first time in far
too long, we are safe.

Miss Bowe is now less worried for direct pursuit, and more
for the local tribes, for not all are certain to welcome our group.
She continues to look for signs of their camps, usually built to
follow the local prey animals, though she believes many will try to
select locations to best protect them from the winter weather. The
days here are not so much shorter than they should be for the time
of year as in more eastern regions, but it is still unusually dark,

and very cold for this region, according to Miss Bowe. We have elected, on her advice, to try to give the local tribes as much space as possible to help prevent any hostilities. But in giving the tribes as much space as possible, we cannot go too far into some of those regions likely to give us the greatest cover from the weather ourselves.

Despite the cold, following the pursuit by many times our number of armed men, constant chance of ambush, and still facing the worst of the winter weather, the weather alone does not seem so terrible for the moment. I am certain I will think differently when we have a day or two more between us and the threat and I am more aware of lack of feeling in my hands and feet, but for the moment, this is a distinct improvement.

December 20th, 1815
46°01'N 118°29'W

Dear Sir,

We have at last made contact with our company again. Eddy made most certain to check the area for any sign, even distant, of the other ship before we signaled our ship, once he had confirmed it was ours. The suggestion that they might have gone north when they caught some sight of the other airship proved accurate. They are not certain if they were seen in turn, and simply lost pursuit, or if they managed to go unnoticed, but they were forced to abandon their intended path partway through, for worry that the other ship would have people on the ground with rockets, or that they might at least be able to track them and put us at risk. They traveled northward around the part of the mountains where we entered, and eventually found a way to travel across that was clear.

According to Miss Bowe, there is another, smaller mountain range to our west. After as accurately as she has led us, and having proved she knows not only the land, but the people of the land, and some of them know her, we are certain that there is no reason to doubt her accounts of what lies ahead still. As such, we will have to put down again in order to make accurate maps, but across open territories, or wooded land, we are trusting in her account and mapping from the air for the protection of our members. The opposing airship, while not in sight, cannot be more than a few days away, and knows that we evaded them, so they have either retreated out of need to restock their supplies, or have given up for the time being, thwarted by our ability to navigate the land and our dirigible's evading them. Given that they have the same accounts as we do of Dr. Bowe's works, we will doubtless encounter them again, but do not currently think it will be here in the American West.

We have elected to carry on with our mission as stated. If they have made some deal with the Spanish, then there is far more good they could be doing with an airship than trying to capture us now, especially with ours being the only air support the Americans of the South could currently expect. Any message sent to England would also be some time in arriving. We also have some engagements lying ahead of us which we cannot afford to miss. While a journey back to New Orleans would be welcome after some of what we have been through in recent times, it is entirely likely that this is part of what they wish to lure us into. Given all of this, Sir James is certain that the best thing we can do is move forward and not allow them to distract us from our pursuits.

For the terms of the wager, we currently have some advantage. Even if they now map the pass and trail over which they followed us, everything there would absolutely confirm Dr. Bowe's accounts of the American West and the trail by which one may travel from east coast to west without needing to move through territory occupied by the Spanish. If we are able to traverse this last obstacle, we can confirm at least that Dr. Bowe did thoroughly search, map, and write of Western America long previous to our movements. This, of course, is only one continent, and we have a long way to go before your bet can be completed. In the meanwhile, no matter that result, the maps included with this and other letters of our travels, along with photographs and descriptions of the things we saw upon our travels, should benefit England and its colonies should there be a push for westward expansion. For now, I will simply hope that the war effort proceeds well, and that in the time we have been away, the colonists have received more direct support and leadership from our armies.

One theory which has been put forth, now that he has been seen, is that the Spaniard and other Europeans among the numbers of our enemy are what they seemed to be, mercenary forces, but his presence among them might afford our enemies an ability to do trade with the Spanish forces, and likely warn them of our ship and align them against us without necessarily forging military alliance. This would still certainly be a betrayal, for our country remains aligned against Spain, and possibly soon will be at war, but does not yet guarantee that any of our secrets have fallen into enemy hands. This explanation, put forth by Sir James after assessing our pursuit and circumstances, would seem to fit what has happened so far, and why they feel so free to move north and south along the mountains, expend energy and fuel hunting us, and still do not put too much effort towards aiding the Spanish forces in more important regions.

I will continue to detail our theories and any evidence we collect as to their actions and alliances as we travel. So far, there is no proof of wrongdoing beyond attempting to murder our members in pursuit of their goals, though that should be quite enough of a problem, but their actions remain most suspicious. Despite the risk we continue on. You have been most generous, and along the way, our actions will serve the whole of England.

Yours,
Gregory Conan Watts

Letter from Heathsville, Northumberland County, Virginia Colony Archives, Wright Collection.
December 21st, 1815

To The Honorable Mr. Wright and Madam Wright,

First, and throughout reading this letter, please be assured of your daughter's health. This letter is not the bearer of bad news. I know that you must be worried about my dear Cousin, with her so far away.

I must admit that your worries are not without any reason. Your brave and sensible daughter volunteered for a most grievous duty. Our mountain party was planned to contain Mr. McBride, Mr. Watts, and Sam Bowe, when your daughter declared that Miss Bowe should not be the only lady in the party and promptly declared she would accompany them. As much as I did not like this plan, Harriet was resolute, and her presence would, indeed, solve the problem. I am ashamed to say that while on this trek, Harriet took a chill and caught fever somewhere on the great continental divide. I count this as a failure in my duties, as you had placed Harriet in my care.

Harriet owes her health to Edward McBride, who bodily carried her to safety, and to Miss Bowe, who knew where in this wilderness one could claim hospitality. Our Eddy is said to have carried your daughter 8 hours a day for 4 days to get her to a village that Miss Bowe could claim as friends. The women of this tribe, assisted by Miss Bowe, nursed Harriet back to warmth and health, and she was able to complete her journey with vigor, if not with full strength.

Indeed, you should be proud of your daughter, as she is now among the first non-native women to have crossed these rock strewn-mountains, and she did so in horrid winter. It may not be a claim banished anytime soon, for many a woman won't even think on the feat.

I also have news directly for Mr. Wright, in his role as Harriet's Father. I would not be too surprised if, once our exploration is done, you receive a visit from Mr. Edward McBride.

He has shown great concern for Harriet, and indeed, she owes him her life. You are, of course, aware of him due to his exemplary war record. James assures me that he owns Lands enough in Scotland to make a suitable match for the daughter of a gentleman farmer. I, however, hesitate in stating this, as I do not think that Harriet recognizes Mr. McBride's regard as the honor that it undoubtedly is. Mrs. Fisher and I will continue to ask her to think of her future, and there is time yet in this voyage.

Your Dutiful Niece,
Jillian Coltrane

The West on Water
Sea to Shining Sea

December 25th, 1815
Columbia River (we think)
45°45'N 120°13'W

My Dearest Cordelia,

Merry Christmas, my dearest! I hope the holiday season is treating you and your family well. Though it seemed like we were forever away from our companions and in the cold, we were returned to the dirigible just in time to meet the season in good company and good cheer. I am including several pictures of the native flora and fauna, which I will hope, though it will reach you late, suffice as gift for now. Though we met with only a partial success in the north, we have found what we were most seeking in the American West, and with both detailed maps and photographic proof of the journey. It seems as if I am well on my way to fame and fortune enough to satisfy your good father's demands of me that we might be married. Though we are far away, the return to warmth and companionship and the joy of the season has had me thinking of you.

Since our return to our fellows, Eddy has taken to spending a great deal of time in training Matthew the ways of his rifles. He is still not teaching him a great deal about actually shooting the weapons, which has been virtually forbidden by Mrs. Fisher, but Eddy assures us that Matthew will soon be entirely capable of cleaning, handling, and reloading the weapons without any need for coaching.

Sir James has also revealed that he hid away some amount of spirits appropriate to the season and insisted that we all come together, crewers included, for a toast to our successes so far and more to come. He has also promised that, when we return to something akin to civilization, we should all be presented with reasonable gifts for our travels. Giovanni Franzini availed himself of a greater amount of drink whenever Miss Bowe came near and he could not avoid it. Julietta Penn, in turn, has stayed closer to Samantha than ever since our return.

Miss Coltrane, in particular, was glad for Miss Wright's

return. Though she seems sometimes aloof, she is still her cousin's teacher, and she was obviously very worried for her health in the time apart. She also received news of the illness Miss Wright suffered, and apparently directly from Miss Wright, some news of the care she had while we were with the Apsáalooke. Though clearly distressed, she seems mostly just grateful for Harriet's return and has promised a shopping trip as soon as they are able.

Though I know I should not pry or report rumors, I feel that I would be remiss if I did not report to you that when they were in private chambers, and I was passing by on my way to play cards with Sir James, I did hear a small bit of an argument between the women. A few words were directed towards wondering why Miss Wright had put herself at such great risk, of course. But also, it seems that Miss Wright has said some small part about Eddy's affection for her, and that she has no interest in him. Certainly the expected gossip among young and unmarried women.

Miss Coltrane was shocked by this, and defended our Scotsman and his value as a match to Miss Wright, but Miss Wright was adamant and spoke instead of gentlemen of England. I cannot be certain, but despite the impropriety of such a match – a baronet's sister is a different thing from a baronet's colonial cousin – Miss Coltrane seems to have the affection for Eddy that her cousin lacks. I am also more sure than ever that Miss Coltrane has no interest in the many dashing and handsome men of money and society that wish her hand, and Miss Wright so fancies. I believe words such as boring, stuffy, and self-absorbed came up, while Miss Wright seemed rather aghast at such a suggestion.

Of course, it goes without saying that such accounts should not be repeated to anyone. It is certain, after all, that once we are returned to England, Miss Coltrane and Sir James alike shall soon have to marry. For the reception we already receive, and the station of the people they have attracted, I must imagine that both weddings will be almost royal events.

In more practical news, one of the finest presents I have yet heard for the lot of us is that Miss Bowe knows a few routes we might travel by to reach the west, but one of these is a river valley which goes all the way through the mountains, with waters which may be traversed, and the way should be viewed and traveled entirely by air. Dr. Bowe did, indeed, note such a route, though some parts are difficult along the river's path, but it would still permit us to complete our mission and map without needing to leave the ship for any long period, save to survey the river's path and ensure that it can be traveled. The thought of trying to move through a mountain valley without support from the air in the midst of this terrible winter, again, was not encouraging me in the least.

I will certainly have more to write later, my darling, but for the time being, I believe Sir James is offering another toast, at least among the gentlemen, and card games and talk shall go well into the night.

My love, always,
Gregory Conan Watts

From the journals of Gregory Conan Watts,
December 28th, 1815
Columbia River
45°56'N 122°51'W

I shall never forget this day so long as I live, and now I think I should not wish to, much as I had thought multiple times as we traveled that my end was drawing quite near. Two days past, we found the riverway Miss Bowe has spoken of a number of times since we set to charting our path. She says that this will carry us all the way to the Pacific Ocean if we wish it, though we elected to move through the mountains, rejoin the dirigible, and then take in the last of the journey from above, at the time, for sake of speed of travel and safety.

She did say she did not think we had a great deal to worry over from the natives here, so long as she was with the group, but Sir James is taking as few chances as possible in our endeavors. The success so far has excited him, and now that we are nearing the end of this quest, I believe he is most eager to move to the next. We have made up enough time in covering much of this country by air and water that we may be able to travel back to New Orleans before we travel southward. We hope to gain some news of the conflict and to determine if we are at war, for we are all quite eager to make certain that all goes well and England has responded before we spend a long period without any means of gaining any word. We are still awaiting the final bit of our travel, ensuring we hit no final obstacles, and seeing what Sir James decides we shall do next, though first, we anticipate a celebration of success in our westward journeys across North America.

When we found the river, Miss Bowe set to making us a small boat, attempting to show myself, Eddy, and Sir James how it might be done. It was a tiring process, but with all of us working, plus two of the ship's engineers, were able to quickly complete our second attempt at the craft, for the first was ruined by inexperience and enthusiasm in woodcraft. It was not the most comfortable of things from the first, with no efforts made towards fine details to permit anyone to ride comfortably, but she felt it would survive the river journey. Within this homemade boat, Miss Bowe, Miss Wright – quite insistent again that our guide should not be alone with unmarried men – Eddy, Sir James, and myself all made the journey, with the others watching our progress from above.

This was not at all like the trips aboard even small craft I have taken at home. The water was fast moving, and on more than one occasion we were having to row not for progress, which the river enthusiastically provided, but to avoid fallen logs, large rocks, patches of ice, and whatever other manner of obstacle it might put in our way. At the places where the water grew more narrow, we were moving especially rapidly, and control was all but impossible. Even with our best efforts, we hit many of the things we would rather avoid, and each time it was all we could do to hold onto the boat and not get thrown overboard, and even then we had a few close calls. At one point, Sir James caught my hand while I was flailing about trying to find some balance and nearly being carried into the water.

Even with all hands remaining aboard, many times, we were certain that this craft Miss Bowe instructed us to construct was going to be split apart when we hit the rocks, but each time, we managed to deflect off them or were carried over them with a terrible scraping noise, with the boat left whole. Miss Bowe has said since that she would have much preferred more time to construct the boat properly, which would have been nice to know beforehand, and that she would much prefer time to instruct us better in river navigation and rowing since, but we were all so excited and eager to get going that she made do with what she had. Despite these misgivings, she seems quite pleased by our successes, and in moving down the river, she was most enthusiastic and seeming to enjoy the journey that had so terrified the rest of us. When we finally set camp for the first night, the rest of us found it quite hard to manage to find our land legs again, and Miss Wright grew quite ill. Thankfully only in the most temporary of senses. I fear I did not fare much better and felt quite nauseous for a good time after we stopped.

Our following ship put down its ladders, and we collected gear, including my camera and writing materials, that I could document where we had come, for Miss Bowe had fortunately assured us we did not wish to bring anything unnecessary along on this journey. I certainly wish the people who will come after us luck, or larger and more sturdy craft, as well as skilled river pilots.

Today was much the same, though the water was calmer, or perhaps it was just that we had our first day of hard lessons behind us, and thus were better able to handle the obstacles that came up, having some idea what to expect. Sir James agreed that when we return to the dirigible, we will make our maps from above, instead of asking me to reliably sketch our path as we travel, but that we need to complete our journey through at least the mountain ways for proof it can be done.

The single most difficult times of the day, in their own fashion, were not the river obstructions, but those times when we began descent. For when we hit larger waterfalls, we had to make it quickly to shore before we were put over the falls, then find a way to travel while carrying the boat. While not so life-threatening as the river often seemed to be, carrying a hastily constructed boat of dense wood down an icy slope is almost precisely the joy it sounds. Miss Bowe had to spend quite a lot of this time navigating ahead, making sure we had the easiest possible path, one large enough by which to travel. With her keen guidance and knowledge of the area, some luck, and the muscle of our combined company, we were at last able to reach the river again each time. It is through greater luck still that no threat found us in this difficult situation, for even if we had warning, between the cold, numbness from effort of carrying the heavy thing, and the many splinters we collected during the trip, I do not imagine anyone would have been eager – or perhaps able – to handle firearms.

Miss Bowe has stated that we are nearing the end. For all its difficulties, following the river has been much swifter than going by foot. I shall be more than glad to see the end of this boat, and in the future, shall give her the time she wishes to construct the craft properly and make sure she is aware that no matter how eager we are to be going, that it is no cause for haste in preparation. I fear that such entreaties will fall upon deaf ears, of course, as Miss Bowe seems to thrill in living in the spur of the moment, and throwing herself into danger and excitement.

For now, I am simply glad for the news that we near the end, and proof of the concept of navigating this way, and seeing the last of this journey from the air. We can travel back the way we came, and in doing so, map the riverway accurately. We shall have to be most cautious in traveling too far back the way we came, however, for another airship, and its troop of men will certainly lie along our return path somewhere.

January 1st, 1816
Pacific Ocean Coast
46º08'N 123º53'W

Dear Sir,

Success at last! We have reached the Pacific Ocean, and flown over it for some time whilst we celebrated our victory. I will hope that this will make up for the bitter news of our partial failure in the far north, which we may try again in a warmer time. For now, I can absolutely state that not only is there certainly a route which one can take by ground from the Eastern reaches of America to the West, but every step of the trip can be found described in Dr. Bowe's journals. I cannot confirm that he moved far from the colonies and Europe yet, but he most certainly traveled the breadth of America.

It is a difficult path, and many skills are required, including good guides, gifts for the native peoples – and ideally someone who speaks or can learn their tongues – and some talent for river navigation, but the entire way can be traveled without need of airships. That we did so under great duress, and still in excellent time is only more testament to the company you have collected here.

When we reach civilization again, I shall be sending you my collected letters and maps and in time shall share what of my journals pertains to these travels as well. Along with all of this are the many photographs you will find collected, in careful order by the region.

Among these photographs you will find a few carefully marked. These are photographs of features of the northern Pacific shores that are unmistakably as Bowe described them in his journals. The first are the great stone arches, his fabled 'gateways from the Pacific.' The others are pieces of native art that the journals referred to as totem poles. Miss Bowe assured us the local tribes were friendly, when greeted properly. Dining with one of these gave me a good opportunity to take these latter photos up close so you can see the detail of the work. In any case, there can be no doubt that Dr. Bowe reached at least these far shores, and did so without benefit of an airship.

I must note, should effort be made to follow our route with a less knowledgeable guide, that our travel was almost entirely in winter, and an exceptionally cold and harsh one at that. In better times, the way will appear different, and while it should seem easier without the snow and ice, our guide assures us that better times would also have given us more trouble with some of the native peoples and other threats which abound along this difficult route.

All cautions and warnings aside, I am most excited for your success, sir, and we will be making haste to complete the next stage of our trip as soon as we have had a chance to renew our supplies, monitor the war efforts against the Spanish colonies, and send off the documentation we have so far.

It is a pleasure to be a part of this effort, Lord Donovan, and I am grateful to you for selecting me to travel with so elite a company as this. We have had our difficulties, certainly, but all are proud to act in the service of England and so fine a gentleman as yourself.

Yours,
Gregory Conan Watts

Letter from Heathsville, Northumberland County, Virginia Colony
Archives, Wright Collection.
January 1st, 1816

To My Beloved Parents, Dearest Fellow Wrights, and to all the
noble Natives of Heathsville,

    I write with glorious news, although I do not know when
you will receive this letter. Just as one cannot send mail for
delivery to the Pacific Coast, one cannot get postal pickup from
the Pacific Coast.

    We have, indeed, reached that most glorious of
destinations, a seemingly endless sea. We followed Dr. Bowe's
journals over vast, empty plains that shame even the largest of
plantations. I doubt there are enough people in the world, let
alone in the American Colonies, to ever tame to cultivation all of
this new area.

    West of the plains is a vast string of mountains, called the
Rocky Mountains by those who dare name such things. These we
covered by foot, to prove the possibility. The snow was deeper in
places then I am tall, and the wind was biting. And yes, I did
include myself in those who covered these mountains by foot, at
least before I succumbed to the cold. My fellow adventurers
carried me onward, and found me warmth and hospitality with a
friendly tribe of the area. While the accommodations were strange
in architecture, they were warm, and I will be forever grateful to
them for taking in a sick stranger. Under their care, and that of
Miss Bowe (the Great Dr.'s daughter!) I recovered, and walked
myself down out of those same mountains.

    As I write, I sit on a most comfortable rock, and stare with
wonder at a rock arch off the coast here. I have been siting here
since dawn, and still am amazed. It is the self same one sketched
by Dr. Bowe, and printed in every copy of his journals. Our
photographer and documentation, Mr. Watts, has found the exact
same angle the sketch was made at, and, in doing so, stumbled
over a cairn of rocks, just as Dr. Bowe said he placed.

    I am now a believer. Dr. Bowe is for real. This trip, and

Samantha Bowe, have convinced me. I plan to spend the trip back to New Orleans re-reading all of his journals, with this newfound perspective. I'm looking forward to our next goal. Lost cities that are not El Dorado sound warmer, at the least.

Your Loving Daughter,
Harriet Wright

Afterward
Dr. Cordelia Bentham-Watts
1887

Readers,

As you well know, this is not the end of the travels of that brave band. As of January 1816, they had barely began to cover the list of Dr. Bowe's claims, as assigned by Lord Donovan.

However, January 1st marks a year since the first letter of my dear Gregory on the topic of these explorations. As well, it marked their first great achievement. Just as the crew of the *Dame Fortuna* stopped to look back over the old year, and look forward to the new, so shall we end this volume here.

It is my hope that this first year of letters has helped you to learn about the people behind the stories. They each had their quirks and habits. They did not always get along like the merry band they projected for the press. They fought and disagreed about the best courses to take. However, they all worked together to try to prove the impossible possible, and in doing so, helped spark the imagination of not only the nation, but a huge portion of the war-torn world.

Their story continues, true, but be sure to not only read for the locations visited, but the friendships forged, and old enmities overcome. This is the true nature of peace, and this is the exploration that any can be master of.

I edit these papers not for myself, and not solely for the memory of my dear husband of sixty-five years, but for those who seek inspiration. I hope you may find it here.

Dr. Cordelia Bentham-Watts

Thank you to the following individuals. Without your aid and support in the process, this book would never have seen the light of day:

Sarah Symonds, my incredible co-writer and the voice of Cordelia and a number of others as the story developed. Kate Perkins, my fantastic editor. The talented Michal Marek for contributing the beautiful cover art. Jennifer Wolf and Matthew Lewis for their support and motivation to keep writing. Kaylin Anderson, Gerry Cook, Carol Wolf, Marci DeLeon, Anne Symonds, and Samantha Hutchison for their invaluable test readings and critiques. Seattle's hydrophobic ducks of Nanowrimo for their own words of encouragement and pressure to keep up the pace that led to Dawn of Steam being written. Finally, Khaya, Gregory, Milo, and sometimes even Osa.

http://www.dawnofsteam.net

Made in the USA
San Bernardino, CA
06 September 2017